The Last Suppers

Center Point
Large Print

**This Large Print Book carries the
Seal of Approval of N.A.V.H.**

The Last Suppers

MANDY MIKULENCAK

CENTER POINT LARGE PRINT
THORNDIKE, MAINE

This Center Point Large Print edition
is published in the year 2018 by arrangement with
Kensington Publishing Corp.

The text of this Large Print edition is unabridged.
In other aspects, this book may vary
from the original edition.
Printed in the United States of America
on permanent paper.
Set in 16-point Times New Roman type.

ISBN: 978-1-68324-673-2

Library of Congress Cataloging-in-Publication Data

Names: Mikulencak, Mandy, author.
Title: The last suppers / Mandy Mikulencak.
Description: Center Point Large print edition. | Thorndike, Maine :
    Center Point Large Print, 2018.
Identifiers: LCCN 2017051608 | ISBN 9781683246732
    (hardcover : alk. paper)
Subjects: LCSH: Large type books.
Classification: LCC PS3613.I474 L37 2018 | DDC 813/.6dc23
LC record available at https://lccn.loc.gov/2017051608

For Andy

The Last Suppers

Greenmount Penitentiary
Inmate Number 6451
East Feliciana Parish, Louisiana
Crime: Murder/Robbery
Execution Date: September 7, 1951

Leroy tells them he doesn't feel right. That his chest's going to explode. They laugh.

"You gonna be dead in two hours anyway." The two guards laugh some more. The larger one shoves him toward the table.

Leroy just wants to sit in his cell with his Bible, but that cook from the prison kitchen has brought over pot roast for his last supper. Says she talked with his mama and got the recipe. It smells like Sundays before church, when Leroy and his brothers would line up for inspection to prove they'd washed behind their ears and didn't have holes in their shirts.

The roast would be in the oven, waiting on them after the preacher turned them loose. That smell got him through many a sermon.

"I hope you like it," the lady says, placing a metal tray in front of him.

The thick slabs of roast and hunks of potato look so familiar his eyes water from the memories. He doesn't want the guards or the

11

lady to see, so he bows his head low and pretends to say grace.

The smell is right, but the tray is all wrong. What day is it anyway? He wants one of those blue-rimmed plates his granny gave his parents for their wedding, the ones brought out only on Sunday with a warning not to dare drop one.

"You gonna watch me eat?" he asks the lady.

One of the guards hits the back of Leroy's head with his fist. "Watch your manners, boy."

"He didn't mean any offense." She looks at Leroy. "I'm sorry to linger. I hope I did your mama's recipe justice."

"Eat, boy!" Another fist connects with his ear.

"Please don't hit him," she says, and turns to leave.

Leroy hacks at the meat with the edge of his spoon and then stuffs a large chunk in his mouth. The heat's gone out of it, but it's tender like his mama's. He chews and chews, but the meat seems to grow, filling his cheeks and cutting off his breath. Leroy's chest pounds faster now, like when his brothers would hold him under the creek till he was certain he'd drown.

Even though he can't swallow, he stuffs in a piece of potato. Then another. Choking would be a mercy, he thinks. The electric chair sits in the next room. Why would they make him eat so close to where they plan to kill him?

The cook is smaller than his little niece, but

dressed like a grown-up. She waves as she exits the room. Like she's gonna see him again one day, walking down the street. He nods his thanks for the food that's choking him.

In his mind, his granny is scolding him for having too much food in his mouth. He sees her, still in her Sunday hat and dress, white gloves clutched in one hand. His lips stay pressed together because chewing with your mouth open is impolite, she taught him.

He slaps at the table with both hands, waiting, waiting for his lungs to give up. The guard hits him square in the back and the mass of food in his mouth is ejected onto the tray.

"Worthless piece of shit," the guard says. "Can't even be thankful for a goddamn meal."

Tears cut shiny lines down his cheeks as the guard shoves his face into the now-cold food.

Chapter 1

Ginny crawled beneath Roscoe's threadbare wool blanket, not caring that the fibers scratched at her bare skin. She'd come to lay with him, as she typically did after the weekday workers returned home or to their barracks and the weekend guards took their posts. The musky scent of Old Spice clung to his pillow. She pressed her face deep into the fabric, breathing in the memories of him that lingered there.

Tonight, he was in the bath, which was also typical right before their visits. He'd once said that the stench of desperation and violence clung to him at the end of the day and he feared it'd rub off on her. Ginny had reminded him that she, too, worked at the prison. To which he shook his head and replied, "The kitchen don't count, Ginny. The kitchen don't goddamn count."

She let Roscoe believe the lie because he needed to think she was immune to the savagery in men's thoughts and actions. But savages existed on both sides of the metal bars, a truth everyone at the prison understood.

The rhythmic sloshing of water between the tub and Roscoe's body would have lulled Ginny to sleep if it weren't for the tiny spasms in her lower back and legs shouting for attention. It had been another thirteen-hour day with only a short break for stale coffee around 2 p.m. If she didn't get out of bed, Roscoe might not be able to rouse her.

She stood before his dresser and eased open the top drawer. It wasn't the first time she investigated its contents, but there were no secrets between them. The act of snooping reminded her of the times she had snuck into her parents' bedroom and investigated their personal belongings. During those foolhardy moments, she held her breath until she almost became dizzy with excitement. Back then, the price of being found out had been her mother's hellfire temper and the bite of a metal belt buckle against her bare legs. No such reproach would come from Roscoe.

He'd added nothing new since the last time she looked. The mainstays were still there: a bottle of whiskey, a small white prayer book that had been his mother's, a change of underwear, and a half-empty carton of cigarettes left over from when he'd quit smoking. The last thing a person should do is lock up his demons in a place he could access at any time, but that was Roscoe. He had impulse control.

As soon as he stepped out of the bath, she closed the drawer quietly and slipped back into bed. He entered the room, naked except for a small St. Christopher's medal he wore around his neck. Other lawmen swore by their St.

Michael's medals. Roscoe never said why he chose St. Christopher, but wearing the patron saint of travelers next to his heart made sense to her. A person's road in this lifetime was perilous enough. A bit of luck might just extend the journey by a few years.

The metal springs shuddered when he sat down on the edge of the bed. His skin, bright red from hot water and scrubbing, radiated warmth. She leaned closer and breathed in the scent of Ivory soap. The smells of the kitchen clung to her own skin and hair—onions, greens, hot grease, perspiration, and industrial dish soap. It crossed her mind to bathe before she met him in his room, but sheer fatigue kept her from worrying about it too much.

"Tough day?" he asked.

She kissed the small of his back before he nudged her to the other side of the bed.

"No so bad. You?"

"Nothing out of the ordinary," he said.

Neither expected a truthful or detailed answer. They always kept their talking to the bare minimum until after—when the lights were out and truth came more easily, like a confessional before the priest opened the curtain for absolution. Still, Roscoe shared only a fraction of what troubled his mind. His darkness played out in nightmares he seemed mostly ashamed of and almost never talked about. The nights they both wrestled with nightmares, they took turns waking the other up with their thrashing and muffled cries.

Ginny rolled on top of Roscoe and let his skin warm her from chest to toes. Aligning their bodies made her feel like they were one entity and that their cells could be merged by the heat and sweat between them. Her mind sometimes went off in odd directions, wondering, for example, if they'd start breathing in unison if they stayed still enough. Or whether a couple could stay completely entwined a whole night without needing to pull away.

His stubbly chin was always a pleasant sensation against her smooth one. She moved back and forth, feeling its roughness. He turned slightly so their lips touched, but only for a moment.

"Enough of that now," he said, rolling her onto her back.

The bedsprings sang for a few minutes while she watched two moths dance in the lamp shade on the nightstand.

Roscoe got out of bed and pulled on the boxers he'd draped over the chair back. His arms and long legs were taut and sinewy, but his belly spilled over the elastic waistband, a juxtaposition Ginny didn't find unattractive. At age fifty, he was more than twenty years her senior and exhibited more vigor than she ever had. She found this strange considering how closely he was tied to the death of others.

He walked to the small dresser and removed a bottle from the top drawer. "Drop of hooch?"

"Sure. A finger is all, though." She sat up, tucking the blanket beneath her armpits.

He handed her a juice glass half-full of whiskey, then poured his own more substantial portion. He set the bottle on the nightstand before he lay back against the wrought-iron headboard. His quarters in the administrative building contained only this sorry bed, a mismatched nightstand and dresser, and a small wooden table with two ladder-back chairs. His clothes hung from nails pounded in the window trim. He rarely stayed in the warden's residence, a three-bedroom, freshly painted, white clapboard house at the far end of the compound. It had a formal dining room and a fully stocked kitchen Ginny envied. He said it was too far from the main prison buildings, that he needed to be closer to "the men." She didn't know if Roscoe meant his guards or the inmates, or both.

It was clear from his face that something troubled him. She traced his forehead with her finger, stopping to smooth the deep lines etched between his brows.

"You sure nothing's wrong?" she asked.

"Just the normal stuff." He took a generous sip of his whiskey.

"Nothing you want to talk about?"

"Nope." He downed the rest of his drink and cradled the empty glass.

Ginny stared at her still-untouched drink. She didn't like the taste of alcohol or how it made her feel, but it seemed more trouble to refuse a taste when Roscoe was drinking. She often thought she'd turn to booze for comfort if she had to witness one tenth of what Roscoe witnessed each day. Even though he refused to talk about it, she'd already heard through the prison grapevine that two men were killed in the fields earlier that day at the hands of Roscoe's guards. Men of questionable nature were attracted to the jobs at Greenmount, and it gave her pause to think even Roscoe couldn't keep their aggression in check.

"There's no more money for the prison larder this month," he said, steering her away from any other questions about his mood.

She never asked for a penny more than was allotted, but he seemed to need to apologize for this thing beyond his control.

"I always make do."

"You could make a meal fit for a king out of spoiled milk, rotten eggs, and flour," he continued. It was one of those compliments he overused, both with her and anyone else he talked to about her cooking.

"Good thing we don't have to find out," she always replied.

It was 1959 and she'd been the lead cook at Greenmount Penitentiary for eight years—the first woman to be allowed on staff. The last warden didn't care if meals were punishment in and of themselves. Said only filth was good enough for filth. She felt her hiring had less to do with her culinary skills and more to do with the Department of Corrections wanting bad press to go away. Just months before Ginny was hired, several inmates cut their Achilles tendons to protest conditions at the prison, including the slop they were fed. Reforms that followed included more staff, better food, and slightly more sanitary living conditions. Roscoe was promoted to warden the same year and had been the one to hire her. She suspected it was a job he wished he hadn't taken, but he never admitted it out loud.

"Goddamned prison board won't leave well enough alone." His voice was tired and low, as if the flu was coming on. "The superintendent and a couple of members are driving up soon."

"It's not near time for their quarterly visit," she said. "What do they want?"

"What do they ever want?"

The superintendent's chief complaint—besides Roscoe taking reform a little too seriously—was he failed to kiss anyone's ass, which was mandatory in the Louisiana penal system.

The visits made Roscoe itch with worry, which

he never showed to his men. The cues were apparent to Ginny, though. He'd chew the skin of his thumb raw and say he was more tired than usual. Another person might be on edge, snapping and grousing, but he did the opposite, retreating into himself. Ginny sometimes felt ashamed for savoring these quiet moods. Still, she worried that the unplanned board visit signaled bad news.

Roscoe reached into the drawer of the nightstand and removed his well-worn Bible. He'd dog-eared almost every page. She wondered how he remembered which pages held significance, unless all of them had at one time or another.

Even though she doubted God's existence, she liked a good story, and the Bible had quite a few of those. She and Roscoe disagreed on whether the work was an excellent piece of fiction or words coming straight from God's mouth. He respected her beliefs—or lack thereof—but said he wouldn't hide his own. She'd never ask such a thing of anyone, much less Roscoe. Her longing for answers didn't mean he hadn't already found his.

"Don't want to talk about work anymore. Want me to read aloud?" he asked.

Ginny always said yes because she loved the power in his voice. He could've been a preacher, the sort who didn't keep people in line with words of fear and shame, but whose voice made the congregation believe he could protect them from Old Scratch himself. That same voice probably commanded more respect from the staff and inmates than anything else about him.

"New Testament or Old?" He put a cigarette in his mouth but didn't light it. During those times he tried to quit, he'd say it helped to have the thing between his lips, even if he couldn't take a draw.

"You pick." She closed her eyes and listened as he started from page one. "In the beginning . . ."

She tried to imagine if they'd be sharing a bed if they didn't work at the prison together, or if he hadn't been her daddy's best friend before he was murdered.

Chapter 2

Ginny followed Roscoe down the hallway of the admin building, although several steps behind because the jackass was on some kind of foot race. He wouldn't turn around, so she spoke to his back. "What do you mean, he won't talk to me? Why the hell not?"

His pace quickened and she struggled to keep up. "Roscoe! Please answer me."

He whipped around on her so fast she almost ran into his chest. "It's Warden Simms unless we're alone. You know that, Ginny."

He towered above her, hands clenched. It wasn't yet 6 a.m. and perspiration soaked through his T-shirt to his uniform. He smelled of chewing tobacco, not Ivory soap as he had the night before, but the scent was just as comforting.

"No one's around to hear," she whispered. "This is important, Roscoe. I have to see him."

The anger drained from his face. He was back to being plain frustrated by the requests she made of him all these years.

"The boy has only days before he meets his Maker and you want to ask him about his favorite foods. He said he doesn't want anything."

"He doesn't know what he wants." She tested Roscoe's patience almost subconsciously. When he failed to give her reason not to, it had only become easier over the years.

"Ginny, let it alone."

Her fingers brushed against his for a second. He stuffed his hands in his pockets and stepped away.

"I can't let it alone," she said.

This wasn't pigheadedness on her part. It was something physical that wouldn't let go. Planning the meals plagued her thoughts and brought on headaches and stomach pains. Ignoring them wasn't an option. She had tried on occasion in the early days.

Truth be told, Roscoe was partly to blame for her fervor. He'd said yes the first time she asked to prepare something special for an inmate's last meal and had agreed another sixteen times in eight years.

"Don't you see how it affects you?" he asked. "You stayed in bed for three days after the last execution. It's wearing on you, girl. You just won't admit it."

Ginny ignored Roscoe's reasoning. She'd just been tired, dog-tired. The execution had nothing to do with it.

"Jesus Christ. If the Superintendent of Corrections knew, I'd be out of a job," he continued. "Then where'd I be? There's already too many folks nosying around."

She wanted to press her face against his chest

and hug away his worry, more for herself than for him.

"We could marry and move to Alabama. I'd have seven kids and you'd sell vacuum cleaners door-to-door." She was only half joking.

He looked up and down the hallway, the furrows easing from his brow. "Ain't nobody want to live in goddamn Alabama."

She leaned in and pecked him on the cheek tentatively. "Ask him again, Roscoe. Please?"

As she ran down the hall, the haunting urgency that came with each execution nipped at her heels.

Dot was elbow deep in flour by the time Ginny reached the kitchen. The old woman's scowl indicated Ginny was in trouble even though she was technically the kitchen supervisor.

"It's 'bout time you showed up," Dot mumbled. Unable to keep up the pretense of anger, her scowl lifted into a grin.

Ginny pulled an apron off the hook near the door. "I guess those sheet pans greased themselves this morning, huh?"

"Well, if you were already here, where'd you run off to?" She put her hands on her ample hips, sending flour onto the cement floor.

A guard arrived with two inmates who ignored the bickering women and got to the business of peeling potatoes. Jess and Peabody were several moons past seventy, their faces like shriveled apples. Their failing health kept them from being useful in the fields. They would have worked in the license plate operation or at the canning plant, but Ginny recruited them. Two guards stood watch over the kitchen because Dot and Ginny were the only women allowed in that part of the prison compound. One guard paid special attention to Jess and Peabody, as if they posed a danger, but Ginny wasn't afraid. Their crimes were unknown to her, but the men exuded gentleness, or maybe just plain resignation.

"You with your boyfriend, huh?" Dot loaded the trays with biscuit rounds, not looking up.

Ginny ignored her and started the gelatinous gravy her daddy had called Shit on a Shingle. It seemed the best use of the prison's ration of fatty ground beef because it could be stretched by adding a roux of flour, milk, and beef broth. Enough black pepper and she could get away with using milk on the edge of sour. She usually served it on plain white bread, but biscuits were cheap to make and the men appreciated it.

"Not talking to me?" Dot continued.

"Talk about something I want to talk about and then we'll see."

"You don't want to talk 'bout anything but the death row boys. Most are headed straight to hell. Worrying about what they eat before they fry is a waste of all our time."

"Uh-huh."

Dot questioned her motivation relentlessly. There weren't words to describe the vicious churning of Ginny's gut when executions were scheduled, or the heart-pounding terror that she might fail the inmate in some way. Dot chastised her for worrying about such details; that a man about to meet his Lord and Savior wouldn't taste the food in front of him anyway.

Roscoe thought she might be a tad touched by madness, maybe inherited from her daddy. But his affliction was brought on by alcohol, nothing more. Ginny's madness started the day she was forced to witness the execution of her father's killer. Roscoe had said no eight-year-old should've been subjected to that horror, but the warden gave his permission since Ginny's mama insisted she be there. Roscoe was just one of three dozen prison guards and other staff who'd crammed themselves into the small, cinderblock room to see justice had been done in the name of their fallen brother. She didn't remember seeing Roscoe, but he said he remembered her being there. And it brought him a greater sadness than the fact his friend was dead.

Dot muttered something to herself, but obviously loud enough to be heard.

"What now?" Ginny asked.

"You're a grown woman and wearing socks instead of stockings," she said, pointing at

Ginny's bare legs. "If I would have caught you before you left your room this morning, I would have said something then."

"It's ninety degrees in this kitchen. And who the hell cares anyway?"

"You should care," Dot said. "Coming up on thirty years old and still dressing like a teenager."

Ginny looked down at her wrinkled cotton dress, plain by anyone's standards, but that didn't bother her a bit. Her shoes were sturdy, leather loafers with rubber soles. The socks helped prevent blisters during the long days in the kitchen. Still, the gentleness of Dot's never-ending observations on her appearance amused Ginny. Probably because her own mama's criticisms stung like the cracking of a leather belt against her thighs.

"You spend entirely too much time worrying about the appropriateness of my wardrobe," Ginny said. "I'm going down to the larder. Need anything?"

"No, but hurry on up. That pot on the stove will start burning."

The cool-storage pantry was just a twenty-foot-square underground room with a dirt floor that was accessible by wooden stairs from the kitchen.

Flour, cornmeal, grits, and lard were cheap. Over the years, Ginny was able to get Roscoe to divert a portion of the crops to the kitchen as well: potatoes, sweet potatoes, beans, greens, and cabbage. The canning factory on the prison grounds also sent its discards, especially beet greens and overly bruised peaches.

She knew she'd done well with the meager ingredients because it'd become common for the guards to eat what she was already making for the inmates rather than demand special meals as they'd done before her time.

Sometimes, she'd buy spices like paprika and cayenne with her own money. The larder housed these and all the other nonperishable items. Now that she had a refrigerator in the main kitchen, she could store the eggs and raw milk that came from the livestock the prison kept. The slaughterhouse, while a revenue-generating operation, sent its leavings that were mostly used to make a fatty ground meat. Ginny had convinced them to also send unwanted pig skin and fat, which, when fried, provided grease for flavoring the thin stews she and Dot sometimes cooked to stretch ingredients.

Ginny returned to the kitchen, a large bag of flour in her arms. "We need cornmeal," she said. "Good on everything else."

Dot bent over to retrieve a large tray of biscuits from the oven. Ginny's stomach growled, reminding her to eat something before they started on lunch preparations.

"Set aside some biscuits for the warden, would

you," she said to Dot. "Walk them over to his office while they're still hot."

"You do it. I ain't his girlfriend."

Jess and Peabody lifted their eyes at Dot's sassing.

"Shut your mouth for once, Dorothy, and do as I say." Ginny's face flushed from the heat of the stove, as well as the flash of anger. She wasn't herself today. Ginny rarely raised her voice in the kitchen. And it had been some time since she spoke so roughly to Dot.

"Well, lookie there. Miss Polk's finally putting that big darkie in her place." Peabody's toothless cackle rang out in the kitchen until the guard nudged him with a billy club.

"Mind your own business." Dot scolded the two men, and they turned their attention back to the bushel basket of unpeeled potatoes.

During Dot's interview for the job five years ago, she'd commented that Ginny was too young and tiny to run a big kitchen all by herself, that she needed a friend more than an employee. The comment had riled Ginny at first and she'd called the woman out on her impertinence. Dot had apologized, but said, "If you want a cook who keeps her mouth shut, I'm not the person for the job. But if you want a hard worker whose mouth sometimes gets ahead of her thoughts, then I can start tomorrow." Recognizing the same trait in herself, Ginny hired her on the spot.

They'd had rough patches, though, trying to sort out their roles. When Dot first joined the kitchen staff, Ginny tried to keep her distance and assert her authority. She didn't need anyone reading her moods or questioning her decisions. It didn't take long before Ginny saw that Dot's age and experience were assets, and she was ashamed she'd dug her heels in so often rather than see Dot's point of view.

In truth, Dot didn't make it easy to compromise. The things they'd sparred over were mostly trivial: whose biscuit recipe was better, whether or not they needed to wear hairnets, whose turn it was to oil the cast-iron pans. Ginny found out the true nature of their relationship on one of the prison's darker days. When violence erupted in the cafeteria and the inmates got the upper hand over the guards, Dot had immediately shoved Ginny into the kitchen's cellar and planted herself in front of the bolted metal door. She shouted for the angry inmates to take their business elsewhere, that to do otherwise was disrespecting someone old enough to be their grandmother.

Even though Ginny regretted her sharp tongue this morning, she couldn't let it go. She moved closer to Dot so no one else in the kitchen could overhear. "You should take your own advice and keep out of my business," she said. "And you might try treating your boss with some respect."

Dot batted her eyes like a repentant child even

though she was three decades older than Ginny. It was her trademark move to gain Ginny's sympathy. Dot wiped her floury hands on the apron and then across her face, leaving a white mustache on her dark upper lip. Any other day, Ginny might have laughed at the sight.

"Don't be trotting out that 'I'm your boss' nonsense. You know I meant no harm," Dot finally said. "Is something else bothering you? I can't remember the last time you raised your voice to me."

"Well, I can't remember the last time you deserved it."

Dot raised her eyebrows and stared.

"What?" Ginny asked, shifting from one foot to the other nervously.

"Deserved it?"

Ginny's hand covered hers. "I know you meant no harm. But I don't want the warden getting into any kind of trouble on account of me," she said. "We can't be public about our . . . relationship."

"Everybody done know you've been with the man for years."

Dot's bit of defiance softened Ginny's ire. She'd grown used to her mothering. Or at the very least, she could put up with it because Dot's intentions were good. When Dot started sleeping at the women's barracks during the week, Ginny found herself happy for the company. Even though the two were always bone-weary at day's end, they'd often stay up playing cards or checkers, and drinking instant coffee Dot made on her hot plate.

The first time Dot asked Ginny to join her family for Thanksgiving dinner, Ginny hesitated, thinking they'd become too familiar. After she gave in that first time, Ginny looked forward to spending holidays with Dot rather than with Miriam. Those afternoons were like being in a Norman Rockwell painting, and the closest thing to a normal family Ginny had experienced. "Maybe everybody knows about me and Roscoe, but they keep quiet about it," Ginny said. "And with the prison board folks making more frequent visits, I don't need anyone to slip up."

"I don't see the problem," Dot said. "Quit your job, marry the man, and stop living in sin. Then you're not sleeping with the boss man and there's nothing to cover up."

"It's not so simple." The biggest complication was Ginny didn't know if she actually loved Roscoe. She had deep feelings for him and hated those times when they couldn't see each other in his room or at the residence. But she had a job to do. And giving it up for a man she wasn't sure she loved didn't seem like common sense.

"Seems mighty simple to me," Dot said. "I'd marry the warden in a heartbeat if it meant I didn't have to work another day. I'd have me some kids and settle down. I sure wouldn't be cooking for dead men."

"Those dead men don't have anyone else," Ginny said. "And Roscoe has never asked. He knows I'm not the marrying type."

"Does he?" Dot pressed. "You're not exactly the best at letting people in."

In truth, Ginny didn't know Roscoe's feelings about marriage. Could be he didn't love her. Could be their age difference or the fact that he was her superior. But if he happened to ask and she happened to say yes, she'd be stuck up at the warden's residence, looking out over 8,000 acres of misery and wondering who was helping Dot in the kitchen and if they were using their resources wisely.

She sure as hell didn't want to raise children in this compound. It saddened her to see the dozen or so kids waiting at the bus stop near the front gate each morning. Were they eager to go to school and have several hours of respite from this place? Did they dread the moment they arrived back at the front gate as she had as a child?

When Ginny was young, she had imagined other students going home to find their mamas tending a flower garden, or waiting with home-made bread and jam. She daydreamed about being invited to birthday parties and sleepovers. But Ginny had been born at the prison and daydreams never kept reality at bay for long. Her mama and daddy may have pretended they had a normal life, but normal wasn't hearing the wails of men being beaten long into the night or watching inmates shuffle in heavy, iron chains on their way to tend the prison crops.

School wasn't exactly easy either. Prison kids bore a stain that couldn't be washed off. She learned that hard lesson on the first day of first grade when the teacher segregated them to one side of the room. As unwelcoming as the students and teachers had been, Ginny saw her time outside the prison gates as an opportunity to reinvent herself. She pretended to be a transfer student from another state, sometimes accidentally writing her made-up name on a test or homework assignment.

Ginny shook the memories from her mind and pointed to the oven, reminding Dot of her original request. "Cover them with a dish towel to stay warm and put some butter on the plate. Hurry now, before he's finished his coffee."

The Shit on a Shingle had already started to scorch, forcing Ginny back to the stove.

Dot had been right. Ginny's mind chewed on something that wouldn't let her be. Less than a week until Samuel LeBoux's execution and the boy wouldn't talk. And Roscoe wasn't eager to serve as the go-between. Other men on death row had been reluctant to talk to her, but they always came around. And it'd never come down to days. She always made sure there was plenty of time to try a recipe, sometimes twice, to make sure it was as close to the inmate's description as possible.

After breakfast, Ginny left the kitchen and walked to the administrative offices. Roscoe wouldn't be there. By midmorning, he and a couple of guards were out checking the crops and then the slaughterhouse. She was there for someone else.

At eighteen, Tim was the youngest and skinniest of Roscoe's newest guards; too young to oversee the cellblocks or fields. He sat hours at the desk, answering a phone that rarely rang and pushing papers that had no urgency to them. Ginny thought Roscoe hired him as a favor to some prison board member, but he never confirmed her suspicions.

"Morning, Miss Polk. The warden's not—"

"How many times have I told you to call me Ginny? And I'm not here to see the warden. I'm here to see you."

His already ruddy cheeks flamed as if she'd said she had come to have sex with him. She pulled up a chair to his side of the desk, which only caused him more discomfort. Ginny found this laughable considering she had the body of a thirteen-year-old boy. But there were only five women working at the prison, so maybe it made sense she could get the same reactions as the girls in the pin-up calendar behind the desk.

"What . . . what can I do for you?" Tim asked.

"I need you to take me to the Waiting Room."

No one could remember when the wooden barracks reserved for death row inmates got its nickname, but it was apt. All those men did was wait. Ginny had never been there on her own before. That is, without Roscoe as a chaperone. But she didn't have time to wait out his stubbornness.

"The day crew is on," Tim said. "John or Terrence can help you."

The guards who watched over the death row inmates during the day shift were good men, calm of mind and spirit, and handpicked by Roscoe. They never questioned why it was important for her to cook the last meals. But they sure weren't about to let her in without Roscoe at her side—or at least accompanied by another guard.

"You know I need an escort or I won't get past the fences," Ginny said.

"But why . . . why does it have to be me?" he stammered. "We could both get in a lot of trouble."

"I promise if Warden Simms ever finds out—and he won't—but if he does, I'll take full responsibility. I'll say I forced you."

Tim's laugh held more confidence than it should have. "I'm a man, Miss Ginny. And I have a gun. Why would he believe someone as itty-bitty as you could force me?"

She leaned in close enough to notice the boy hadn't bathed in a couple of days even though he was freshly shaven and his nails were clean. Made her think he was reluctant to go into the men's communal showers and relied more on the washbasin in his room.

"But, Tim . . . Lord knows what you might have tried when you realized the two of us were alone in the admin office. After all, you're a man and you have a gun."

Tim backed away so quickly his chair scraped against the wall behind him.

"I'd never do such a thing!"

"Oh, I know," she assured him. "We're just talking hypothetically here. Because I know you'll agree to help me."

Ginny stood and walked out of the office, hoping Tim would follow. He did.

The Waiting Room wasn't a single room, but a long, narrow, wooden building with twenty-two cells. Each five-by-seven-foot cell contained an iron cot with a one-inch pad, a small stool and desk, a metal washbasin with rank water, and a metal bucket for a toilet. The structure was attached to the cinderblock execution building at one end, forming an L. The paint on the white clapboards had chipped away, leaving gray rotting wood exposed to the sun and humidity. No one seemed inclined to spruce up a place that held the likes of murderers and rapists.

"I can't let you in the cellblock." Tim shuffled two steps behind Ginny as she walked across the compound. "It wouldn't be right. No lady should see that."

Tim held the door to the execution building open for her. Each time she entered the dank death house, she became an eight-year-old again, overwhelmed by the bloodlust the prison guards exhibited at the execution of her daddy's murderer, deafened by the shrieking of Silas Barnes's soon-to-be widow, and jealous his young son was allowed to sit outside on the dusty ground.

She'd passed the boy on her way in to see his father executed. He had a lazy eye that pointed in toward his nose. His stare had given her the shivers, as did his slight smile that told her he had no idea why he was there.

Even though the room had been hosed down after the last execution and the windows had stayed open for much of several months after that, her brain called up every vile scent that permeated the room the day she watched Silas die: the body odor of too many people crammed in one room in July, burned hair and blistered skin, feces and urine from a man as his body gave up life. At the time, she was sure that's what hell smelled like.

"You all right, Ginny?"

John, the lead guard, stood right inside the door, arms crossed. His slight smile said he knew she was up to no good.

Ginny dipped her head. "I'm fine. How are you this morning?"

"Got yourself a new escort, I see. The warden busy or something?"

"Something like that." She pinched the back of Tim's elbow to remind him to keep his mouth shut.

"You sure you want to be doing something the warden might disagree with?" John asked.

Her stare said to mind his own business. John wasn't the type to cause unneeded conflict, so she didn't worry too much.

"She's here to see LeBoux," Tim said. "I told her she can't go in the cellblock."

"Ginny knows that, boy. I'll bring Sam to the corner room."

The corner room served as a buffer between the two buildings, a space for the death row inmate to wait that was separate from the cellblock and from the room that held Gruesome Gertie, the state's lone electric chair. A cruel purgatory. It was also the room where the inmate could eat a last meal, if he chose to have one. In her time at the prison, they all asked for one and she complied.

Tim followed Ginny into the room. An old

41

metal kitchen table with two ladder-back chairs anchored the center of the twelve-by-twelve-foot space. A bare lightbulb hung above the table. Tim dragged one of the chairs over so he could reach the two transom windows. The heat was stifling and she appreciated he thought to open them.

Ginny sat down and placed her hands on the metal tabletop, which stayed cool despite the heat. Her fingernails were either bitten to the nub or cracked and peeling from too much time in dishwater. She couldn't remember the last time she painted them, even though she'd purchased a bottle of Vixen Red at the pharmacy in Boucherville last month. Ginny felt so foolish after, she shoved the unused polish to the back of a dresser drawer.

Retrieving Samuel caused a ruckus, which gave Tim a fair amount of anxiety. He paced the room, one hand on his holster. Inmates' voices could be heard through the door. Some shouted lewd things for Samuel to do to the "crazy cook lady." Others just called out their favorite foods and begged him to tell her. John shouted for everyone to calm down and the mutterings trailed off.

"How can you stand hearing those shameful things?" Tim asked.

"I don't take it personally."

The remarks riled Ginny when she was younger, but now they seemed wholly unconnected to her, just the rantings of madmen. Anger seemed a normal consequence of living one's last days like an animal.

The door finally opened and John led a hand-cuffed Samuel toward the table. Tim stepped forward and shoved him into the chair.

"Sit!" Tim's hands shook visibly. He'd perspired through his uniform and his face had become slick with sweat. Ginny prayed Samuel made no sudden moves or Tim might come completely unhinged and kill him on the spot. Roscoe was right to keep Tim doing office work until he gained some sense and experience.

John moved between Tim and Samuel. "Boy, no need to get hot and bothered. You go on back to the admin building. I'll bring Ginny around a little later."

"If something happens to her, it'll be my fault," he said.

"Ain't nothing going to happen. Sam's a good kid." John withdrew a pack of chewing tobacco from his pants' pocket and leaned against the wall. "And it ain't like this is Ginny's first time meeting with an inmate. Go on. You look like you need some air."

Still frantic, Tim looked at her for assurance. She nodded and he practically flew from the room.

"Sorry about that, Samuel. My name's—"

"I know who you are. Every dead man knows 'bout you." The nineteen-year-old lowered his head. His dirty blond hair fell like a veil over his eyes. "I told the warden I didn't want to talk to you."

"Yes, but—"

"Yes, nothing," he said. "I want to be left alone."

Samuel sat at a table where seventeen men sat before. Ginny could recall each and every dish she'd prepared and carried across the prison grounds on a covered tray. The meals were never piping hot because it took so much time to walk from the warden's residence, where the last suppers were prepared.

She never stayed to watch them eat. Never dared to hope they enjoyed the meals. When a man was hours from dying, how could he enjoy anything? Dot reminded her of that constantly. Panic attacks sometimes gripped her when she thought she might be force-feeding them memories they'd sooner forget. Yet, something deep in her gut told her it was the gesture that meant something to them, not the act of eating. The cruelty and darkness in that place sometimes overwhelmed her. Dot and Roscoe were the light Ginny needed to keep on working there. Maybe Ginny's meals were the light those men needed to make it through the final hours before death claimed them.

"You're due a last meal of your choosing," she said. "It's supposed to be something we already have on hand in the kitchen, but I can get other ingredients on my own."

"Are you hard of hearing? I don't want nothing." He used his cuffed hands to swipe at the sweat on his brow. The sharp metal had already reddened his wrists.

Last year, Samuel had been convicted of killing a pharmacist in Baton Rouge. He'd broken into a pharmacy after hours to steal morphine. The pharmacist had gone back to fill a special order and happened upon Samuel. The damn fool should've run. Instead, he shot the pharmacist and busted through the back door, where the pharmacist's wife waited in the still-running car. Panicked, Samuel shot her in the head and dragged her body from the car before driving off in it himself. She lived.

"Your people still live in Catahoula Parish?" Ginny asked.

"What do you know about my people?"

She knew just about everything there was to know about every man on death row in Louisiana. Many of the details she could scavenge from the prison files and court records in Roscoe's office or from local newspaper accounts. Ginny had researched Samuel's family some time ago, when he first resisted the idea of a last meal. If Samuel wasn't going to talk, she'd damn sure find someone who would.

"I know enough. Like you have twin sisters

45

who are sixteen years old. And you were raised mostly by your grandmother," she said.

The hardness around Samuel's eye softened. "Yeah, the girls are still living with Grammy in Jonesville."

"Are they coming to the execution?"

"Why you ask something so stupid? 'Course they're not. Little girls ought not to see something so horrible. Neither should my grammy."

Samuel exhibited the good sense her mama had lacked twenty-one years ago when she dragged Ginny into the execution room even as she pleaded to just wait outside. Her mother's ludicrous excuse was that she'd suffocate in a hot car.

"Will you have anyone there?" Ginny envisioned the small area partitioned for family and wondered if the bench would be bare when Samuel died next week.

"I want to go back to my cell," he said to John, whom she'd almost forgotten was in the same room.

The ringing in her ears drowned out Samuel's continued rejections. *Calm down, Ginny. He'll come around,* she told herself. The panic usually dissipated with deep breaths. In and out. In and out. She damn well knew that last suppers weren't going to change anything: They wouldn't make bad men good, they wouldn't make up for any brutality exacted by the guards, they wouldn't ease the suffocating fear of meeting death. The closest thing she could liken it to was bringing a casserole to a family after a funeral. For her, food did what words could not. It said, "I'm sorry for the loss. I'm sorry I can't do more to help."

"Please, Samuel." She reached for his hand and he jerked away. "If you change your mind, tell one of the guards to come get me. Do you hear?"

John lifted Samuel by the elbow and led him back into the barracks. Ginny didn't wait for John to escort her back to the admin building. She took off at a trot. Dust from the road puffed up around her ankles with every step, turning her black shoes a dingy gray-brown. The midday sun had baked the road until you could smell the actual dirt. The stench from the Waiting Room was stronger, though, and would linger on her skin and in her nostrils until she could find a stronger or more pleasant scent to take its place. Ginny understood why Roscoe scrubbed his skin raw at the end of each day.

Chapter 3

Ginny was almost certain Tim hadn't told Roscoe about her meeting with Samuel. When she entered Roscoe's office the next morning, he appeared distracted by work, but otherwise uninterested in her.

"I'm thinking of visiting Mama today, then maybe going into Baton Rouge to do some shopping." She searched his face, wondering if he was biding time before chastising her.

Roscoe continued flipping through some paperwork on his desk, not looking up. "Dot can handle things in the kitchen alone?"

"Of course she can. But having free rein can give her a big head," she joked.

"Uh-huh."

"Well, I'll be heading out then." She waited tentatively, still not believing her good luck.

"Borrow Miriam's Cadillac if you're driving as far as Baton Rouge," he called after her. "Don't need you breaking down."

She had already decided to borrow her mama's car. Three years ago, Ginny had purchased a used Chevy Styleline based on the color alone—a soft powdery blue called Twilight. It was a beautiful thing on the outside. She should've had someone check under the hood before laying out $700 for it. Three times in the last year alone, Roscoe had to send a deputy warden to pick her up from Boucherville because the car wouldn't start.

While it was only thirty miles from her mama's house to Baton Rouge, it was ninety miles to Jonesville, which was Ginny's real destination. She didn't know how Roscoe would react to her visiting Samuel LeBoux's family, but she didn't want to find out by having to call him because the Chevy was broken down on the side of Highway 84.

Ginny got in the front seat and positioned a small pillow beneath her rear so she had a better view out of the window. At times she felt foolish for doing so, but hated the idea of other drivers thinking she was an underage girl driving a car. As she turned onto Highway 66 to Boucherville, a hot breeze lapped at her face. It'd be a good day. She could feel it. Having a purpose gave the day some order.

She hadn't bothered to phone Miriam she was coming. The door was open, so Ginny let herself into the house and made her way to the kitchen. Her mama, concentrating on a crossword puzzle, shrieked when Ginny spoke.

"Jesus Lord in Heaven! You scared me to death!"

"Fling that pencil any harder and you could put out someone's eye." Ginny kissed her on the cheek. Her mama smelled of talcum powder and drugstore perfume, and wore a full face of makeup. "I called out when I opened the screen door. You must've been concentrating on a word."

"What the hell are you doing here?" Miriam asked.

"Do I have to have a reason to stop by?"

"I guess I'll make a second pot of coffee, although I've probably had enough. It would've been brewed already if you thought to call first." She was annoyed and clearly suspicious of the unannounced visit.

Ginny hadn't planned to stay, but it seemed rude to just ask to borrow her mama's car, considering she hadn't made a proper visit in some weeks and only called when she had the energy to endure Miriam's naggy comments without biting back. The least she could do was wait for the coffee to brew and drink a cup.

Ginny retrieved two clean coffee cups from the cupboard and sat down.

"So tell me why you're really here," Miriam demanded.

"I need to borrow your car, if that's okay. I'll fill her up before I get back."

"Where you headed?" she asked.

Ginny's hesitation was answer enough.

"Not again." Miriam closed her eyes, visibly dismayed over Ginny's visits with inmates' families. "Where this time?"

"Jonesville."

Ginny offered no other information while her mama retrieved stale sweet rolls for them to dunk in their coffee. Peculiar as it sounded, they both preferred day-old pastries to freshly baked ones. It gave Ginny a sense of home the physical house couldn't. She still considered her parents' housing at the prison as home, even though she only spent the first eight years of her life there.

During those years, she still had her daddy. When they were together, Ginny could almost block out the harsher realities of the fenced world they occupied. They'd douse the dusty front yard with water from the hose, churning the dirt into a delicious muck perfect for making mud pies. Sometimes, her daddy would lift her onto his shoulders and they'd walk through the long rows of corn after the inmates had stopped work for the day. Ginny would pretend to be a scarecrow protecting acres of crops from the menacing blackbirds. He was the one to kiss her good night. He was the one who cared when she cried and worried when she didn't laugh enough.

After his murder, Ginny felt the best part of herself had been cut away. Miriam must have felt the same because she really didn't feel up to parenting anymore. Theirs was not a shared loss. A house without her daddy would never be home. It didn't matter where Ginny lived after their years at the prison.

She soaked her pecan roll in the coffee and stuck half of it in her mouth, chewing openly, but Miriam didn't laugh.

"That won't work on me," she said. "You're not a girl anymore."

"No, I'm not. But you're a morose old bird," Ginny said.

"What do I have to be happy about? My own daughter rarely visits me. And she's living in sin with a man old enough to be her father, working at a godforsaken prison, no less."

Their conversations were the same each time they saw each other. Her mama rarely bothered to mix up the order of her grievances.

"It's a shame I'm the sole reason for your unhappiness." Ginny picked at pieces of pecan floating in her cup. "Maybe you should try living in sin."

"Virginia! That is exactly what I mean. No respect for me at all." She got up from the table and pretended to attend to dishes in the sink.

Ginny looked at her mother's wide hips and movie-star curves. No one would have guessed they were related. Miriam had more height, weight, and roundness to her. She didn't pass down her shiny blond hair to her daughter either. This upset Ginny considerably as a child because she idolized Veronica Lake and wanted to look just like her. Instead, Ginny got stuck with her daddy's wiry dark brown hair, which required wrestling into a single braid or ponytail each day.

Another daughter might have gotten up and hugged her mother from behind, maybe even nuzzled against her neck. A good daughter might have lied and said she applied for a respectable job in Baton Rouge after all, or considered moving home and attending church regularly. But Ginny wasn't that kind of daughter.

Most days, Ginny could barely abide with their strained truce to remain civil. She couldn't remember the last time she told Miriam she loved her. Surely it was in the days right after the funeral when Ginny needed her mama the most. Miriam's usual hardness had only intensified. She had no time for Ginny's foolish pleas for hugs or comforting. And she wouldn't tolerate any talk of the murder, or the murderer's execution. Sometimes, the eight-year-old Ginny would find Miriam staring at her, accusation in her eyes, as if Ginny had pulled the trigger herself. It didn't take long for Ginny to withhold her affection even though that was a risky undertaking. After all, Miriam was the only family left to take care of her.

As an adult, Ginny allowed the visits to her mama to grow less frequent until she was about to cut her out of her life for good. It was Dot and Roscoe who encouraged her to make an effort; they said that's what you did with kin. She dreaded disappointing them more than she dreaded the visits with her mama.

"I'll leave my keys on the foyer table. Just in case you need to drive somewhere today," Ginny said, wishing she had another option than borrowing Miriam's car.

"Don't you let anything happen to my car in colored town." Miriam didn't bother turning around.

Even though Samuel's family was white, Ginny decided not to waste her breath.

The hot breeze that felt so good against her face midmorning was suffocating by noon. Ginny used the air-conditioning only intermittently, fearing the car might overheat. She kept to the speed limit, although she wanted nothing more than to floor it and get to Jonesville and out of the car.

Mercifully, it wasn't hard to find Samuel's grandmother's place in a town of 1,600 people. Ginny had to ask for directions only once before she found the faded blue clapboard house at the end of a dirt driveway.

Her dress clung uncomfortably to her back and thighs. The swamp-like Louisiana humidity made that an everyday occurrence. Dot's admonishments about her wardrobe came rushing back to her. Ginny was embarrassed she hadn't thought to wear stockings or a proper hat for a visit, but regret was pointless now. It was more important that she not arouse Roscoe's suspicion by wearing Sunday clothes on a work-day.

The sight of a Cadillac on a normally deserted road signaled her arrival before she could even knock. A young black teenager with a crying toddler on her hip appeared at the screen door. She wore a skimpy yellow halter and shorts, but still looked miserably hot.

"I'm sorry. I might have the wrong house," Ginny said. "I'm looking for Mrs. LeBoux."

"Grammy? Someone's here to see you," she shouted, then disappeared.

Ginny took a seat on one of the three rocking chairs on the porch and waited until the screen door screeched again. There stood a frail-looking woman who'd lost half her height to old age. Her pale face was covered with a web of deep lines that grew deeper when she scowled. Although her hair had gone mostly gray, Ginny could tell she'd had sandy blond hair as a young woman. Samuel's hair.

"It's actually hotter in the damn house. We'll have to talk out here," she said.

"Mrs. LeBoux?" Ginny extended her hand and the old woman shook it.

"That's me. But the real riddle is, Who is you?" She sat in the adjacent rocking chair and pointed to the Cadillac as if the car could give some clue to Ginny's reason for showing up at her doorstep.

"My name is Ginny Polk. I'm from the prison."

"Mighty fancy car for prison folk."

"Oh, it's not mine, ma'am. I borrowed my mama's car because I was afraid mine wouldn't make a trip this far out," Ginny said.

"Jonesville isn't a place people visit on purpose. Most of us are here because we always been here."

"Yes, but I'm here to talk about your grandson."

"Samuel will be dead this time next week," she said.

"That's why—"

"We won't be going to the execution if that's what you're here about." The woman's lips disappeared into a hard line.

Frustrated by the interruptions, Ginny blurted out her mission in one breath. "Yes, ma'am, but I'm a cook at the prison. I wanted to fix something special for Samuel's last meal, but he said he doesn't want anything. I was hoping you might tell me what foods he used to like."

The old woman appeared to be chewing on Ginny's words. Soon her soft laugh grew into a hoarse cackle that held more rancor than humor. "Why the hell you care what a man eats the day he dies?"

"It's what I do—"

"Oh, it's 'what you do,'" she mimicked. "You go all soft on the young inmates? Have pity on them?"

"It's not like that." Ginny looked away from Mrs. LeBoux and toward the car. She tried to put herself in the woman's shoes. How'd she feel if a complete stranger appeared at the door wanting to talk recipes when one of her loved ones was about to die? Ginny thought to tell her about the other death row inmates and the dishes they'd asked for, but couldn't see how that'd persuade the old woman to listen.

"You here about Samuel?" The young black girl joined them on the porch, but she'd left the child inside. "I'm his girlfriend, Eileen."

Ginny stood and offered a hand, but the girl backed away, sticking her hands in her shorts' pockets. She may have been Samuel's age, but looked closer to fifteen or sixteen.

"Yes, I work in the kitchen at the prison. It's customary to grant a prisoner one last meal of his choosing. I thought I'd ask his family for advice on what he might like."

"He won't tell you himself?"

Ginny shook her head and sat back down.

"Ain't that just like him, Grammy?" Eileen sat down on the third rocker and reached for the older woman's hand.

"Mrs. LeBoux?" Ginny asked.

"Call me Aida."

"Ma'am, I don't really know why the last suppers are so important to me. Maybe it's a sign of respect. You know . . . acknowledging the person's a human being no matter what crimes he may have committed."

Aida held tightly to Eileen's hand. She'd clearly taken the black girl in as family. That was a risk in the South and especially a small town like Jonesville. But Eileen's son was a remembrance of Samuel and something they'd always share. Ginny found the sight comforting. That kind of compassion was rare.

"I can't really think of him being there. The heartache is too much," Aida said.

"Have you seen him lately?" Ginny asked.

"No, his sisters are afraid of the place, and I just can't bear it," she said. "Eileen thought about visiting. You know, to tell him about the child."

"I thought it'd break his heart. Make it worse." Eileen held a hand to her chin to stop its trembling. "But maybe we made a mistake."

"Samuel was a good boy," Aida said. "Really became the man of the family when his folks died. Those sisters of his, though, they're wild and sometimes mean-spirited. Not Samuel."

Ginny's conversations with inmate families often took this turn. They wanted her to know there was goodness in their son's or husband's or grandchild's heart. It's as if they wanted to make them more human even though she never saw them as monsters. Not even those who committed the most heinous acts. When Ginny cooked for them, she tried to honor that little piece their families always recalled.

"He never hit me once," Eileen said. "Nope, not once. My other boyfriends did, but not Samuel. He was kind to me. Made me feel good about myself. He wasn't ashamed I was black."

Ginny let Aida and Eileen share their memories for several minutes before bringing the conversation back to why she'd come.

"Samuel ate everything I put in front of him," Aida said. "I don't recall him liking one thing more than another. He had an appetite, though. He always wanted seconds or thirds."

It was easy to picture Aida over a hot stove, preparing suppers for her grandchildren. What were those meals like? Did those aromas bind their memories to Aida and the home she made for them? Ginny thought back to her own mother's kitchen and the absence of feeling in that space. Miriam's cooking rarely brought comfort and sometimes not even sustenance.

Some of Ginny's fondest memories were of her daddy enjoying a good dessert, his mouth open in a wide grin as he devoured cakes and pies and cobblers. Miriam would chastise him that his sweet tooth was as long as summer and that they'd go poor buying so much butter and sugar.

A year after her daddy's murder, Ginny decided she'd learn to make a different dessert each week to honor him. She developed a knack in the kitchen and rarely had to throw out a recipe gone wrong. Miriam's hips grew wider with each month until she forbade Ginny from baking altogether. She told her she might as well learn to cook suppers instead. Ginny's confidence soared with each successful stew or roast or meatloaf. Instinctively, she knew when she could alter a recipe to make it her own and when she needed to follow it faithfully. Miriam rarely complimented her. That was all right with Ginny. She had been cooking for her daddy all along. She pictured him at the table, digging into her meals as if they were the best thing he'd ever eaten.

"Your pork neck stew," Eileen said, interrupting Ginny's thoughts.

"What about it?" Aida asked.

"It was his favorite."

"And how do you know that, child?"

Ginny sat forward in the rocker.

"One day after football practice, I asked Samuel to come to my house," Eileen said. "I remember he said nothing could keep him from his grammy's pork neck stew. I asked, 'Not even this body?' He said, 'Not even you, sweetheart.'"

"Could I have a copy of the recipe?" Ginny asked.

"Recipe? There ain't no recipe." Aida's smile returned.

"Well, could you tell me a little about it? I'd

like to try to duplicate it." She was close to getting what she wanted. Although Ginny's heart beat faster, she found her breathing was much easier. She wouldn't let down Samuel after all.

The woman's laugh was genuine this time. "Just 'cause I tell you what to put in a pot, don't mean it'll taste the same as something I've been making since I was twelve years old."

"Then show her, Grammy. Please?" Eileen knelt by Aida's rocker, almost in supplication. "Let's do it for Samuel."

Ginny couldn't believe her ears and almost knelt at Aida's knee as well. "Would you really consider teaching me? I'd be honored. And I'm happy to pay for the fixings."

Eileen didn't wait for Aida to answer. She got up and pointed at the Cadillac. "I know where to get the pork necks. You drive."

Eileen and Ginny followed Aida around the hot kitchen as she prepped the ingredients. Her movements were swift and decisive, but her gait was slow as she shifted from one foot to the other. Ginny scribbled down what she saw and would've written more except she was worried about missing a step. First, Aida seasoned the pork necks before browning them in lard. The sizzling pork fat danced from the pot onto the skin of Ginny's arm. Aida swatted her away when she added onion, celery, and water, but Ginny hovered close enough to guess the quantities of each. Salt and pepper were added in quick dashes. When she asked how much, Aida just shook her head. The old woman then covered dry lima beans with boiling water and left them soaking before suggesting they all sit on the front porch to cool off.

Eileen brought out checkers, so they played several games. The aroma of stewed meat drifted out, teasing Ginny's already growling stomach. When it was time to add the soaked beans to the pig necks, she trailed Aida back into the kitchen, not caring if she was being a nuisance.

They returned to the porch with hard salami and saltines to snack on. The women finally asked questions Ginny figured they'd have already asked by then.

"You stay and watch 'em die, when you could just make the food and be done with it?" Eileen asked.

Miriam asked the same question every time Ginny attended an execution. Even though she'd been responsible for making her daughter witness the first one at age eight, she now seemed horrified Ginny would subject herself to such gruesome proceedings as an adult.

"I think of it as bearing witness to the end of a man's life," Ginny said. "I'm not family or law enforcement. I'm just a fellow human being."

Some years ago, she started taking down

the inmates' last words and adding them to the official records. Roscoe felt better knowing there was a valid reason for her presence in the chamber. He didn't have to explain over and over why Ginny insisted on staying.

"You saw seventeen men go to the electric chair?" Eileen's eyes were large and wet.

"Eighteen if you count the man who murdered my daddy."

"When your daddy die?" Eileen asked.

"Many years ago. I was eight."

"And they let a little girl see something like that?" she asked.

Ginny nodded.

"I'd have nightmares if I had to watch such a thing." Aida shuddered.

It was too difficult for Ginny to explain the nature of her nightmares. Rarely were they about the act of killing. Instead, she was haunted by the families who watched their loved ones die. Their fear and anger usually surpassed that of the death row inmate's emotions, and it was a horrible thing to witness. Yet, she could always tell from their eyes the exact moment they let go of the terror they felt leading up to the execution. After their husbands or fathers or brothers slumped lifeless in the electric chair, loved ones could get on with the process of grieving and leave Greenmount behind for good. Or, that was Ginny's hope.

Aida and Eileen went silent. Most folks did

when they learned a child had been allowed to view an execution. Or, they'd start in on Miriam being an unfit parent to insist on such a thing. In those instances, Ginny grew tired of coming up with excuses and let them judge her mama all they wanted.

The morning of her daddy's execution, ignorance kept Ginny from resisting much. The day took on the flavor of an Easter morning. They ate a hearty breakfast of eggs and ham steak before putting on their best Sunday dresses and shoes. Miriam swept her hair up in a tight chignon and affixed her church veil with a pearl-tipped hat pin even though they weren't headed to mass. Ginny's uncles arrived that morning with much fanfare, whooping and hollering and honking the horn as they pulled up. Ginny and her mother treated the occasion with the solemnity of Easter, while the men treated it with the raucousness of Independence Day.

Once they'd arrived at the building where the execution would take place, a crowd of people blocked the view of the door. As soon as they recognized Miriam, they parted as if she and Ginny were celebrities. The guards and some wives grabbed for her hand while others screamed out, "Justice for Joe!"

All these years later, Ginny wondered if taking one life for another meant justice had been served.

"So, Samuel will be number nineteen?" Eileen asked.

"Pardon me?"

"The nineteenth person you'll see die." Eileen began to cry softly, so Aida pulled her to her breast. They hugged each other across the arms of their rocking chairs.

"I don't mean to upset you," Ginny said.

"No worries, child," Aida said. "She has a lot of crying to do and it won't stop after next week."

"You think God forgives us when we die?" Eileen wiped her wet cheeks, but new tears just took the place of those she'd cleared. "I don't want Samuel to go to hell."

Ginny didn't have an answer. But Roscoe believed in God, and he believed enough in forgiveness to minister to men on death row who wanted to make peace before the end.

"The warden thinks so. He often sits with the inmates and reads Scripture," she said, divulging a piece of Roscoe's private life she probably shouldn't have. "He said many of the men are truly repentant."

There was another reason Ginny stayed to view the men die, but she could never find the right words to explain it, even to Roscoe. When she was a child, her grandma Nan had said a person's soul drifted up from his body at the moment of death and some folks could see it. When Ginny watched her father's murderer die, she prayed to see a wisp of smoke, a flash of white light, *anything* to prove there was a merciful God. Perhaps it was a foolish notion, but at every execution since then, her eyes sought out such signs.

"I have to believe Samuel's sorry for what he done and that he's going to a better place," Aida said. "I have to believe it."

"Will you be picking up the body?" Ginny asked. The prison gave families the option of retrieving their loved ones for private burial or having them interned at the prison.

Eileen winced at the word *body,* causing Ginny to regret her question instantly.

"No," Aida said. "He'll be buried at the prison. There will be a little service here at the Baptist church. Don't need no casket and don't need no grave to visit every day. We'll keep Samuel in our hearts."

Aida's hand lingered over her chest, and Eileen mimicked the gesture almost subconsciously.

From time to time, Ginny wondered if her daddy's death would have been easier to handle if she just believed he was in Heaven, as Miriam insisted. Ginny resented having to visit his grave at the Boucherville cemetery as if they were calling on a relative for Sunday tea. Still, if he wasn't in the grave and wasn't in Heaven, she had nowhere to place him in her mind. As a child struggling with the finality of death, she soon formed her own beliefs. One being it was more important to do something worthwhile when she was still alive than to mourn those who were already gone.

Samuel's younger sisters were due back any minute from their summer jobs at the feed store. Aida begged Ginny to stay and eat dinner with them, but she was already woefully late in getting back to Miriam's. Before leaving, Ginny did, however, take a few bites of the delicious stew and made notes on the final blended flavors: earthy, oniony, a tad on the salty side. Aida hadn't bothered to skim off any excess fat, so the tender lima beans were oily on the tongue—perfect if one had cornbread to soak it up.

"You do a good job for my boy," Aida instructed. Her voice cracked slightly, but she didn't cry. Most older folks Ginny had met were hardened by life and thought tears pointless. At her daddy's funeral, her own grandmother had pinched Miriam's elbow and told her to hold it in.

"I'll do my best." Ginny hugged Aida first, then Eileen.

She had already started the car when Eileen jumped off the porch and ran toward her waving something.

"Please, Ginny. Give this to Samuel when you see him." She thrust a creased photo through the window. "Tell him he has a son. Thaddeus.

Named after my granddaddy. Tell him we won't ever forget him."

Ginny nodded, too choked up to speak. As she turned out of the driveway, her eyes avoided the rearview mirror and the two women she'd spent an afternoon with. She wondered just how many years of this work she had in her.

The sun had set by the time Ginny got back to Boucherville. She'd forgotten to add gasoline to the tank. Her mind had been preoccupied: where to purchase the pig necks, whether she had time for a dry run of the recipe before Samuel's execution just three days away, when to give him the photo of his son. Miriam was the least of her worries. She'd just have to leave her mama some money and put up with whatever chastising awaited.

Ginny's stomach turned a somersault when she saw her car wasn't the only vehicle in the driveway. Roscoe's prison truck was parked so close to her Chevy their bumpers appeared to touch. She eased the Cadillac past both vehicles and under the carport.

Even with her eyes trained on the steering wheel, she could still make out Roscoe standing near her mama's porch, his arms crossed. Ginny got out of the car and walked back toward the front yard to face him.

"What you doing here?" she asked, going on the defensive.

"I got worried when you didn't return to the prison before dark, so I called your mama. She told me you didn't make it to Baton Rouge after all."

"That's my business, Roscoe."

"When you lied to me this morning, you made it my business."

Frustration, more than anger, tinged his words. It seemed like the weight of their relationship made him more tired than he'd ever been.

"I only lied because I didn't want to upset you." She took two steps toward Roscoe, but he backed up to keep distance between them.

"Look where that got you." Miriam offered her commentary from the front porch.

"Shut up, Mama."

"This isn't her fault." Roscoe took off his hat, revealing sweaty dark hair plastered close to his scalp.

"Why would anyone be at fault?" Ginny asked. "I didn't do anything wrong. I'm a grown woman and can do as I like."

He shook his head as if he had a retort, but it never made it to his mouth. The sinking feeling in her stomach grew heavier. It pained Ginny to think she'd upset Roscoe. He struggled with enough at the prison without seeing her as a nuisance or an outright problem.

"Can we talk later?" she asked. "This is none of Mama's business."

"See how she disrespects me, Roscoe? Joe would never have stood for it."

"Joe's dead, Miriam, so you don't know what he would and wouldn't have stood for."

Ginny smiled at Roscoe's retort, but his scowl said, *Watch yourself.*

"You have no right to talk to me that way," Miriam told him. "Not after what we've been through."

"Been through what?" Ginny asked.

"Nothing. Just your dad's death and all," Roscoe said.

Ginny looked from Roscoe to her mama to try to decipher what hidden language they might share.

"And you got no right to be mad at me for telling Roscoe you went to Jonesville," Miriam said. "Shouldn't have lied and told your boyfriend you were going to Baton Rouge."

She used the word *boyfriend* the way another person might use a curse word. Not a hundred words spoken between them and she'd riled Ginny up to the point she wanted to rip the blooms off all the black-eyed Susans along the fence line.

"Why does it always have to be like this?" Ginny asked.

"Like what?"

"Like this! What do you have against me and Roscoe? It has nothing to do with you."

Her mama's jawline hardened. "Nothing to do with me? Oh, little girl. Your father and I were friends with Roscoe long before you started up with him."

"Miriam—" Roscoe pointed at her mama, almost as if in warning.

"It doesn't matter now, Mama. We really do need to be going."

Roscoe touched Ginny's shoulder. "Come on and ride with me in the truck," he said. "I don't want you on the road at night. I'll have Tim get your car tomorrow."

She wanted to keep her car so she could sneak away after breakfast to find those pig necks for Samuel's meal. Not wanting to rock the boat, she nodded and headed toward the truck. She could always drive back to town the next afternoon.

"And good night to you, too!" her mama called from the porch. Neither of them said a word back to her.

Roscoe flicked ashes from his cigarette out the window. Since Ginny couldn't read his face in the dark, she watched the end of the cigarette flare with every draw he took. He'd started smoking again. Stress always loosened his resolve.

She couldn't get her mama's words out of her mind. *Your father and I were friends with Roscoe long before you started up with him.*

Her mother hadn't really said anything Ginny

didn't already know. Roscoe and her daddy had been inseparable, at work and in the evenings, too. Roscoe was always over at their prison residence drinking beer or having dinner. As a young child, Ginny recognized that both her mama and daddy seemed happier when Roscoe was around. She'd come to look forward to his visits just so Miriam wouldn't be so short. Ginny tried to remember whether or not her mama flirted with Roscoe or he with her. The laughter they shared was the strongest memory, not their faces.

After her father was killed, when she and Miriam moved from the prison housing and into town, Roscoe would check in on them. He'd stay for dinner sometimes, but they didn't laugh the same way they had when her daddy was alive. Roscoe loaned Miriam money from time to time. Ginny used to think he had purchased the Cadillac for them as well, but Miriam insisted the money for it came from the prison, in reparation for her father's death. If the prison had intended those payments to help with living expenses, they didn't know her mama that well.

Ginny fondly remembered Roscoe always giving her a dollar and a pat on the head as he left the house. But he stopped coming by after a couple of years. He did show up for her high school graduation, but by then he seemed more a stranger than Uncle Roscoe.

Now, his anger seemed a wall between them.

"I wish you'd understand," she said.

"You ask a lot of me, Ginny."

She scooted across the seat and laid her head on his shoulder, hoping he wouldn't push her away. He didn't.

"Are you worried the prison board's going to find out about the meals?"

"They already know," he said.

The news caught her off guard. She moved back to her side of the truck, trembling. "What's going to happen?"

"Let me worry about it," he said, roughly.

"You have to worry about everything. Tell me what I can do."

He stared at the road, not even turning occasionally to look at her. "Short of stopping those meals, nothing."

Closing her eyes, Ginny shut out Roscoe and the conversation, listening instead to the hum of tires against asphalt. She couldn't stop cooking. Her heart would break if Roscoe outright asked her to quit. Surely, he knew better than most how much it meant to her.

"There was another death today," he finally said. "And another inmate almost dead. Probably won't make it through the night."

By death, he meant murder—a beating that went too far. Either by his guards or the inmates who were given power to serve as guards themselves.

Somewhere along the way, some genius thought it was a good idea to arm inmates and allow them to keep their own in line. Their violence far surpassed those of civilian guards and created its own power structure. Roscoe had always thought inmate guards were a bad idea, but didn't voice his opinion when he was just a guard himself. After his promotion to warden, he recommended doing away with inmate guards and hiring more civilian staff. The state was big on reform talk, but not on action. The recommendation was soundly denied.

"I'm sorry, Roscoe."

"Nothing to be sorry about. It is what it is."

With each year Roscoe served as warden, he grew less hopeful one man could make a difference. In 1951, he had a dozen paid guards and 600 unpaid convict guards, which took far less money from the state's pocket than Roscoe's original plan for 150 guards overseen by ten captains. Eight years later, he'd been allowed just under eighty guards total.

"I'm more worried about you," he said.

She lifted her head from his shoulder. "Why me?"

Even in the dark, she could see he shook his head.

"You take things too far. You don't even know why."

"This isn't about Daddy." She'd said those

words so often she'd almost begun to believe the lie. But the last suppers were tied to him, or at least his killer's execution. Roscoe thought Ginny was trying to make up for something—like she believed the family of her daddy's murderer blamed her somehow.

"Roscoe, if I'm not hurting anyone, why does it matter why I do the things I do?"

"You don't think straight."

"I don't know what you mean—"

"Tim told me you coerced him into taking you to see LeBoux," he said. "I told you to leave it alone, but you went behind my back. Tim's probably flapping his mouth to anyone who'll listen."

Her face burned hot. She didn't intend to undermine Roscoe's authority. She pushed it too often, thinking their relationship gave her privileges.

"You make me look weak, Ginny. It's got to stop," he said.

"I don't know why Samuel's indifference bothers me so much. His family was just so grateful I wanted to do something special for him. I was late getting back because his grandmother was showing me how to cook pork neck stew—"

"Listen to yourself. You're getting excited all over again. This is about how it makes you feel. Not how it makes Samuel feel."

She would have insisted it wasn't true, but she

knew otherwise by the tightness in her chest. Ginny was just too embarrassed to admit it. Every death row inmate accepted her offer of a last meal. Samuel's rejection felt personal.

She thought back to what she'd told Aida. *It's what I do.* The line between doing something kind for a desperate man and doing something solely for herself had blurred along the way.

"Sam asked to see me today. He wants you to leave him alone," Roscoe said. "*I* want you to leave him alone."

They asked the unthinkable of her. What about Samuel's baby son? And his favorite dish? She'd promised his grammy she'd do a good job of the recipe. She'd promised.

She slid back over to her side of the seat and leaned her head against the window, trying to slow her breath. "He doesn't know he has a son. His girlfriend asked me to tell him."

"Can't you please let this one go?"

Ginny wondered what that meant—to let one go. She never thought one inmate was less deserving of a last meal than another. She never took into account their crimes. Giving up on Samuel—on any one of them—was unfathomable.

She wanted to erase the image of Eileen clutching that photo, begging her to tell the man she loved he was a father. It was no longer clear what Samuel deserved to know. He'd murdered a man who was also a father, and stole precious time he could have spent with his children and grandchildren.

"He just wants it to be over. And that's his right," Roscoe said. "Did you ever think having a meal that reminds him of his grandma and learning he has a boy of his own might make it even harder on him?"

"I don't know," she said. "All I can do is imagine being in their position, and ask myself what I'd want. And I'd want one last human connection."

"That's because you don't think something better is waiting after we die," he said.

"Then let it be about human decency."

"You act like these men are the same as you and me. Don't forget they're on death row for a reason. They're the ones lacking human decency."

They didn't speak the rest of the drive, and he didn't kiss Ginny good night when he dropped her off at the women's barracks.

1951

She Won't Make It Easy on Anyone

Roscoe Simms felt older than his forty-two years. He'd only been warden for two months and the job had stooped his shoulders and caused a permanent case of sour stomach. It had been a particularly rough week, and the last thing he wanted to do was meet with Miriam's daughter.

Miriam had called just two days earlier asking if he'd consider hiring a woman for one of the kitchen jobs. He figured she was asking for herself and was surprised when she said her daughter, Ginny, wanted the post.

"She's a hell of a cook. You won't find better," Miriam had said. "But she won't make it easy on anyone."

Roscoe hadn't bothered to ask what she meant. He hadn't spoken to Miriam since the night of Ginny's high school graduation three Junes ago. That was the last time he saw the girl, too. Even though he promised Joe he'd look after them both, it got too complicated and soon months turned into years.

He sent a guard to meet Ginny at the main prison gate and escort her to his office. After a few minutes, she was standing in his doorway, holding out her hand for a formal handshake.

"I suppose I need to call you Warden Simms," she said.

"Probably best."

Roscoe couldn't get over how much she looked like her father had at twenty-one. Hair like a squirrel's nest, a strong chin, eyes a little too large for her face. She didn't get Joe's height, though, or Miriam's curves for that matter.

"May I sit down, or should we stare at each other a little longer?" she asked.

He laughed out loud. "You have your daddy's mouth."

The girl turned ten shades of purple. "I'm sorry. I didn't mean for it to come out that way," she said.

"Don't matter to me. At least when we're alone," he said. "But if you get this job, I'd be your boss. I can't have the people who work for me smarting off or being disrespectful."

"I understand." She sat straight up, her fierce eyes locked on his. "It won't happen again."

Miriam's comment came rushing back to him: She won't make it easy on anyone. Roscoe began to wonder what can of worms he'd opened in even agreeing to see her today. The least he could do is describe the nature of the job and why he'd let the former head cook go.

"I read about the prison reforms in the paper,"

Ginny said. "Terrible about those men who maimed themselves."

He winced. The incident would be the first thing everyone remembered when the prison was mentioned. Truth be told, Roscoe almost didn't accept the promotion to warden because of it. The new governor had used prison reform in almost every damn stump speech. Even the folks in town began to treat the guards differently, as if they were criminals themselves. Hypocrites. Everyone knew what went on. Louisianans had long scared their boys into behaving by threatening prison time. They looked the other way until the press got involved. Suddenly, Boucherville was best known as the town closest to the penitentiary.

A few of the men quit rather than deal with a new warden, whom they were sure would come from the outside. No one was more surprised than Roscoe when the prison board recommended his appointment.

"Ginny, I have to ask . . . why in the hell would you want to work in a prison?" *And especially this one?*

"Do I even have a shot at this job, or are you meeting with me as a favor to Mama? If it's the latter, I don't want to waste any more of your time explaining my reasons."

Of course he'd agreed to it to appease Miriam. But now, for reasons he couldn't comprehend, he found himself wanting to hear more from this young woman who reminded him so much of his dead best friend.

"Let me show you the kitchen," Roscoe said. "We can talk on the way."

Once given free rein to speak, Ginny took every advantage, peppering him with questions until he was exhausted. She tested the stoves and inspected the pantry. She asked intelligent questions about the farm and the canning facility, the kitchen's budget, how many prisoners worked in the kitchen and how they were selected, how many hours the cooks worked, and whether the cooks had some say in what and how much the prisoners ate.

By the end of an hour, he felt she'd interviewed him and not vice versa. He suggested they take a drive in his truck so he could show her the grounds. She'd lived in the guard housing until she was eight, but he didn't know how much she remembered.

"There's sandwich makings at the warden's residence," Roscoe said. "Let's grab a bite to eat and finish talking there."

"You say warden's residence as if it's not your house," she said.

"I don't stay there much. There's a small room with a bathroom in the admin building. I just sleep there."

"Hmmm."

She didn't expand on her muffled grunt and he wasn't about to ask what she meant by it. He drove them past the houses where guards with families could choose to live. Most didn't.

"Is anyone living in Mama's and Daddy's old house?" she asked.

"Nope. Why do you ask?"

"Can we stop there?"

Ginny jumped from the truck as soon as he cut the engine. She ran up to the small front porch and looked through the window.

"Go on in," he said. "I'll wait out here."

Roscoe sat on the porch steps he and Joe had sat on many an evening, drinking beer and listening to baseball on the transistor radio. They hardly ever spoke about what had happened during their shifts, as if they'd made a pact not to speak it aloud. Miriam would usually be inside making dinner while Ginny, then only six or seven, would play in the front yard. Calling it a yard was being generous. The dusty patch of hard ground had nary a blade of grass. Sometimes she'd jump on Joe's lap and beg for a slug of beer. He'd oblige if she promised not to tell her mama. In those moments, Joe almost seemed a decent man, capable of at least loving his daughter.

Now that the house was empty, Roscoe could hear Ginny's footfalls as she walked from empty room to empty room. Her voice echoed as she yelled out her observations about the place needing paint and a good scrubbing.

When she rejoined him a few minutes later, he edged over so she could sit beside him on the stoop.

"I remember you and Daddy out here," she said. "You ate with us a lot, didn't you?"

"Quite a bit." He kicked his heel against the dirt. "You haven't been back here since, have you?"

"Nah, Mama said there was no reason to come back to a place that had killed her husband."

Joe hadn't died at the prison, but rather just outside of Baton Rouge, in the dark of night and off duty. Yet, Miriam blamed the prison and probably would until the day she died.

"Your mama says you know your way around the kitchen," he said.

"I bet she had a lot more than that to say." Ginny cut her eyes away from him. "She gave me a piece of her mind when I told her I wanted to work here."

"I'm a bit curious myself. I figured you'd have bad memories of this place. Maybe never want to come back." Roscoe was surprised how much he enjoyed being in her company and wanted her to keep talking. He regretted he'd stopped checking on her just because he and Miriam had split ways. He'd let Joe down. Still, the girl seemed to turn out all right—confident and smart. It's not like he would have had much influence on a strong-willed teen.

"It has nothing to do with having good or bad memories," she said. "I need a job and I can cook."

"You have other options."

"Most jobs require experience, and you can't get experience without having a job," she said. "It'd give me a start. Don't guess you have people beating down your door to take the job."

"You'd make only $180 a month," he said.

"That's $180 more than I make now."

That mouth again.

"I don't see how working in a prison kitchen's going to translate to the real world," he said. It sounded like he was trying to talk her out of wanting to work here, but nothing was further from the truth.

"It'd show I could run a large kitchen, manage supplies, and handle supervising," she said. "If I'm tough enough to survive this place, I can make it anywhere."

Ginny was gutsy, but he wondered how she'd manage in such a cruel environment. She'd always have less than she needed to do her job, she'd be ridiculed for her size and sex, and she'd be exposed to the side of man's nature prisons were supposed to keep locked away.

"It'd be hard on you, girl." He looked out at

the dull white buildings that blended into the dirt around them. "It'll change you."

"Has it changed you?" There she was again, staring at him with those too-big brown eyes, challenging him to answer. Poking at him, like Joe used to do.

" 'Course it's changed me," he said. "You got to worry about the people it doesn't."

"Did it change Daddy?"

He stood and pointed to the truck. "I'm getting hungry. Let's get those sandwiches."

She was smart enough to stop pressing him, and he appreciated the silence while he gathered his thoughts. If he decided to hire Ginny, he'd be entering dangerous territory. Her questions about her daddy wouldn't stop. And there were too many Roscoe didn't dare answer. Like the real reason Joe died that night outside Baton Rouge.

Chapter 4

Just before daybreak, Dot stirred in her room, clearly not caring how loud her movements were. Ginny grabbed a blouse and was just buttoning it when Dot entered her room without knocking.

"Heard you hollerin' in your sleep last night," she said.

"Pay me no mind. It's nothing," Ginny said.

"It ain't nothing if you can't get away from it."

Both Roscoe and Dot worried that two decades after the murder of Ginny's father, she still had nightmares a couple of times a week. They figured the worst ones were about watching a man being executed. That wasn't it at all. The worst ones were those where she ran toward the young son of her father's murderer and begged his forgiveness. He'd just stare at Ginny with accusation in his eyes. She'd say, "It's not my fault. Please don't hate me. Your daddy killed my daddy." And he'd say, "And now you've killed mine."

Ginny shook off the memory of the dream and pulled a skirt over her slip. Her hair stuck out in every direction. She tried to smooth it with her palms, but its strong will frustrated her to no end.

"Here, let me," Dot said. She worked the hair into one braid and wound it into a low knot at the base of Ginny's neck. "Hand me those bobby pins."

Dot grabbed several, storing them between her lips while her hands were occupied. The hair was soon secured so tightly it'd not come loose in a hurricane. Ginny shook her head a few times to prove its staying power. Sometimes she wished Dot would take her time. Just the act of being touched made Ginny feel safe and loved.

Ginny liked that Dot was sleeping at the barracks more often. She mostly stayed at her son's home on the weekend so she could be near her grandchildren. Lately, though, Dot remained at the prison all week to avoid her daughter-in-law, a woman whose temperament made the prison feel almost inviting.

"Let me make the bed and then we can go," Ginny said.

Dot didn't mind waiting. Ginny was sure her friend understood that little things mattered a lot. That's why she helped Ginny paint her room a ghastly shade of pink she'd warned was too bright, and why she helped her hang floral curtains only Dot and Roscoe and Ginny would ever see, and why she brought books from the library every time she returned from her weekend visits to her son's. Ginny's room was home. And Dot helped make it feel that way.

"We making cornmeal mush for breakfast?" her friend asked.

Ginny nodded. "Yes, plus let's add some pork fat."

They walked along the gravel path to the kitchen, a brisk ten-minute walk because the women's barracks was isolated from the rest of the prison buildings to ensure their safety. But she and Dot didn't mind. It gave them time to prepare mentally for the day ahead.

As the two women worked, Ginny described her afternoon with Samuel's grandmother. Dot listened raptly to the list of ingredients that had been jotted down in great detail.

"I make a similar stew," she said. "But there's okra and tomatoes in mine."

"Where do you get the pork necks?" Ginny quit stirring the cornmeal.

"Any butcher shop should have 'em. The one on Lester Avenue usually does. Didn't your mama ever cook pork necks?"

Ginny laughed. "Mama doesn't like to cook, but she was a fine baker. Boy, did Daddy love her pies. After he died, she stopped baking altogether. I guess she thought it was pointless with just me in the house."

"How'd you get to be such a good cook then?"

"I started baking desserts, pretending they were for Daddy. But Mama grew tired of that and said

I should be cooking supper instead. So I started to read cookbooks like they were storybooks. I remember borrowing cookbooks from the ladies in the neighborhood," Ginny said. "I'd hurry and copy some of the recipes in a notebook before they came around asking for them."

Those women weren't Miriam's friends and would have never come around otherwise. Ginny had thought they felt sorry for her because of her daddy's murder. As an adult, Ginny wondered if they had felt sorrier that Miriam was her mama. Just as prison kids were ostracized at school, Miriam bore the stigma of being a prison guard's wife. It didn't matter that she and Miriam had left Greenmount behind. Once part of the prison, always part of the prison.

"You have that notebook still?" Dot asked.

"Maybe. It'd be at Mama's house, I guess. Why?"

"Because those recipes could give you ideas for your own cookbook."

Ginny suspected Dot would not let it go, no matter how much she protested.

"I promise to think about it, but let's concentrate on that cornmeal mush."

Together, they cooked several large pots. The one Ginny worked on stiffened up too quickly, so she added some beef broth, not wanting to waste what little milk was left in the icebox. Dot finished frying up bits of fatty pork leavings and then added them to each of the pots. Ginny sampled some from each batch and added quite a bit more salt.

"Wish we had some maple syrup or honey," she murmured.

"This ain't a restaurant," Dot said.

"I know, but a little sweet would complement the pork fat."

Dot shook her head and smiled.

"What?" Ginny asked. "I think of cooking like solving a puzzle. Certain ingredients just fit together better than others. Sometimes it's one last piece that makes all the difference."

"Well, I been cooking a hell of a lot longer than you and you still manage to surprise me with what you throw together, or how you can stretch a little bit of something into a meal."

Dot's good opinion mattered to Ginny and she blushed, although she knew the compliment was mainly to bolster the argument for that damn cookbook.

"I really need to get those pork necks," Ginny said, looking at the clock.

"Go. I can finish up breakfast," Dot said. "And we have plenty of cabbage soup leftover from yesterday to serve for lunch."

Ginny kissed Dot on the cheek and hung her apron on the hook near the door. When she turned, she ran headlong into Roscoe, who stood in the kitchen doorway.

"How long have you been standing there?" Her face flushed.

"What does that matter?"

The air between her and Roscoe hung heavy with unfinished business from the night before, but they both knew it wasn't the time or place to get into it. Things would get much worse, though, if he'd overheard her comments about leaving to buy pork necks.

"Good morning, Dot." Roscoe tipped his head in greeting, but then turned back to Ginny. "Tim's in the truck. He'll take you to Miriam's to get your car."

Dot's soft chuckling caused Roscoe and Ginny to turn with puzzled looks.

"What's funny?" Ginny asked.

"You two, that's what."

"Go on," Roscoe said, not understanding as Ginny did that Dot's honesty was rarely filtered with niceties.

"You're both acting uppity, like two badgers waiting to see who strikes first," she said. "You've been together too long for such foolishness. I guess it's expected given that you're both pigheaded."

"Dot, you forget your place," Roscoe said without a trace of ire in his voice. He liked Dot as much as Ginny did, and was happy for her influence in Ginny's life. But he couldn't let insubordination pass without at least saying something.

"Yeah, yeah. That's twice in one week I've been reminded who my boss is. Don't think I don't know it." She moved closer to them, making Ginny think Dot might start shaking a finger at them. "My son and his wife don't like me meddling in their affairs. I guess it shouldn't be any different with you two."

"Well, Ginny isn't your daughter," Roscoe said.

Dot grunted and turned back to her work. "Uh-huh."

Ginny smiled as she followed Roscoe outside.

Tim's ingratiating politeness had worn on her the whole way to her mama's. Really, he just wanted forgiveness for telling Roscoe she'd gone to talk to Sam. Then he yammered on and on about Roscoe inviting him to have dinner at the residence when some of the prison board members visited next.

Mercifully, the drive was short. After leaving her mama's house, Ginny purchased the pork necks and headed straight back to the warden's residence. It wasn't the kind of day anyone in her right mind would want to spend in a kitchen, but the heat didn't bother her as it normally would.

She'd purchased six pounds of the meat, figuring it'd be enough for two batches: one for practice and one for Samuel. Leftovers always went to the guards on duty. They appreciated anything she cooked or baked.

Ginny laid out the pages of notes on the counter and put on an apron. Her heart beat soundly as a nervous feeling invaded her belly. Not a bad feeling, but like excitement and anticipation and worry all mixed together. The same feelings used to overwhelm her when she took exams in high school. Ginny knew the work and was a good student, but the anticipation of starting the exam almost made her throw up each time. Then, she'd get into a rhythm of answering the questions and her confidence would grow.

Trying new recipes gave her similar feelings. Angst and worry at the start, then pure joy in the middle, and finally an exhausted euphoria when the dish turned out as planned.

After the necks were simmering and the lima beans soaking in a separate pot of hot water, she took off the apron and retreated to the front porch. It became a game to identify the familiar sounds of the prison. As a cook, she used her sense of taste and smell so much, she worried the other senses would diminish if they weren't exercised once in a while.

The men working the fields were singing hymns. They were far enough away that the words were unintelligible, but a deep melody carried; as if all the men sang bass and were in need of a baritone or two. The singing could almost mask the sound of the beatings.

When temperatures topped 100, the birds rarely

sang. But today, a flurry of squawks rose and fell somewhere near the administration building, where the three largest trees on the prison property grew. Most likely, a predatory bird veered too close to the guarded nests.

Ginny opened her eyes and gazed across the gravel paths connecting the prison buildings. The heat distorted her vision, making the road appear shiny like melting lard. She didn't worry too much about losing her sense of sight because it was about as acute as her sense of taste. Still, she'd practice by trying to notice one new thing about a person every time she spoke to him or her. Folks often grew uncomfortable at the stares. Her observations might include one gray hair nestled in bushy black eyebrows, or a slight variation in color between two pupils, or that one cheek had more freckles than the other.

Roscoe sometimes worried that by working at the prison, Ginny had made her world smaller than it should be. But her senses gave her multiple worlds to explore. And as she'd told him many times, the prison wouldn't be her home forever. Although some days she wondered if that was true.

Once the lima beans had cooked with the pork, Ginny dared to taste the broth. She licked the greasy film from her lips and smiled. It was damn close to Aida's. It just needed more salt and black pepper. It was best to be stingy with the seasoning because she'd learned the hard way you couldn't truly undo oversalting, even by adding a potato.

She turned off the heat under the large stew pot and placed the pork necks on a cutting board to remove the meat from the bones and return it to the pot. That's when the front door slammed and Roscoe called her name.

A swinging door connected the kitchen to a formal dining room and they reached it at the same time. His brute force won out and the door met Ginny's face. The smack almost sent her to the floor. Regaining her balance, she reached for a dish towel to catch the blood rushing from her nose.

She sat down, holding her head back. "Goddamn it, Roscoe. Be careful, would you?"

"Why isn't the dining room table set? And why are you still in your work clothes?"

She thrust the bloody towel at him. "Don't worry about me. It's only blood. And my nose is probably not broken. Now what the hell are you jabbering about?"

"The prison board dinner. *Tonight*."

The dish rag dropped from her hand. She'd forgotten she had been tasked with cooking dinner for eight—and the guests would be arriving in less than an hour.

"Shit, are you sure it's not broken? Let me get some ice to help with the swelling," Roscoe said.

"Not now. Grab a tablecloth from the buffet and set the table. I'll make cornbread."

Roscoe did as he was told, but grudgingly. He grumbled and cursed under his breath. Ginny's hands shook every time a plate clanked against the tabletop. She was sure the dinner wasn't until next month. Had Roscoe mentioned the board was coming earlier?

When he came back into the kitchen, he was perspiring profusely. "If you forgot about the goddamn dinner, what's cooking on the stove?"

Ginny poured the cornbread batter into two round baking pans and didn't dare look up. "I was practicing the pork neck stew I told you about—you know, for Samuel."

She'd really done it this time. Her shoulders tensed and she waited for him to blow. Instead he walked over to the icebox and peered inside.

"What can you throw together for dessert?" He wiped his brow nervously. Gone was the urgency in his voice, as if he'd already determined the evening would be a disaster no matter what they did.

"Stop letting out the cold," she said. "We have fresh strawberries. I'll make some shortbread while you all eat. I'm sure we have whipping cream."

He closed the door to the icebox and pointed to the stew. "Is that any good?"

"Yes, I think it is. It'll have to do."

"I guess it will."

Roscoe stood stock-still while she put the cornbread in the oven. His stare bored into her skin.

"I can't find the words to tell you how sorry I am," she said. "I know how important this is to you."

He backed away when Ginny reached for his hand. "Obviously not as important as Samuel," he said.

As much as she wanted to curl up on the kitchen floor and cry, there was still too much to do. She didn't dare look at the clock as she finished pulling the pork from the bones and measuring out the ingredients for the shortbread. When Roscoe left in his truck, Ginny went to the dining room to check the table.

He'd done a pretty good job with the place settings despite all the noise he'd made. She added a napkin to each and retrieved the fan from the parlor. Set in the open window, facing out, perhaps it could draw some of the heat from the room.

She stepped out onto the porch for some fresh air. That's when Roscoe's truck careened up the dirt drive, clouds of dust in its wake. Dot sat in the front seat.

"He said you needed my help." She rinsed the strawberries and set the colander in the sink.

"He probably wanted you here so he wouldn't be tempted to kill me."

The attempt at a joke failed and Ginny's lip trembled. Dot hugged her, although the heat made the gesture sticky and uncomfortable.

"That man has been nothing but patient and gentle with you all these years, unless he gave you that bloody nose," she said, stroking Ginny's back.

"No, just bad timing with a swinging door."

"You're just having a bad day all around, aren't you?"

Ginny swiped at her tears. "A doozy and it's not over yet."

"Well, no time for crying," Dot said. "Let's see how the stew turned out."

Dot slurped a taste from a teaspoon, then tossed it in the sink. A few years back, Ginny had told her that chefs never lick their stirring spoons. Dot had been insulted and said, "I may have been raised in the country, but I know a thing or two about the real world. And I also know that when I'm cooking for inmates, they don't give a shit whether I lick a spoon or not."

"So, how is it?" Ginny asked anxiously.

"You know it's fine," Dot said. "Don't go fishing for compliments."

As delicious as the stew tasted, it wasn't the type of food usually prepared for the quarterly prison board dinners. Depending on the time of year, Ginny would make standing rib roasts or roasted pheasant or lamb shoulder chops. In the warmer months, they'd sometimes move the table under the big tree in the yard and have more simple fare like fried catfish and hush puppies.

Occasionally, board members invited their spouses to attend. They'd shower Ginny with compliments and ask for recipes. Once, a board member's wife asked if she'd consider becoming her personal cook. It was anyone's guess how tonight's dinner would be received.

Dot surveyed the kitchen, a keen eye assessing what else needed to get done. "There any iced tea in the fridge?"

Ginny shook her head no.

"Let's make some and add lots of lemon and whiskey to it. That'll make everything seem a little better," Dot said.

"You get the water boiling. I'll find the whiskey."

While Ginny mixed the tea, Dot chopped up two heads of lettuce and emptied a jar of chowchow over it. The vinegary mix of yellow squash, peppers, and cauliflower would serve as the dressing. She set a bowl of salad at each place setting and hurried back into the kitchen.

"Folks are driving up now," Dot said. "Two cars."

Ginny looked down at her wrinkled dress.

Despite wearing an apron, she'd managed to get grease stains on the bodice as well as a few drops of blood from her injured nose. Roscoe would be embarrassed if she set foot in the dining room this evening.

"You'll have to serve the stew and cornbread," Ginny said.

"Why me?"

"Look at me. And why do you think Roscoe asked you to change from your kitchen clothes?"

"Then you think I look nice?" Dot posed seductively, one hand on her hip and one on her head. She did look nice. The navy-blue dress camouflaged the curves Dot hated and played up those she liked.

"Thought you vowed never to wear that dress since you wore it to your husband's funeral," Ginny said.

"Seems a shame not to after all these years," Dot said. "And besides, I think he'd agree I look damn fine in it."

"Stop horsing around. We both have a job to do."

As Dot filled glasses with the spiked tea, Ginny kept her ear close to the door, listening to the guests. She held a hand against it, though, in case Dot stormed back into the kitchen.

"Something smells mighty good." A booming male voice stood out above the rest.

"We're not here for the cuisine," another male said. "And Roscoe knows it."

The scraping of chairs against the floor signaled the start to dinner. Ginny backed away from the door just as Dot returned.

"Five men, one woman, Roscoe, and that skinny boy who works in Roscoe's office," she said.

Tim. If Ginny had been listening more closely this morning on the drive into town, she would have realized he meant he was attending the prison board dinner *tonight.*

She opened the door just a crack. Roscoe paid inordinate attention to his salad as Russell Dunner, Superintendent of Corrections, spoke to him in a private conversation. Roscoe's face remained placid. The look was familiar. He'd retreated to a peaceful place in his mind, probably reliving a fishing trip to Catahoula Lake. Yet, if asked, Roscoe would still be able to repeat every word Dunner said. His brain worked like that.

The rest of the men ate their salads and made small talk. Ginny recognized a few faces but couldn't recall their names from previous dinners. Tim didn't say much, but appeared pleased as punch Roscoe invited him, like a child finally asked to sit at the grown-ups' table at Thanksgiving.

The woman had to be Dunner's new wife. Roscoe had mentioned some time ago that he remarried after his first wife died. She sat stiffly in her crisp linen suit with a pinched look on her face. She sniffed at the chowchow on her fork and set it back down without taking a bite.

Roscoe muttered a few more "yes, sirs" before the loud man spoke again.

"You hired Roscoe to be warden, now let him do his job." Salad dribbled down the man's chin as he spoke.

"We got no business keeping a warden who doesn't have the stomach for corrections," the superintendent said. "This ain't no hotel."

A bitter laugh escaped Ginny's lips. The prison was the furthest thing from a hotel. Just because Roscoe worked to improve living conditions and cracked down on the brutality of the guards, didn't make him a weak man or an ineffective warden.

Dunner continued his tirade. "And now he wants to separate first-timers. They're all god-damned convicts and they can live together."

It wasn't Roscoe alone who recommended the system. The thirty-four-member Citizens' Reform Committee proposed classifying inmates according to the types of crimes they committed—segregating the most violent. The prison nurse backed the recommendations. After all, she saw the men who suffered the repeated rapes and beatings. The eventual guidelines had three categories: the incorrigibles, the occasionally but not continuously turbulent and obstructive, and the majority.

"The incorrigibles? What a load of bullshit," Dunner said.

"He's just doing what the governor expects of him," the loud man continued. "He has to at least appear to implement reform. Now, where's dinner? My stomach is hollering for whatever's in that kitchen."

Dot and Ginny backed away from the door and filled bowls with steaming stew, making sure to put generous amounts of pork in each serving. Dot opened the swinging door with her backside, expertly juggling three bowls. She returned to the kitchen twice more until all the guests had their dinner.

"The cornbread," Ginny whispered. "You forgot the cornbread."

Dot hurriedly placed the pie-shaped wedges onto a serving platter and returned to the dining room. Ginny peered through the door just in time to see the superintendent's wife push back from the table and stand.

"I didn't agree to visit this godforsaken place just to eat nigger food!"

"Patricia, sit down," the superintendent said firmly.

"Don't tell me what to do!" She jumped to her feet, causing her chair to crash to the floor.

Two of the men suppressed smiles while Tim's cheeks flamed.

The woman's face grew as red as Tim's as she continued her rant. "All your wives kept on about how the little white gal at the prison kitchen was some world-class chef and the first time I come to one of these dinners, this slop is what's served? And cooked by a darkie?"

"It's mighty tasty, if you ask me." The loud man eyed Dot apologetically.

"Well, ma'am, this here stew was actually cooked by the little white gal you mentioned," Dot said in an icy tone. "It's only served by a darkie."

Roscoe stood up quickly. "Dorothy, not now."

"You're going to let her talk to me like that?" The superintendent's wife now directed her ire at Roscoe. "You're as weak as Russell said you were. You can't even control your colored staff." She accented her words with a rude finger poke each time.

"Dorothy, go see about dessert." Roscoe nodded to the swinging door to the kitchen. Ashamed that she'd been spying, Ginny pulled away from the door before he spotted her.

The superintendent's wife stormed out of the house and headed straight to the car, where she sat, seething. Dot and Ginny stood at the kitchen window watching the tirade unfold, while Roscoe and the superintendent exchanged words on the porch.

"World-class chef, huh?" Dot snorted. "And why's Roscoe calling me Dorothy all of a sudden? It's like he's putting on airs."

"Shhh. I want to hear what's being said."

"This night has been better than a picture show," Dot said. "Roscoe sure seems to be taking it well."

That remained to be seen, but he did seem the calmest of the whole lot of them, a trait that had attracted Ginny to him a long time ago. Her stomach, though, was the opposite of calm, churning at the thought of repercussions from Mrs. Dunner's reaction.

"I wouldn't want to be trapped in a car with that woman for the next two hours. No sirree." Dot stifled a giggle. "She's just like my daughter-in-law. Has a corncob stuck up her—"

The creak of the swinging door to the dining room startled them both and they turned at once.

"Any chance I could get seconds on the stew?" The loud man, a toothy smile on his face, stood with a bowl in his hands.

"Yes, sir, of course," Dot said. "Give me that bowl."

While Dot was at the stove, the man extended his hand to Ginny. "I'm Herbert Levy, one of the new board members. I've heard about your cooking skills and you didn't disappoint."

She wiped her hand on her apron before shaking his. "Nice to meet you, sir. I'm sorry I look such a fright. I didn't have time to freshen up before you arrived. The day got away from me."

"Don't worry yourself," he said, accepting his refilled bowl from Dot. "You get into a scrap today?"

"Excuse me?"

Herbert pointed to his nose.

"Just the dang swinging door into the dining room." She touched her nose gingerly.

"Well, I'll be extra careful heading back in there."

Before he returned to the dining room, he glanced back at them and winked.

"And, ladies? The rest of us wouldn't dream of missing dessert just because Mrs. Dunner lost her appetite."

Chapter 5

The rest of the dinner was uneventful. Dunner's wife couldn't be placated, so the couple had left almost immediately after her fit. The rest of the men finished off most of the stew and then all of the strawberry shortcake before bidding them good night. Ginny and Dot cleared the table and washed dishes while Roscoe sat on the porch, a glass of whiskey in his hand. He hadn't said a word, but was unlikely to do so while Dot was still around.

The women stepped outside when they were finished.

"Let me drive you back to your quarters," Roscoe said, standing.

"That's okay," Ginny said. "I have my car from earlier."

"I was talking to Dot," he said. "You're staying here tonight."

"Back to calling me Dot, are you?" She winked at Ginny.

"Go on ahead. I'll see you first thing in the morning." Ginny nodded toward the door. "And thanks for the help tonight." Dot's cool head had salvaged an otherwise disastrous evening. Ginny had never felt so grateful for her friendship.

After Roscoe's truck was out of sight, Ginny

went back inside. Exhausted and dehydrated, she was also famished. She ladled the rest of the stew into a bowl. Only cornbread crumbs remained, so she crushed saltines in the broth to thicken it instead. Ginny carried her bowl onto the porch and sat in the chair where Roscoe had been earlier. She downed the last of his whiskey before digging into the stew. The heat of the alcohol burned her throat, but warmed her belly in a pleasing way.

Ginny took a big spoonful of stew and closed her eyes, savoring the way the flavors had melded over the evening. It occurred to her to cook Samuel's batch a day early and let it sit in the fridge until the day of execution. Maybe that would make it as rich as his grandma's version.

Before Roscoe even reached the house, he killed his headlights, sparing her eyes, which had already adjusted to the dark. He sat down on the chair next to hers while Ginny refilled his whiskey glass.

She slurped the last of the stew from the bowl and set it on the porch.

"My mama made a pork stew that was similar," he said. "Yours was much better."

"I'm sorry Mrs. Dunner didn't like it."

"Did you see her turn up her nose at the chow-chow?" he asked. "How can she say she's from Louisiana?"

Ginny smiled in the dark.

"Good idea about the iced tea," he said. "That something extra was good planning."

"Dot's idea. She's smart like that. And thanks for fetching her. I needed her help after all."

They sat for a long time without speaking. The night air was considerably cooler than it had been in recent weeks and the perspiration on her cotton dress began to dry. She slipped off her shoes, enjoying how her bare feet felt pressed against the still-warm porch boards.

"I wish I could make it up to you somehow," she said.

"What's done is done."

"What about the superintendent? He didn't seem happy."

"That had nothing to do with what you served." His matter-of-fact tone betrayed none of the emotion Ginny hoped he'd show.

"I heard a little of what was said. You're a good warden, Roscoe." The superintendent had said he doubted Roscoe had the stomach for corrections, but she couldn't tell from the conversation whether Roscoe's job was truly in danger.

"I don't know if there's such a thing as a good warden." A heavy sigh punctuated his words. "Especially here."

Ginny got up and sat on his lap, wrapping her arms around his neck. She didn't worry anyone would see them because it was so dark out.

"You're a good man and that affects all your decisions. You've done so much to turn things around."

"It's too damn little and too damn late."

Their foreheads touched. "Then why stay?"

"Most days I don't even know," he said.

He'd lost so many battles this past year. The system for separating convicts, the elimination of the inmate guards, and most recently incentive pay for inmates. Roscoe felt releasing an inmate without a dime to his name only encouraged more criminal activity. He proposed paying prisoners four cents an hour, half of which they'd save for their release and the other half they'd use to buy incidentals like cigarettes or magazines while they were still locked up.

"Sometimes it's easier to stay in a bad situation because you're too tired to envision an alternative." She ran her hand through his hair before resting her head on his shoulder.

"You talking about me or you now?"

"Probably both," she admitted.

Roscoe didn't appear eager to talk anymore. And since he wasn't admonishing her for forgetting the prison board dinner, she should've just suggested they go to bed. But the obvious absence of anger made her itchy, like a scab just begging to be picked at. No matter how often Ginny tested his patience, he seemed willing to forgive and forget. Why? He wasn't so generous with his men, but then again, he wasn't sleeping with them.

"Roscoe?"

"Hmmm?" He'd started to doze.

"I know I say I'm sorry a lot, but I do mean it. I'm mortified I forgot the dinner tonight."

"I already said to forget about it."

"I know . . . but you let so much slide. And I appreciate it, considering my knack for getting under your skin. But I wonder why it comes so easy to you?"

"Who said it was easy?" He lifted her off his lap. She stood in front of him, not knowing what to do.

"Sit down," he said. "Please."

She couldn't see his eyes or mouth in the dark. They usually helped her gauge how their conversations might unfold. Feeling utterly alone and disconnected, she regretted tearing at this one particular scab.

"You try my patience more than the prisoners do most days, and I'm left shaking my head after many of our conversations," he said. "But I promised your daddy I'd look after you if anything ever happened to him. And I can't do that if I let my pigheadedness get in the way."

Her heart sank to think their relationship was more about a twenty-year-old promise to a friend than it was about loving her, faults and all.

"Daddy, huh."

"You know I didn't mean it that way," he said.

Ginny didn't know what Roscoe meant. Their relationship befuddled her. They were an unlikely couple, and neither of them had seen it coming. About four years ago, she'd asked Roscoe if she could make an inmate's last meal in the kitchen at the warden's residence. It was homier and gave her a calm the main prison kitchen could not. She'd pleaded until he finally agreed.

The next day she'd made two batches of clabber cake and both had fallen when taken from the oven. Ginny had been standing at the counter, her arms weary from beating a third batch of batter that used up the last of the sour, clotted milk. Tears streamed down her face and rolled off her chin as she thought of the inmate who only wanted one last taste of the cake his mama had made every Sunday when he was a child.

Her tears fell faster when she thought of all the men she'd cooked for in the previous four years—men who already had their dance with the state's electric chair—and all those still awaiting their turn. And there she was, a blubbering fool, foiled by the simplest of recipes and thinking it was the end of the world.

Even though Roscoe had entered the house without a sound that day, she didn't startle when he wrapped his arms around her waist and kissed her neck. It was as if Ginny had been waiting for just such a thing to happen even though she couldn't remember ever desiring it. Among the many emotions she'd felt when sleeping with him the first time, the strongest was relief. Like a century's old puzzle had been solved; one that ensured her survival. The reasons for staying in the relationship eluded them. They just continued, the way they'd always done—as warden and cook.

Throughout the years, she refused to entertain the thought that love was even possible. She recalled the way she yearned to be held, how she sought him out time and time again. She had been the pursuer. Ginny had told herself many stories: that it was just about sex; that it was connecting to another human being in an inhumane place. She didn't believe their affair was a way to remain connected to her father, or as a way to hurt her mama, as Miriam often suggested. Her detachment from her emotions became so acute, it was as if she was watching herself in a picture show, one where she'd never know the ending. Yet here she was, wishing with all her heart that Roscoe saw something in her apart from being Joe's daughter. That together, she and Roscoe could be that happy ending she'd never envisioned before.

"Do you remember that first day?" she asked. "In the kitchen?"

" 'Course I do," he said.

"Were you afraid I wouldn't feel the same as you?"

An answer didn't come. Instead, Roscoe stood and led her into the house and up the stairs.

The largest bedroom had an antique bedroom set donated by the widow of a prison board member some years ago. The woman had said she wanted the warden and his wife to have something lovely in a place that was mostly ugly. She might be disappointed to know Roscoe remained a bachelor all these years and preferred the creaky, iron bed in his quarters at the admin building.

Ginny, however, loved the bed with its soft mattress and fluffy pillows. But the mirrored makeup table was the real gem. It had three panels; the two smaller mirrors flanked the large one in the middle and could fold inward. She sat on the small, upholstered stool and pictured herself like some New Orleans socialite who brushed her hair 100 strokes every night and slathered her whole body in expensive creams.

Roscoe stood behind her and began removing bobby pins from the braid Dot had wound so tightly at the base of her neck.

"There's blood and pork grease on your dress, and a bruise is coming up on the bridge of your nose," he said. "But not one hair is out of place."

Ginny smiled. "Dot got carried away."

"I noticed it earlier. I should've said you looked nice."

"You were busy having a heart attack when you realized I'd forgotten dinner," she reminded him. Still, hearing his words now made her breath quicken.

He helped her up and she wrapped her arms around him, nestling her head under his chin, where it fit so perfectly.

"About your earlier question . . . whether I worried about your reaction that day in the kitchen," he began. "I wasn't thinking at all. I just had to hold you."

Ginny kissed his chin, hoping he'd meet her mouth with his, but he just kept talking.

"You know, just because I promised your daddy I'd look after you, doesn't mean I don't love you, Ginny."

Those words—heard for the first time—were a shock. She almost thought she misheard him.

"Thank you, Roscoe." She nuzzled closer. While Ginny thought about saying she loved him, too, the words stayed lodged in her throat. She wanted to say them back. Didn't she? Her heart beat wildly. She panicked to think she might be missing the one opportunity to change the nature of their union.

Roscoe saved her from the awkward moment by kissing her roughly and lifting her onto the bed. Their lovemaking seemed different now that he'd said the words out loud. Not better, but maybe sacred, as if they both took their relationship more seriously.

Later, Ginny wondered if her hesitancy was because she feared giving everything of herself to him. No matter. Her heart sang that Roscoe finally said he loved her after all these years. She fell asleep thinking she was in the very place she needed to be.

Lawrence Grimes
Father of Death Row Inmate Thomas Grimes
Thibodeaux, LA
November 17, 1956

Lawrence is ashamed he's not bathed in a week and that his nails need clipping. Since Esther's passing and the eldest boy going to prison, he doesn't feel up to doing much but sitting in his rocker. Still, he's combed a neat part in his unwashed hair and put on his Sunday shirt. He hasn't worn it since Esther's funeral. The thought of that dark day causes his hands to shake.

"Please call me Ginny," the young woman says as he pours her a cup of coffee.

Esther always made the coffee, so Lawrence is worried the pot he's brewed is bitter. Miss Polk sips it politely anyhow.

"Thomas sends his best," she says.

Lawrence grunts in reply because he doesn't know how to respond. He visited his son only once since he got sent up to Greenmount. He tries not to think of Tom much. He blames the boy for Esther's death. Her heart broke to learn her son had killed a man. The sorrow put her in the ground, Lawrence was sure of it. Tom would be in the ground in just a week. Lawrence would let him rot in the prison graveyard. No way he'd let that boy be buried in the church cemetery next to his mama.

"Thomas said your wife used to make a coconut cake each Easter when he was a boy," Miss Polk says. "He said you might have the recipe handy."

"Why do you want a recipe, miss?" He refuses to call the girl by her first name. Esther would have said it wasn't polite to be so informal.

The coffee tastes burnt even with milk and three heaps of sugar. He drinks it because it helps him stay focused. Otherwise his thoughts would drift back out to the front porch, where he longs to be: in his rocker next to Esther's empty one. It's where he feels closest to her.

"Thomas asked for the cake as his last supper," Miss Polk says. "I like to make something meaningful for the inmates if at all possible. It seems to ease their fear in the final hours."

Lawrence's eyes grow shiny as he remembers his young son's sticky face covered in Esther's seven-minute frosting. Tom would sometimes eat three or four pieces before Esther would finally shoo him out of the house. His wife would beam proudly as she wrapped up the leftover cake.

"I don't know if she had a recipe, but I can look." Lawrence is grateful for the chance to turn his back to Miss Polk. His sudden memory of Esther in her faded, checkered apron, a bowl of batter in the crook of her arm, is almost too much to bear.

From the cupboard, he pulls down a familiar tin box filled with scraps of paper. He sifts through the unorganized recipes: pickled okra, molasses cookies, divinity. His mouth waters at the foods he'll never eat again because his Esther is gone.

"Here it is." He rubs his shirtsleeve across his cheeks before turning around.

Miss Polk cradles the paper carefully, as if he's given her a sparrow with a busted wing.

"May I make a copy?" She opens her purse and pulls out a pencil and folded piece of paper.

"Take it," he says. "Not like I'm going to need it. In fact, take the whole box." He pushes the tin across the table.

She lays a youthful, unblemished hand over his ancient one. "Thank you for the gesture, sir. But I think it's important for you to hang on to those memories."

Lawrence no longer cares if his guest sees him cry. He prays Esther will not be ashamed of him.

Chapter 6

Ginny got up early the morning after the prison board dinner and showered. Without a change of clothes, she had to put on the grease-spattered and bloodstained dress of the day before. It felt like putting on a piece of the past. Today was a new day; the day after Roscoe said he loved her. Surely, most things would feel different now.

Roscoe had risen earlier than she. In the dark, he'd planted a gentle kiss on her forehead and left the residence. More than once Dot had urged her to become a proper wife, to make this house her own, to give up her job. She'd be adrift if she didn't have to report to the prison kitchen by 5:30 a.m.

Ginny drove her car back to the women's barracks. Lights were already on in Dot's room, so she didn't bother to tiptoe into her room to dress. She was pulling her damp hair into a side braid when Dot entered, dressed and ready to walk to the kitchen.

"Not knocking these days?" Ginny asked.

"We're well past that and you know it." Dot grabbed a brush from the bureau and pointed to the bed.

The braid Ginny had fastened just a minute prior was now loose. Dot pulled the brush through her hair with a vigor that suggested it could be tamed. She then pulled it into a single tight braid and gave it a good-natured tug.

"If you'd worn your hair to the side like that, it would've ended up in the soup pot," she said.

"Thought I'd try something different today."

"Uh-huh." Dot studied her as if she were some new creature.

"What? Is it wrong to want to look nice?"

Dot snorted and shook her head. "We spend our days in a suffocating kitchen, sweating until we're soaked through and through, taking on the smell of sour cabbage and greens. Not exactly a beauty pageant. Who are you trying to impress?"

Ginny ignored her and turned to the mirror, searching her face for some sign. If she felt this different, maybe she'd look it, too.

Her mood was lighter as the day progressed, and she didn't get upset at things that usually sent her over the edge, like spilling a bowl of flour or scalding her fingers on a pot handle. Every time she'd catch Dot staring, she'd stick out her tongue and make cross-eyes.

The thought of taking lunch to Roscoe made her feel strangely shy. Had those words been stored up for a long time, or was his declaration spur of the moment, surprising even him? More importantly, would he be wondering why she hadn't said the words back to him?

"Do I even want to know what's gotten into you?" Dot finally asked.

It was a powerful thing to be loved. Ginny's daddy had been free with the words, but her mama withheld them or doled them out on rare occasions. Regardless, she hadn't felt loved since before her daddy's murder. Two decades later, she could scarcely believe she'd survived so long without the feeling.

"Roscoe said he loved me," Ginny admitted.

"What's new about that? Hadn't he been saying it all this time?" Dot stopped what she was working on, her mouth gaping.

"Nope, neither of us had."

Dot let out a low whistle. "Hard to believe. Most men will say they love you so you'll drop your drawers faster."

"Guess it was important enough to wait."

"What happened last night?"

"I really don't know," Ginny said. "Sometimes there's no rhyme or reason to things."

"Or sometimes things happen at exactly the right time," Dot said. "I'm wondering how things will change around here. For all of us."

"Well, I can't think about that now. I'm heading over to the warden's residence to cook that batch of pork neck stew." Ginny removed her apron and smoothed her dress. "That'll give the flavors some time to meld before Sam's execution tomorrow."

Ginny didn't know if she imagined it, but she thought Dot's brow furrowed for an instant.

"Go on, then," she said, shooing Ginny from the kitchen.

The first step was stopping by the barracks to retrieve the photo of Samuel's son Eileen had given Ginny. Now, in the warden's kitchen, it claimed a spot on the counter far enough from the ingredients and the stove so it wouldn't get harmed, but close enough to serve as inspiration.

Do a good job for my boy, Aida had said. Those words lay heavy on Ginny's heart. Typically, trying out recipes was a delicious chance to lose herself, but today, each and every step was important and deserved close attention. Her senses were on high alert: crisp onion and celery crunched audibly under the blade of the knife. The stew pot radiated heat as the lard melted. Her eyes drifted time and time again to the photo of Samuel's son and his toothless, beguiling smile.

Once the stew appeared under control, she began prepping Roscoe's supper. She'd left a note in his office saying he was expected to dine at the residence with her this evening. Consciously or not, Ginny had decided to make his favorite—pan-fried pork chops in brown gravy with dirty rice—as if they were celebrating a special occasion.

Cooking meals for both these men at the same time created a queer feeling in her stomach. One man had a future with her, if he wanted it, while the other had no future at all.

The photo of Samuel's son wasn't the only thing she'd picked up from her room before arriving at Roscoe's. A floral cotton sundress and a pair of seldom-worn sandals made their way into an overnight bag. On a whim, she'd also grabbed a tube of lipstick and the bottle of nail polish from the back of her bureau drawer.

After dinner was made and warming in a low oven, a scalding hot bath loosened Ginny's cramped muscles. She let the towel linger over her body, which no longer responded to the afternoon's earlier urgency. Her hair fell into its normal state of unkemptness, free from braids or ponytails or bobby pins. She dotted lipstick on her lower lip and then rubbed it in until only a faint pink stain remained.

The front porch was her favorite place, especially in the early evening when the sun was low in the sky. She grabbed a big glass of lemonade and the red nail polish and sat on the stoop. With so little practice, she did a fine job of painting her toenails. The lemonade was overly tart, made the way Roscoe liked it. After the polish had dried, she walked barefoot across the lawn to the edge of the field to pick some black-eyed Susans for the table. Roscoe drove up before she could make it into the house to find a vase.

"You look nice." He leaned against his truck and waited for her to reach him before they walked onto the porch together.

"You smell nice, too," he added, and kissed her on the cheek.

"I made pork chops." The grin on Ginny's face made it apparent the evening was about more than dinner.

He eyed her strangely. "Let me wash my hands and I'll join you in the dining room. Then you can tell me what's up."

The pork neck stew was still simmering, so she gave it a final stir before filling their plates with pork chops, rice, and fresh green beans. Roscoe entered the kitchen with a vase in hand.

"You forgot to put your flowers in water. Since you went to so much trouble to set a fine table, I figured we shouldn't let them wither on the counter."

She and Roscoe returned to the dining room and he placed the flowers between them. He'd noticed the nice tablecloth and good china, and complimented the smells permeating the house. They spoke little as they devoured their supper. He ate two large pork chops and most of the rice. She had no trouble polishing off her portions either.

"I'm not certain why I deserve such a fine meal, but I appreciate it." His face was more at ease than it'd been in months.

Ginny squeezed his hand, uncertain how to voice her reasons, which were unclear even to her.

He leaned to the side and peered under the table. "Nice toes."

"Well, shit. I forgot my good sandals upstairs."

"Tonight warranted *good* sandals, huh?"

She playfully punched him in the arm. "Let's have our coffee on the porch."

Roscoe didn't tease further, which surprised her. Instead, he talked about the ups and downs of his day, and asked about hers. For someone usually quiet, he seemed to want to fill the space with words.

"About last night . . ." Ginny began.

"The dinner turned out fine. Don't worry about it."

"I meant what happened after dinner."

He leaned forward in his wicker chair, hands clasped in front of him. "Something bothering you?"

"No, not at all. Well, I . . . I mean, I wanted to tell you . . ."

She swiped at the sudden tears, so he reached over and grabbed her hand.

"Jesus, girl, what happened to upset you so

much?" Roscoe lifted her chin, but she couldn't meet his eyes. "Did I do something wrong?"

"No! I did something wrong. Or rather I didn't do something I should've done. Or rather, should've said."

"You're making no sense. Let's walk a bit."

He led her to the grassy area in the front of the residence. They leaned into one another so he could envelope her with one long arm. When Roscoe kissed the top of her head, she hugged him tighter and spoke into his chest.

"Last night . . . you said you loved me. But I didn't say it back."

"You didn't?"

She pulled away from him. "You mean you didn't even notice? I sure as hell noticed it was the first time you'd said it in all these years."

"Good Lord, Ginny. Why are the words so important?"

She didn't know why. But after last night, they seemed more important than anything.

"Don't you want me to say it back?"

"It'd be fine if you did," he said.

"It'd be fine? What kind of cockamamie answer is that?"

He stared at her blankly as if he couldn't understand a word she uttered. Fuming, she affixed her fists to her sides to keep from boxing his ears. How could he be the same man who had her walking on clouds all day?

"What do you want me to say? I figured you loved me because you've stayed with me all these years."

Roscoe's reasoning made some sense. He'd not been privy to how much she struggled with the reasons for staying in their strange relationship. It was natural to think that a woman who had sex with you regularly had at least some feelings for you. Especially since she'd been the one to seek Roscoe out.

"I don't know." She shifted her feet in the cool grass, but didn't feel like holding him.

"You can always tell me what you want, Ginny."

The sheer pain of the conversation probably played out on Roscoe's face, but mercifully, the darkness hid it. Feeling sorry for him in this moment wasn't a priority.

"I shouldn't have to ask for what I want," she said.

"Well . . . I said it last night without you asking. But now, the whole conversation is about what I'm not doing right."

The exchange made her think they'd lasted all these years because they failed to speak any feelings aloud. Now that they had, both were doing a miserable job of it. She feared opening her mouth might result in something even more harmful being said.

Ginny turned her back to Roscoe and stared

131

out at the lights of the prison, the strongest being those atop the watchtowers. While almost every path through the maze of buildings was lit, the warden's residence was shrouded in blissful darkness.

"The size of my mouth exceeds the size of my body," she said.

Roscoe's muffled chuckle eased the tension.

"I'm guessing that's something Miriam told you a time or two?" he asked.

"Well, you know Mama. Words are actually her strong suit."

Moving behind her, Roscoe draped his long arms across her shoulders and rested his chin on her head. She pulled on his arms as if they were suspenders.

"I asked your daddy once how he could stand her constant chatter and he just asked, 'What chatter?' I don't know if he was pulling my leg or if love gave him a deaf ear."

She felt queer inside hearing her daddy might have loved Miriam. As a child, she just assumed her mama vexed him the same way she vexed her; that she and her father were bonded against a common enemy who was out to spoil their fun in whatever way she could. Miriam had always swooped in and demanded that Ginny clean up, or do her homework, or go to bed—anything to stop an activity her mama had not been invited to join. Even when the three of them played cards or marbles together, Ginny thought of herself and her daddy as a team trying to beat Miriam. It must have been apparent to her mama, who often stomped off in a huff when things weren't going her way. As a child, Ginny also believed her daddy's drinking got worse in response to Miriam's nagging. Only as an adult could she now see the real reasons a Greenmount guard might turn to drink and why his wife might be so unhappy.

Ginny's face colored at the childish thoughts boiling up. Her daddy was dead and there she was, jealous he might have cared about the woman he married and had a child with.

"I didn't mean to spoil something you wanted to be special," Roscoe whispered in her ear. "God knows I do love you, Ginny Polk."

His attempt to say the right words thrilled her and eased the jealousy about Miriam from her mind.

"I love you, too, Roscoe Simms."

With eyes closed, she paid attention to the chirping of cicadas and the steady thrumming of Roscoe's heart against her back. She longed for a camera that could capture feelings and sensations like a photograph because she worried her feeble memory would never be able to reassemble all the pieces of this important moment.

Roscoe let her stand there against him in the

silence, whereas another man might have grown uneasy or thought the moment too awkward to bear. He cradled her expectations as well as her body.

"Ready for bed?" he finally asked.

She nodded and followed him into the house. They stopped at the bottom of the staircase.

"I need to put away some things in the kitchen," she said. "Be up in a minute."

He gave her hand a quick squeeze and took a few steps before turning back.

"Ginny? We have any cornflakes?" he asked.

"Thinking about breakfast already?"

"Nah, I meant to tell you earlier. Sam says all he wants tomorrow is a box of cornflakes, milk, and lots of sugar. If we have that on hand, you don't have to run to town tomorrow."

The humming in her ears grew loud, as if the cicadas they heard outside now swarmed the room. Still cooling on the stovetop was Aida's pork neck stew, yet all Samuel wanted was cereal for his last supper. *Do a good job,* his grandmother had instructed.

"Ginny? The cereal?" Roscoe pressed.

"Um . . . yes, I think so. Almost a full box."

"All right then."

Roscoe made it to the top of the stairs before she sat down on one of the dining room chairs. Ginny leaned over the table and rested her cheek on her arm. *Cornflakes.* Goddamned cornflakes had dispelled the magic she'd felt with Roscoe in the yard. The memory of the night she first told Roscoe she loved him would always include death row inmate Samuel LeBoux.

Chapter 7

Execution days were generally of two types: the kind where the energy of the guards and prisoners was ramped up so high you expected a riot; or the opposite, when things were so damn still the place appeared to be a ghost town. There was no rhyme or reason for it, just that the two types existed and you wouldn't know which until the day of.

Today, the prison was the latter. The men at breakfast seemed to renounce speech altogether. Even trays, cups, and spoons went mute, failing to clank against tabletops. Dot lowered her normally boisterous voice to match the solemnity in the air.

"I'm just saying if I was you, I'd serve the boy his grammy's stew with some spoonbread and forget about the damn cereal," she said.

That was Ginny's belief as well, but her stomach churned in warning. In the past, it'd been perfectly normal for her to go against Roscoe's wishes for the right reason. Now, pushing him seemed a bad idea. Not that he'd retract his feelings, but she owed him more. Like thinking things through. In truth, though, she was bound to do something one day that would raise his ire again. Why not today? Especially since Aida's request seemed worth it.

Dot made it seem so clear-cut. "The boy deserves more than cornflakes," she'd said, and those words bolstered Ginny's feelings.

"And would you tell him about his little son?" The photograph rested in her apron pocket, heavier than the paper it'd been printed on.

" 'Course I would," she said. "That was his girlfriend's wish. You ain't doing it on your own accord."

The unsettled feeling wouldn't leave Ginny. Perhaps it was just how one was supposed to feel on execution day.

Since Dot said she could handle things in the kitchen, Ginny walked over to the death row cellblock. The door to the Waiting Room stood open, so she let herself in and made her way to the corner room. It was just as stifling as the day Samuel told her to mind her own business. Not a sound came from the prisoners' cells. What was Samuel doing at this very moment?

The creak of the door sent shivers through her body. John, the lead guard of the unit, stepped in.

"What are you doing here, Ginny?" His voice was as low as Dot's had been, as if he, too, felt some reverence was in order.

"I don't know. I have a peculiar feeling about today."

"Yeah, I know what you mean. Seems to have hit Roscoe pretty hard as well."

John using Roscoe's first name didn't strike her as strange. They were friends. And John knew Roscoe had feelings for her. She and John would have both been less familiar if anyone else had been around.

"Why do you say that about Roscoe?" she asked.

John pulled at his collar and then put his hands on the back of the chair. "Maybe I shouldn't be saying anything."

Ginny sat down at the table and motioned for him to do the same. He looked back at the door as if someone might object.

"John?"

He sat down. "Roscoe's in there right now with Sam, reading Bible verses."

"That's not unusual. He often reads to the men."

"Yeah, but he's come every day for the last three weeks. And when he leaves, he carries with him a weariness like I've never seen before. Like he's dreading this boy's death more than others."

Roscoe hadn't shared this with her. They rarely spoke about Samuel except in regards to his last meal. And those conversations weren't pleasant or lengthy. Had she been so wrapped up in the details of Aida's wishes and the damn pork neck stew that she hadn't seen a change in Roscoe?

"Weary, huh?" she asked.

"With every year that goes by, it seems those executions get harder and harder for him. Which is natural, I suppose. If I didn't have my wife to talk to about it, it might drive me a little crazy. Although some of the boys around here look forward to it like it was the World Series."

Ginny had volunteered to witness every execution and take down the prisoners' last words, although all she had to do was drop off a tray of food and leave. Every one of her actions seemed wholly separate from the act of killing. She assumed Roscoe felt the same detachment. They hadn't talked about it, not the way John and his wife did.

"Didn't mean to upset you, Ginny."

"Oh, you didn't. I just went somewhere else for a moment." She smiled to reassure him. Usually, she was inclined to squeeze a person's hand, but thought it too forward, even with John. Samuel had recoiled when she reached for him that day in the corner room.

"You know, Roscoe could be upset about a hundred other things besides Sam," he said. "He's had a lot on his mind lately, including the damn Superintendent of Corrections. Sorry I said anything."

"No, I'm glad you did."

"You staying for the walk-through? We'll be starting any minute."

The walk-through was rehearsal for the night of the execution, although each man knew his part by heart. Still, some wardens were superstitious that without the walk-through, things might not go smoothly. It couldn't be risked with the press and public present, and especially if family members of the death row inmate attended. Death by electric chair was horrific enough. A botched execution would be disastrous given folks' negative feelings about prison goings-on in general.

Ginny had heard the words so many times they were etched in her consciousness: *A jury of your peers has found you guilty of the crime of murder. A judge has imposed a sentence of death as your penalty. As warden, I am charged with carrying out that sentence according to the laws of the State of Louisiana. At this time, do you have a statement for the witnesses present?"*

Most men had little to say. Some apologized to their own families or to the families of those they'd harmed. Others wept and whispered prayers for mercy. Only once, in her presence, had anyone screamed out he was innocent: that was Silas Barnes, her daddy's murderer.

"I think I better just go," she said.

"You want me to tell Roscoe you were here?" John asked.

"No, please don't. He has enough to worry about."

Some summer days, the residence could feel almost cool inside. The large oaks in the yard shaded the porch and front rooms, and fragrant lilac bushes blocked sunlight from the kitchen. She tried to guess whether the inside temperature was ten or fifteen degrees cooler than the outside, but realized it didn't matter one bit as long as it was cooler, period.

The air held remnants of last night's pork chop dinner and the stew she'd made and put in the icebox. Ginny still hadn't decided whether to bake cornbread or spoonbread to go with the stew. Spoonbread was denser and wouldn't crumble in the broth as quickly. Yet, most folks associated cornbread with family gatherings.

"Stupid woman!" Her frustration echoed in the empty house.

Samuel would be dead in a few hours and she was comparing recipes like a spinster at a county fair baking competition. Maybe there was something wrong with her that she couldn't feel the gravity of the situation as Roscoe and John did. What did a goddamned recipe matter?

Roscoe worried that seeing the execution of Daddy's killer broke her. But it was always more of an observation. He never probed further, trying to needle out what was unhinged in her mind. Ginny envied John and his wife, lying in bed at night, the two of them able to sort through their feelings. Hers had never been looked at squarely. Yet she'd allowed them to drive her actions all these years.

The weariness John described seeing in Roscoe overtook her as well. She wanted nothing more than to climb the stairs to the master bedroom, strip down to her undergarments, and lie down on the top of the voluminous bedding, sinking down until it swallowed her whole.

Instead, she walked into the kitchen to search the pantry for yellow cornmeal.

With the oven on, the room felt as sweltering as the prison yard. As soon as Ginny mopped the perspiration from her face with a dish towel, beads of moisture formed on her brow and trickled off her nose onto the counter.

Her dress had lost its starch hours ago and instead clung like a desperate child. She leaned away from the stove to stir the stew, wishing her arm was longer. Yet, when the spoonbread came out of the oven, she scooped a serving into a bowl for herself despite the heat. For a split second, Ginny regretted taking any. It was Samuel's, after all. But she couldn't help herself.

After dotting it with cold, salted butter, she doused it generously with maple syrup. The dish reminded Ginny of her mournful baking period after her daddy's funeral. Even savory dishes somehow ended up sweet. Ginny's fear of toothaches had been so grave she brushed after every meal and sometimes in between. Her mama would admonish her for ruining the taste of perfectly good food. But even if Ginny hadn't brushed like a crazed person, Miriam would have scolded her about something else—like the fact she seemed unable to gain weight and her mama couldn't keep it off.

The dining room was slightly cooler, so she put a place mat on the cherry tabletop and sat down to eat the sweet, cornmeal custard with a spoon from the good silverware in the hutch. Each bite became a silent meditation.

Gone was the usual fervor she felt on execution days. She'd not yet retrieved the wooden tray from the pantry; the tray that carried steaming plates of food covered with bowls or dish towels to keep them warm on their trip from the stove to the corner room. Ginny stopped using the metal trays from the prison's cafeteria. They seemed cold and punitive. The wooden tray also held tall glasses of tea or lemonade with extra ice, or a cup of coffee if that's what the prisoner preferred. With two guards present while the prisoner ate, she didn't think a real plate or glassware posed a danger, and Roscoe finally gave in to her wishes.

She'd gotten expert at balancing the heavy tray during transport, her hands gripped tightly around the metal handles, so not a drop of food or drink was spilt. The tray had been painted white at some point in its history but was now worn at the edges like it was a much-loved family heirloom. Except for execution days, though, it remained high on a shelf, as if being tainted by death gave it only one purpose.

With her thoughts so scattered, Ginny found herself scraping her spoon at the empty bowl. Eating the steaming-hot spoonbread only added to her flush. She needed a bath something fierce. It'd have to wait. The stew needed tending. It had begun to stick, but not scorch. She turned down the flame beneath the pot and went to the pantry to retrieve the tray.

A lone lightbulb hung from the pantry ceiling. Roscoe had affixed a long piece of twine to the chain because she was too short to reach it. Yet, the damn fool had put the tray on the highest shelf. Instead of getting a chair to stand on, Ginny tested her weight on the bottom shelf and it held. She moved her foot to the next shelf, holding all the while to a higher shelf. The top shelf tilted toward her, sending the wooden tray and several empty pickling jars onto the floor and her on top of it all.

"Lord Almighty, what's that racket?" Dot called from the kitchen.

Ginny's eyes grew wide. Like a child who suddenly remembered to cry after being startled, she began to sob.

"You're not a stupid girl," Dot said, extending

her hand. "But some days, it seems you try mighty hard to convince me otherwise."

"Why . . . are . . . you . . . here?" Ginny's words were interspersed with great draws of air and more tears.

"To help you."

"I've never needed help with the last suppers." She wiped her hand across her dripping nose and noticed a finger had been cut by the broken pickling jars.

"Today's different." Dot picked up the broken tray, one of its handles a casualty of the fall. "Now go wash up. You might even have time for a bath."

"How will I carry the food?" Reeling with emotion, Ginny couldn't think of a substitute for the tray. Its role seemed essential to the last suppers.

Dot moved loose strands of hair from Ginny's face, then tugged at her chin gently. "Calm yourself. There's a crate of peaches in the corner of the kitchen. We'll empty it and it'll do fine."

At Dot's touch, Ginny wanted to fall into her arms and disappear. She daydreamed that Dot would then rock her gently and tell her she didn't have to bring the meal to Samuel after all. She'd lead Ginny to the sofa and insist she lie down. Dot would hum soothing hymns until Ginny dozed.

Tiny pieces of glass that were stuck to the back of Ginny's damp dress now dropped to the floor with delicate clinks, bringing her back to the task at hand. She brushed off those that remained. Small hiccups, brought on by her earlier sobbing, peppered her breathing as it finally slowed. The bath was probably a good idea after all.

The peach crate was bulkier than the wooden tray but had higher sides and handholds cut out. With leaden arms, Ginny loaded up a mixing bowl with spoonbread pushed to one side and then filled it full of pork meat torn from the bone and a generous helping of the thick broth. No sense bringing just one serving in case Samuel wanted more. Nestled against the bowl were a glass of tea and a glass of lemonade since she failed to ask his preference.

Although the bath had refreshed her physically, her spirit seemed heavy as she prepared the meal for transport.

"You want to bring the cornflakes and milk just in case?" Dot asked.

"Now, why would you go and say that?"

Ginny felt wrung out, through and through. While she didn't think Roscoe would make a scene about the stew and her completely ignoring Samuel's wishes, his consternation might prove too much to bear. And now, she no longer felt confident in her decision.

"Hells bells, Ginny. I only meant it didn't hurt to bring the cereal just in case he really does prefer it to his grandmother's dish. Can't he have both?"

"Am I doing the wrong thing? Is that what you're saying?" She looked from side to side anxiously, her jittery movements out of her control.

Dot grabbed Ginny's hand and sat her down firmly on a kitchen chair. Sitting directly across, she looked Ginny in the eyes. "I'm worried about you, child. You've worked yourself up good. Maybe I should bring the food over."

"No, it's my job." The words echoed off the walls like the wails of a screaming two-year-old. The shrillness probably just worried Dot more. Ginny breathed and exhaled slowly, counting to ten to calm herself.

She never seriously thought of relinquishing this duty. Dot wouldn't want to stay for the actual execution, or take down Samuel's exact last words, which Ginny promised to share with Aida and Eileen.

"I'll be all right, Dot. Hand me my apron."

"I won't," she said. "Something horrible has gripped you. I always thought these meals were a poor idea, but now I'm certain of it. You're the last person who should be messing with the death boys."

Ginny grabbed the red gingham apron from the

pantry doorknob herself and cinched it tightly around her waist.

"Here," Dot said, handing her the photo of Samuel's son that had been lying on the countertop. "I hope you know what you're doing."

Ginny put the photo in her apron pocket and picked up the crate. It felt solid in her hands. Everything else in that moment, though, seemed amorphous. What used to be a straightforward process felt like a dark hallway filled with unnamed perils.

"Open the door for me, Dot. I need to be going." She straightened her shoulders and drew in a deep breath.

Death row prisoners took their meals two hours before the execution and well before the execution room began to fill up with guards or press or family members. Ginny appreciated not having an audience when delivering the food. Victims' families objected vehemently to those final gestures of compassion, and she really couldn't blame them. Ginny knew firsthand the pain of having someone you loved murdered.

The walk never seemed so long as it did today. Her hip bones ached from the heavy crate. The tea and lemonade sloshed about, but never crested, because she'd only filled the glasses two-thirds full. Several executions ago, Roscoe had asked why she just didn't drive. She found it impossible to explain that walking was her way of honoring the gravity of the day.

John saw her coming and rushed to take the crate off her hands.

A thousand pins and needles covered her skin. She shook out her arms to bring back some feeling into them.

"This smells mighty fine, Ginny. You bringing us leftovers tomorrow, right?"

"I always do." She followed him through the execution chamber and into the corner room. Her forehead beaded with feverish perspiration.

"I'll get Sam," John said. "He's with Roscoe."

He placed the tray on the table. Ginny stood a few steps away, wringing her hands, which still felt prickly. The photo of Samuel's son lay heavy in her pocket. She considered the best time to give him the news. While he was eating? Right before the execution? Roscoe's words came back to her. Perhaps it was more cruel to tell Samuel about a boy he'd never see grow into a man, a boy who'd probably be ashamed his father was a murderer.

The creak of the metal door to the execution room startled her. Dot entered with a shopping bag in her arms.

"What are you doing here?" Ginny paled at her friend's appearance.

"I thought you could use the help."

"I told you this was my job."

"Please, Ginny." Dot's worry sucked the air from the room. Her presence there was more than just a desire to be helpful. She was frightened about something.

Ginny turned her attention to the shopping bag in Dot's arms. A box of cornflakes and a bottle of milk peeked out of the top.

"You told me I was doing the right thing!" Pain gripped her temples and pounded behind her eyes. The floor became less solid, wavy, and unsure like a carnival funhouse.

"What does it hurt to give him a choice?" Dot asked.

Before Ginny could protest further, the door to the cellblock opened. Roscoe led the way, his hand clasped around Samuel's upper arm. The top of Samuel's head had been shaved, revealing enough bare skin for electricity to be conducted properly. It gave him a clownish appearance, intensified by the redness in his cheeks and nose.

Both warden and inmate stopped abruptly, eyeing the tray and then Ginny at the same time. Roscoe's eyes shone with defeat while Samuel's held disbelief, then condemnation. The disappointment of both men hung in the air.

"What have you done?" Roscoe asked. The words, although soft and resigned, slammed into her as if they were shouts.

Samuel wrenched his arm from Roscoe's grasp and ran straight at the table. Hooking his shoulder under the table's edge, he lifted it like a football linebacker lifting an opponent. The table hit Ginny square in the belly, sending the tray and its contents down her body before shattering on the floor. The hot stew and ice-cold lemonade created an odd sensation as they soaked her apron and dress.

She didn't move, even when it looked like Samuel was rushing directly at her. But she wasn't his target anymore. He dove at the floor near her feet instead. Picking up a large shard of the broken mixing bowl, he stabbed viciously at his neck, looking at her all the while. Roscoe and John lunged for him, slipping on the stew and lemonade and blood that slicked the floor. Samuel's movements slowed as the blood rushed out of him. His eyes no longer focused on Ginny but on some distant place beyond the room they occupied.

The three men were joined in a horrific wrestling match, their clothing absorbing the copious amounts of blood Samuel was losing. Ginny groped at the wall behind her as if digging through the cinderblock was her only escape.

"Dorothy, get her out of here. Now, Dot!"

Roscoe's voice had an underwater quality, muted and protracted. Ginny became a rag doll in Dot's arms. The large woman supported most of Ginny's weight while her feet dragged behind, almost useless. Darkness overtook her before they even left the building.

"Lift your arms, Ginny. We got to get you outta this dress."

She ignored Dot's instructions and slumped against the mattress. Dot had gotten her across the prison yard and into her room, but Ginny didn't remember the journey. All she wanted was sleep.

Dot yanked at the wet clothing covering Ginny's unresponsive muscles. She turned to the desk, rifling through the drawer until she found a pair of scissors.

"Hold still," Dot said. Carefully, she cut away the dress and apron.

"The photo," Ginny mumbled and pointed to the floor. "The photo."

"What are you talking about?"

"Samuel's son. My apron."

Dot knelt and searched the strips of cloth. She withdrew the photo Eileen had given Ginny, looking at it only for a second before swiping it across her dress. The stew had soaked through the apron, reaching the photo hidden in the pocket.

Dot set the warped photo against the lamp on the nightstand and pulled the bedspread over Ginny's shoulders.

"You get some sleep. I'll just be in the next room if you need me."

She lingered for a moment, then closed the door quietly. Ginny stared at Thaddeus's tiny, smiling face until it melted beyond recognition.

Chapter 8

Ginny's life became long periods of stillness punctuated by occasional activity like going to the bathroom, sipping broth, or eating toast. Roscoe, Dot, and her mother came and went, but she lay in bed with her back to them, eyes and heart closed.

Miriam had been by almost every day since the incident with Samuel. Incident was her mother's word, not Ginny's.

It's been a week since the incident, Ginny. You need to get up.

It's been two weeks since the incident. Act like an adult.

It's been a month since the incident. Are you going to stay in bed forever?

Ginny had not been able to sit with what happened long enough to name it. Awful images would flit across her consciousness and she'd sit bolt upright, as if from a nightmare. Then her mind would mercifully push them to a place where they held less power.

Some days her mother didn't speak. Only Miriam's perfume told Ginny it was her and not Dot who swiped a cool washcloth across her forehead or stroked her back through the blanket.

Today, her mother's voice rose and fell in the hallway in a familiar exchange.

"You should've known something like this would happen. Her foolishness has gone on long enough."

"What do you want me to say, Miriam? How in the living hell would I know Sam would react the way he did?"

"You're the warden. You could've stopped her ages ago."

Roscoe's voice dipped lower, sparing Ginny the rest of the conversation. In the past week, he'd become increasingly angry at her mama's accusations. Some were as ludicrous as saying Roscoe seduced her all those years ago and she had no choice but to remain working at the prison "under his spell." Or that their relationship had sickened her mind because she was essentially sleeping with her father every time she slept with someone as old as Roscoe. Or that Ginny's insanity would surely rub off on Roscoe, bringing heartache upon them both.

The door opened and closed. Not Mama this time. The smell was yeasty and fresh, as if someone just opened an oven door.

"You're going to eat today or we're going to have ourselves a proper fight," Dot said. "With the weight you lost, no way you'd win."

Her large hands grabbed Ginny's shoulder and forcibly turned her. Then Dot pulled her to a sitting position and pointed a finger. "You stay put."

Dot dragged the desk closer to the bed. On it was the basket she'd brought. Its contents included a loaf of piping-hot bread wrapped in a dish towel, a small plate and knife, a stick of butter, and a jar of jam. She moved the desk chair over and sliced a thick hunk of bread.

"You always clamoring for the end piece. Here. It's yours. Eat it," Dot demanded.

Ginny's hands rested limply in her lap. She stared at the items but couldn't look in Dot's face. Her friend's eyes were sure to show the searing disappointment so apparent in her tone.

"Fine." Dot pulled the knife across the stick of butter and slathered the bread. She thrust the slice in Ginny's face. "Now eat it."

Dot looked full of anger and exasperation at her unwillingness to cooperate. Ginny had been mute for more than a month. Nothing she could say would make any difference, so she shook her head no.

Lightning-fast, Dot smashed the butter-laden bread into her face and ground it with her palm until Ginny sputtered in protest.

"Goddammit, girl. It's time to end this foolishness. That man of yours is heartsick, beside himself because he can't help you. Your crazy mama is stepping on our last nerves. And I need you back in the kitchen. I need you, period."

Dot's chest heaved with the pain Ginny caused her. Every muscle in her face and neck tensed. Even her artery bulged with exertion.

"Do you even know what you mean to me?" Dot asked, breathless. "I would've left this place ages ago if it weren't for you. This place makes a person hard, but you manage to make me smile almost every damn day. Now look at you. Where's my Ginny gone to?"

Ginny wiped her face with the edge of the bedspread and brushed the bits of bread from her lap onto the floor. Tears stopped at the back of her throat, although she wanted them to escape in a deluge, filling the room until grief poured out the window and floated away for good.

"I ain't going to come back until you pull yourself together," Dot finally said.

At the sound of the door slamming, loud hiccups of air escaped from Ginny's chest. She tore a piece of bread from the still-warm loaf and gouged the butter with it. The soft dough filled her mouth only for a second before she swallowed and stuffed in a second and third piece. Holding the jar near her lips, she used two fingers to scoop the preserves onto her tongue. Then she sucked the red, sticky fingers, catching her breath before attacking the rest of the loaf.

Night and day passed. The room was dank and stifling. Even with her face against the pillow,

Ginny couldn't escape it. Roscoe came that evening and carried her down the hall into the barracks' shared bathroom, where he'd drawn a scalding-hot bath. He lowered her into the water, keeping a hand under one armpit so she wouldn't drift below the surface. The rough nap of the washcloth traced every inch of her, causing the skin to prickle to life. Never had anyone touched her so gently. Her mama's baths were rough and obligatory. After her daddy died, Miriam would just point at the tub and tell her she was grown enough to take her own baths and she better not slosh dirty water over the clean tile floor.

"Ginny, you got to come back to me." Roscoe's lips touched her ear as he spoke. "Put Sam behind you. It wasn't your fault."

She looked into his face for some sign he was telling the truth. How she wished his words could absolve her from the sins committed against Samuel, against Aida and Eileen.

A soft knock on the bathroom door preceded Dot's muffled announcement she'd changed the sheets and that the bed was ready.

"Bring something to put on her, would you?" With one arm, Roscoe lifted Ginny from the tub like she weighed nothing at all. The other arm reached for a towel.

Dot entered without knocking and set the cotton gown on the toilet lid. "Girl, you're bright red like a cherry. You got any skin left?"

Dot had lied earlier when she said she wasn't coming back. Even when a person felt pushed beyond a breaking point, friendship had a fiercer tug on the heart. And Dot had a big one. Both of them loved Ginny without reservation, yet no matter how hard she tried, a dense fog still separated her from life.

Together, Dot and Roscoe worked to pull the nightgown over her still-damp body. They each took an arm, forcing her to walk the few steps back to her room. The window was open and a breeze had dispelled some of the stale air. The sheets, smelling of detergent and bleach, were crisp and slightly scratchy, as if they'd just come off the clothesline on a hot day. Ginny burrowed into the comforting scent.

Roscoe bent over and kissed her wet hair. "I'm ready for you to come back to me."

Sometime during the night Ginny woke up and found herself sitting on the floor with a pair of scissors in her hand. Scattered around her were pieces of black scrapbook paper, newspaper clippings, notes written in her own hand. Her screaming woke Dot and drew her into Ginny's room.

"What have I done? What have I done?" Ginny grasped at the triangular pieces, putting them together, hoping they'd form a whole picture, but none of the edges matched up.

Dot knelt down, tears marring her cheeks. "Thank God you're ready to talk again."

"Help me," Ginny whispered. "Help me put it back together."

Once Dot got over her shock, she insisted on making instant coffee using the hot plate she kept in her room. She said she couldn't be expected to act civilized at 1 a.m. without something to fool her into thinking it was morning. Ginny gladly accepted Dot was in charge and waited for her instructions, keeping her eyes averted from the carnage she'd wrought while not in her right mind. What other reason could there be for such destructive behavior?

Dot set two cups of coffee and a sleeve of saltine crackers on the floor between them. "What happened here?"

"I don't remember." Ginny's body shook so visibly Dot touched her arm to steady it.

"Well, it's obviously some kind of memory book you've been working on," she said.

"I know what it is. I just don't know *why* I did this . . . and why I can't remember doing it."

"You've not been yourself these past weeks. Who knows what you were thinking."

Dot put on her reading glasses and pulled her robe tighter. She picked up the pieces, a few at a time. Her brow crinkled as she deciphered their meaning. Recognition became disappointment.

"This ain't about you, girl. This about the dead men."

Ginny nodded. The scrapbook didn't hold photos from her childhood or newspaper clippings about her school honors or magazine articles about the movie stars she'd idolized as a teen. The pages were memorials to the men executed by the State of Louisiana. Sometimes she'd included their mug shots, arrest records, and bits from their official prison files. Sometimes there were newspaper articles from the trials. Every inmate's section included the recipe of the dish he requested as his last supper and the words he uttered seconds before dying in the electric chair.

Thirteen men were black, four were white. Six were in their twenties, five were in their thirties, five were in their forties, and one was seventy-nine. They had committed crimes like murder, rape, and robbery in parishes across the state: Vermilion, St. Charles, East Feliciana, Madison, Orleans, Tangipahoa, St. Landry, Jefferson, Caddo, West Carroll, West Baton Rouge, Franklin.

Eight had kin present when they died.

Nine had asked for savory dishes, most times a favorite food prepared by their mama or grandma like pot roast or gumbo or greens. Three asked for breakfast food like eggs or biscuits with sausage gravy. Four asked for desserts they'd remembered having as children. One asked Ginny for hard butterscotch candies. As a child, he'd been caught stealing a handful from a drugstore counter and felt too ashamed to eat them after that. On his last day on earth, he couldn't think of anything else he'd rather have.

"This ain't right, Ginny." Dot shook her head. "You holding on to these men like they is your own family."

"It's not like that."

"What's it like then, huh?"

Ginny touched the pieces of paper tentatively. "No one else was going to remember them."

"And that's how it should be," Dot said. "They did terrible things. Things those victims' families won't never forget."

"Those men had family, too, Dot. Wives and mothers and children and friends who also had to go on with their lives. But I'm too tired to argue with you. Will you just please help me?"

"I'm not arguing," Dot said. "I'm concerned. Can't I be concerned?"

Ginny held several pieces in her outstretched hands.

Dot huffed, grabbed them from her, and started arranging the pieces on the floor. With a keen eye, she could see patterns Ginny failed to see. Within an hour, full pages had been reassembled. Ginny ate saltines and drank cups of coffee while her friend worked magic.

"You have any glue?" Dot asked.

Ginny stood carefully, aware her legs were still wobbly and unsure, and retrieved the rubber cement from the desk drawer.

"You have lots of blank pages left in the scrapbook. Just glue all these cut-up pieces onto new sheets," Dot ordered. She pointed at an open spot on the floor where Ginny could work alongside her. "I don't know the exact order, but I expect you do."

She assembled the pages reverently, almost in penance for the damage she'd done with the scissors in a fit she couldn't even recall. Faces and names and recipes came together again. Oscar Facianne: clabber cake. Donald Beauchamp: hot pepper shrimp with grits. Orville Dowdy: dry toast with a soft boiled egg.

Dot had laid a few pieces of paper to one side on the floor, then seemed to change her mind. She folded and stuffed them in the pocket of her robe instead. "I'm not going to let you put Samuel's page back together. No sense in reliving any of it. Not like it'd be complete anyways."

Ginny's stomach clenched as Dot took the ruined photo of Samuel's son from the night-stand and put it in her pocket as well. She was right, though. What happened to Samuel shouldn't be remembered.

Dot held her lower back while she eased up from the floor. Sitting cross-legged for three hours had both of them cramped up and stiff.

"If Roscoe knew about this, he'd think you were a madwoman."

"He doesn't have to know," Ginny said.

"Secrets have a way of eating at a relationship," she warned.

"You already said he was beside himself. I don't want to hurt him anymore."

"So, you heard me when I said that."

Ginny nodded. "And that Mama was stomping on your last nerves. No one needed to tell me. I could've guessed she'd wear out her welcome."

Dot laughed soft and low. "Roscoe's face ballooned up like a ripe berry the last time she visited. I was certain he was having a heart attack. He told her she wasn't welcome back until you asked for her."

It was Ginny's turn to laugh. "That's unlikely."

Dot sat on the bed while Ginny leaned up against the wall. A damp breeze entered the window screen above her, causing a chill to run the length of her spine. It was almost 4 a.m. She longed to drift back to sleep, although she was fearful about what else she might do and then not remember.

"I also heard you say that you needed me," Ginny said.

"Well, that kitchen is a big place to take care of," Dot said. "And you left me all on my own."

"I think you meant something else."

Dot fidgeted with her housecoat. "If you're trying to egg me into saying I love you, then I will. Ginny Polk, I love you like a daughter. And I'm mad as hell that you worried me to death these past weeks."

"I love you, too."

Caretaker was a role that fit as naturally as Dot's own skin. Because of Miriam's deficiencies in the parenting department, Ginny gladly accepted a mother hen in a prison yard of roosters. She'd always known she meant something special to Dot. Her daughter-in-law's inability to love or accept Dot created a chasm of pain Ginny hoped to fill in some way.

From time to time, Ginny used to think she'd been too hard on her mama. After all, Miriam had had a rough life, which could make anyone hard. But Dot hadn't had an easy life. When her husband was injured at the sawmill, Dot eked out a living cleaning houses, doing laundry, and washing dishes at the elementary school in Boucherville. After her husband passed, Dot raised a fine son all on her own and thought him to be her finest achievement. While Dot exhibited a sharp tongue, she never complained about her circumstances and she never belittled anyone. Ginny had been vigilant, always trying to assess when Miriam might go on a tirade or exhibit the meanness that marked so many of their interactions. Ginny never feared that around Dot.

She felt accepted for who she was. It seemed natural that Dot saying she loved her meant almost as much as Roscoe's earlier declaration.

"I don't think you should be making any more of those meals," Dot said. "Roscoe don't think you should either."

They'd likely had a few conversations about her and she couldn't blame them. They didn't have anyone else they could talk to, and neither trusted Miriam enough to have a conversation about Ginny's well-being. 'Course, it probably seemed easier to blame the *incident* on the last suppers instead of some damaged part of her.

"Silas Barnes never got a last meal," Ginny said, rubbing bits of glue from her fingers.

"What are you talking about?"

"The man who killed my daddy. He didn't get a last supper."

Dot closed her eyes, visibly exasperated by the turn in conversation. "You weren't but an itty-bitty gal. There's no way you could know such a thing."

But Ginny did know. Silas's wife had brought fried chicken with her in the hopes the prison would allow him to have a last meal with her. At the time, Ginny hadn't known the warden denied the man that last bit of comfort from his kin. But she had noticed the covered basket sitting on the bench next to Mrs. Barnes throughout the execution. The smell of deep-fried chicken, once

Ginny's favorite, turned her stomach as she'd tried to distinguish it from the horrible smells of death. After the execution, as the widow sat there weeping, one of the guards spit in her face. She'd thrown the basket at the wall, missing Miriam by a hair.

"It was a big scene. When I asked Mama about it afterward, she said a guard killer didn't deserve a last meal of his choosing and that Mrs. Barnes and her goddamned fried chicken could go to hell with her husband."

After everything her mama had forced Ginny to witness, she'd cried more for Mrs. Barnes than she had for her own daddy. When she couldn't stem the flow of tears, Miriam shook her until her teeth rattled. Her mama said she'd never been more ashamed of her daughter than in that instant.

"Why are you remembering Silas now?" Dot asked.

"When Samuel threw the pork stew on the floor, it reminded me so much of the basket of food Mrs. Barnes had thrown at the guard," Ginny said, recalling the anguish in both their faces. She felt their utter despair in her nightmares, the ones that haunted her both day and night.

"Lord in Heaven," Dot mumbled. "It's too much. It's all too much."

Ginny didn't ask her if she meant the story, or the last suppers, or the scrapbook of all the men who'd been put to death during her time at the prison. But she agreed with Dot. It did feel like too much.

"You coming back to work today?" Dot asked.

"I expect it's time. Especially since you need me so much."

Chapter 9

Ginny's blue chambray dress hung about her like a flour sack. She'd lost ten pounds over the past month, but her puny frame didn't have five to spare. At least her apron cinched it in, giving the appearance her clothes fit. Dot vowed to make it her personal mission to ply Ginny with the fattiest, most sugar-laden foods imaginable until she reached 100 pounds again.

Her strength had atrophied as well, making the workday even more exhausting than normal. Dot took up the slack, joyful her friend and boss was back in the kitchen at all. She chattered almost nonstop, telling stories about how she whipped the inmate kitchen helpers into shape and they were doing a better job because of her stern guidance.

Of course, Jess and Peabody took it in stride. Ginny winked at them to let them know they'd been doing a good job all along. Their grins welcomed her back to an old and comforting routine.

"You have any trouble getting the supplies you needed while I was gone?" Ginny asked Dot.

While she was gone. Seemed a safer way to describe what happened. Miriam had vacillated between using the words *breakdown* and *spell.*

Ginny wondered if her mama knew she'd been overheard in the hallway outside Ginny's room. Miriam had told Roscoe she always knew her daughter was off in the head and it was only a matter of time before Ginny totally lost it. That had to have been the day Roscoe told her she wasn't welcome at the prison anymore. Or, at least Ginny liked to think it was.

"Roscoe made sure I had everything I needed," Dot said. "He even got a couple of ladies from town to come in and do some baking."

"He's a good man."

"That he is. So, why not give him what he wants?" Dot asked.

"And that would be?"

Dot dropped the baking sheet on the counter. "Quit this job. Marry him."

Ginny threw her arms up. "How's that supposed to solve anything? And he hasn't exactly asked me to marry him."

Had Roscoe and Dot had a conversation about this very subject? If they had, it wasn't one she'd overheard while cocooned in her bed. Even after he told Ginny he loved her, marriage hadn't entered her mind because it would mean leaving the kitchen.

"One thing your mama and I agree on is this job isn't good for you," Dot said.

The guard at the kitchen door seemed overly interested in their conversation, so Ginny pulled

Dot closer. "Forcing me to leave this job is the worst thing you could do for my sanity. I need this place. And I hate that you agree with Mama about anything."

Dot put both hands on Ginny's shoulders, getting flour and shortening on her dress. "It's a sad state of affairs if you feel you need this place."

"Then why do you stay?"

Tenderness filled Dot's wet eyes. "I've told you many times. To watch after you, child."

"Well, I guess *you* won't be leaving anytime soon, because I'm not." Ginny turned back to the cutting board and the bag of onions waiting to be chopped. "And let's not mention Roscoe and marriage in the same sentence again. There're ears everywhere, and I don't want him getting the idea I planted rumors."

Dot dropped the conversation and instead chastised Jess and Peabody for their slowness in peeling potatoes. Their peeling skills weren't the problem. Dot was agitated, but probably thought she couldn't press it anymore. She and Roscoe had deemed Ginny fragile, if not truly crazy, as Miriam insisted. She'd likely get a free pass for the near future.

Breakfast and lunch passed without Roscoe stopping by the kitchen. He wasn't expected to, but Ginny assumed he'd heard from the guards that she was back at work. People might think of women as experts at gossip, but they hadn't seen how fast news could travel in this prison.

Dot insisted Ginny take off around two. She'd handle supper on her own. The walk to the women's barracks didn't bother Ginny. Her aching back appreciated the opportunity to stretch. The muggy Louisiana air slicked her skin with sweat, but it was better than being cooped up inside. She passed a few guards on the path. Most wouldn't meet her eye, as if her breaking from the world had been a shameful thing. There was no point in trying to convince anyone she had no choice in the matter, because even Roscoe, Dot, and her mama thought she had. Their pleas for her to get better always felt like a judgment that Ginny wasn't trying hard enough. Maybe she hadn't.

Only Dot and Ginny resided in the barracks anymore. Two other women had worked as part-time housekeepers at the admin buildings but quit when they were concerned they'd be enlisted to work full time in the kitchen. Or, maybe they grew tired of the vigil at the madwoman's bedside. No matter. She and Dot now had the bathroom to themselves.

The door to her room was ajar. She pushed it open slowly and found Roscoe seated near the window, blowing cigarette smoke through the screen.

"Thought you'd quit again," she said.

"Couldn't think of a good enough reason not to start up."

He wouldn't look at her, so she walked over and sat on his lap. He buried his face into her neck. His skin felt feverish.

"I'm better," Ginny said.

He nodded, but didn't speak. The heaving of his shoulders told her he couldn't have come to the kitchen to see her. Only here, in private, could he release the emotions holding him hostage. She stroked his hair, wrapping her fingers around the longish pieces at his neck. He needed a haircut and a shave. Both their lives had been on hold during these past weeks.

She couldn't remember putting the scrapbook away, but was relieved it was out of sight. Roscoe didn't need one more thing to convince him she was tainted with her daddy's madness.

"Last night, I woke up from a bad dream and called out for Dot," she said, concocting a story for her recovery that had nothing to do with scissors and dead men. "She brought in some coffee and crackers. We sat for hours. Then she asked if I was ready to go back to work and I said I was."

"You probably should have rested today. I could have sat with you." He ran his hand across his face and then through his hair. Tears had made his eyes a deep cobalt blue. She could have lost herself in them for hours.

"Work kept my mind occupied," Ginny said. "Until I could see you."

She bent down so her lips brushed against his wet, stubbled cheek. He smelled of sweat and sun. He aroused a passion she'd not felt in a long time. His kisses, tentative at first, became more urgent. She swung her leg around, straddling him and the chair. He pushed her skirt up and pushed aside her panties as she groped for his belt, then his zipper. Her hips moved in sync with his breath and she forgot how exhausted she'd been earlier.

Later, when they were on the bed, Ginny draped her arm across his chest. It looked like a child's arm, thin and without defined muscles. For Roscoe's sake, she'd make an effort to eat more and gain back her strength—to prove she was really better, at least in physical health.

"Thank you for the times you sat with me." She ran a finger through the hair on his chest, tracing a heart like a teenager might. "I knew you were there even if I didn't speak it."

"I wish I was the one to bring you back. Not Dot." His arms drew her closer so her head nestled at the base of his neck.

"Dot didn't bring me back. I don't know what did. I just came back." That was the truth. Ginny didn't know why she'd pulled out the scrapbook and destroyed it. Those acts came from a primal place that frightened her. And she dared not look at it closely.

"You need to get back to work?" she asked.

"Nah, something I got to show you. Let's get dressed."

They walked back to Roscoe's truck at the admin building. Where they were going was still a mystery to her, but he thought it best she not walk the whole way. The truck wound its way past the Waiting Room and death row cells, and up the hill toward the warden's residence. Ginny thought they'd stop there, but he kept going, circling back past the barracks where the unmarried guards slept and then to the row of seven houses set aside for guards with families. All but two had been vacant in recent years as more families opted to live in Boucherville.

Their white clapboards had been baked in the Louisiana sun for decades, leaving very little of the original paint. The sad grayness blended into the dusty landscape so that the lot of them looked like a ghost town in a black-and-white movie. Except for one. The house she'd grown up in.

It had been freshly whitewashed and seemed a brand-new addition instead. A splash of color drew her eyes to the porch. Two lemon-yellow metal chairs were flanked by pots of geraniums and spider ferns.

"What's this, Roscoe?"

He squeezed her hand. "You'll see."

They parked in front of the life-size dollhouse. It looked nothing like the house she'd lived in with her parents. Her skin tingled with a child's excitement on Christmas morning.

"Can I go inside?" she asked.

"You better. It's yours." He waved his hand toward the porch.

Hers? Ginny didn't wait for an explanation, but instead bounded up the steps. The door was unlocked; its squawky hinge remedied since she last visited the house on the day of her interview for the cook's job.

She braced herself, thinking the sitting room would unleash a flood of memories, but it looked completely unlike it had twenty-one years ago. The walls had been stripped of the wallpaper and the bare boards painted a creamy yellow. All the trim had been freshened with white paint.

"Hope you like the furnishings." Roscoe stood behind her. She hadn't heard him enter.

"Where did you . . ."

"Secondhand shops. A few things from the warden's residence," he said. "Do you like it?"

She sat down, unable to process it all. "But why?"

"Your mama's right. This prison is a god-forsaken place. Some days, I just can't bear you're a part of its ugliness. I think that's why things happened the way they did with Samuel."

"Oh, Roscoe . . ."

"Let me finish. I figured you'd be too stubborn to quit your job no matter how much I begged. So, I wanted you to have someplace special you could go that didn't seem a part of the prison," he said.

Some men were good with fancy words, telling you how much they loved you and such. Words didn't come easy to Roscoe, so he'd made this house a declaration of his devotion. She'd never be loved by someone as much as she was by Roscoe in this very moment, and the realization made her sad as well as happy.

Nothing Ginny could utter—no words of gratitude—would ever measure up to what this gesture deserved. So, she hugged him, wrapping her arms tighter and tighter around his shoulders until she couldn't squeeze any harder.

Roscoe led her into each room and then waited patiently as she took notice of every little detail: the small dining table covered with a delicate, crocheted doily; a painting of a fox-hunting party that had previously hung above the buffet at the warden's residence; the kitchen pantry stocked with every spice and ingredient she could imagine needing. Her hands touched every surface as if to confirm she wasn't dreaming.

"Come look at the bedroom," he said, pulling her away from the kitchen.

She quickly realized why he was so anxious for her to see it. He'd moved the cherry bedroom set from the warden's residence here, including the vanity with the tri-fold mirror she adored. The bedroom was fit for a princess and left her with her jaw hanging.

She jumped onto the fluffy duvet. "I can't believe this is all for me. When, Roscoe? When did you find the time?"

"You were in such a bad state, I couldn't sleep at night. Couple of times I was certain I was having a heart attack. Coming to this place gave me peace."

"I'm so sorry for what I put you through," she said. "What happened . . . it was just so awful. I couldn't bear to face what I'd pushed Samuel to do."

"No matter how mixed up the reasons, your cooking has meant something to those men and their loved ones," he said. "It's something you had to do for yourself as well. Sam . . . that wasn't your doing, but I suspect it has changed things for you. And for that, I'm sorry."

In his quietness, Roscoe had developed a sense for what went on deep below her surface. It was probably why he'd been able to put her stubbornness and other faults into perspective.

Roscoe stood and pulled her to her feet. "Got something else to show you."

He led Ginny back to the sitting room and

pointed to a small desk situated underneath the front window. It was small, but well-proportioned to the room. On it rested a Royal portable typewriter with a turquoise case.

"What's this about?" she asked.

"Dot said you wanted to write a cookbook . . . you know, share your cooking secrets with other folks," he said. "She said old as she is, she still learns something new from you almost every week."

Ginny sat on the desk's mismatched chair and rested her fingers on the keys. She'd learned to type in high school, so the apparatus wasn't foreign to her. All her recipes, though, were either carried around in her head or scribbled on bits of paper in handwriting that looked more like chicken scratch. Still, she was suddenly comforted by the idea that Dot had been pushing for so long. The project would occupy her mind and she needed that right now.

"The man at the store said you could get it in four other colors . . . if you don't like this one." Roscoe laid his hand on the typewriter. "Oh, and he said it was especially quiet. That way you won't step on Dot's last nerves."

Dot. Ginny hadn't thought about how it might hurt Dot if she moved.

"She'll be alone in the women's barracks, Roscoe. I can't do that to her."

"She could stay here, in your old bedroom,"

he said. "She stays at her son's place over the weekend, so we'd have the house to ourselves then. You know, she helped me get the place ready."

"She did?"

"Yup. She was kind of bossy, but we settled into our roles. I provided the manual labor," he said.

Although this had been her parents' house, Roscoe had transformed it into a place where Ginny could make different memories. His pitiful, makeshift bedroom in the admin building wasn't theirs, and he'd never grown accustomed to sleeping at the warden's residence. They could both use this place to escape the ugliness of the prison.

"I want to see my old room." It'd crossed her mind earlier, but she pushed away the thought. Roscoe may have expertly painted over any bad memories in the rest of the house, but it'd take a magician to stop her mind from reliving those awful nights listening to her mama cry after her father was killed. Those same nights she knew she couldn't call out after having a bad dream. Comforting Ginny had been her daddy's job, even if it took some doing to rouse him after he'd had too much to drink.

Some of the guardhouses had two and three bedrooms. Miriam, though, had insisted on the one-bedroom style because she said she'd never have a child while Joe still worked at the prison. Ginny had been a surprise, or a mistake, depending on what kind of mood her mama was in when she told the story. The other housing was full at the time of Ginny's birth, and her father made it clear he wasn't quitting. Thus, the prison converted the screened-in porch into a bedroom right before she was born.

Ginny never minded sleeping on the converted porch. Sure, they'd neglected to add insulation, so the walls and floor let in the winter cold. Three layers of quilts usually did the trick, although she'd sometimes lie awake at night thinking the weight of them might accidentally smother her considering she was an underweight child.

"Why in God's name did you paint this room pink?" she asked.

Roscoe followed her into the small space that now reminded her of a stomach coated in Pepto-Bismol.

"Well, this is the color you painted your room in the women's barracks," he said. "And there was leftover paint. I thought you'd like it."

Dot had been with her at the hardware store when she chose the color: flamingo. Her friend warned she'd regret it, but still agreed to help paint the room. After the first few brushstrokes, Dot began to laugh. Ginny had been too stubborn to admit her mistake, so she told Dot she liked it; that it was cheery and reminded her of a Florida beach house. And really, what did Dot expect from a woman who bought a car based on its color alone? Mostly, Ginny figured it didn't hurt to leave the hideous shade since her eyes would be closed most of the time she spent in the room.

"Why are you laughing?" Roscoe asked.

"Oh, no reason. Has Dot seen this yet?"

"Nah, I painted it last. Why are you still laughing?"

"It's perfect. Dot's going to love it."

Nothing else in the room was familiar. And by painting the room such a hideous color, Roscoe had unintentionally made it easier for her to return to this house. She could accept his wonderful gift without reservation.

1938
Truth, Lies, and Birthday Cake

Miriam demanded Roscoe come for dinner and birthday cake. She'd said Ginny begged her—that she wanted things to be like old times—and Miriam wasn't about to disappoint a child whose daddy died just a month earlier.

Roscoe didn't give a shit about his twenty-ninth birthday, but he'd do anything to make Ginny happy. Still, it took three glasses of whiskey to steel his nerves. He'd not been the one to tell Miriam about Joe's death. Two other guards volunteered, so Roscoe stayed away from the grieving widow—that is, until she showed up in the fields yesterday and ripped him a new one.

"Pull yourself together, you drunken coward," she'd screamed at him. "I don't care what you think of me, but that little girl adores you for some goddamned reason. And if she wants a goddamned birthday party, then Jesus Christ, she's going to get one."

The other guards and the inmates working the fields had heard her tirade and stopped to watch it unfold like the latest picture show. Roscoe pleaded with Miriam to lower her voice. She'd always considered herself a woman of God. When she started using the Lord's name in vain, he knew turning down the request would only invite a world of hurt for himself and Ginny.

Pulling up to the house, Roscoe remembered he hadn't washed out his mouth with Listerine. Miriam would smell the whiskey and give him hell for his drinking. He hoped she'd be on her best behavior for Ginny's sake.

The little girl ran to the truck to greet him. "Uncle Roscoe! Uncle Roscoe! Happy birthday," she called out.

He scooped her up and she burrowed her face in his neck. Ginny was eight but was small for her age and light as a feather. She was dusty from playing outside.

The bruises on his face caught her attention. They had faded some over the last few weeks, but the beating was severe enough that the marks would be with him a while longer. She touched his cheek and forehead softly and then poked a swollen spot near his eye. "You got hurt."

"Oh, just got in a scrape at work. Nothing to worry about," he said. "If I weren't so damn skinny, maybe the other guy would look like this and not me."

She smiled at his joke, but worry still clouded her eyes.

"I hear birthday cake's on the menu this

evening," Roscoe said, and put her down on the ground. Grass wouldn't grow on the hard, packed earth around the guard housing and he thought it especially sad that kids had to play in dirt. Only the warden's residence had a lush green lawn, making it seem like a mirage in a desert.

Ginny grabbed his hand and tugged him toward the house, quick to put aside talk of his injuries. "Mama made pork chops, too. Your favorite."

"Good. Both of us could stand to put on some weight," he said. "Hope there's mashed potatoes, too."

Miriam stood just behind the screen door to the porch. Her arms were crossed and her face was just as stern as it'd been in the fields yesterday.

"Wash your hands, Ginny. You're a hot mess," she said, and faded into the darkness of the room behind her.

Miriam almost bristled that Ginny could be in good spirits. She felt that the girl ought to be displaying the grief Miriam and Roscoe felt at Joe's passing. But it's a tricky thing to make a child look reality squarely in the face.

Roscoe kept his comments light, although Ginny's resemblance to his best friend made it hard to keep from asking for a beer. Hell, Miriam might have thrown out all the liquor by now. Joe's drinking had always been a sore spot in their marriage. And although Joe was the heavier drinker, Roscoe imagined Miriam thought him to be the bad influence.

"Remember the one birthday when Daddy smashed your face in the cake," Ginny asked. "That was messy. We ate the pieces with our hands. Remember?"

"Your father ruined a perfectly good lemon cake," Miriam said. "No sense in remembering that fondly."

Ginny's face fell, so Roscoe gave a conspiratorial wink. She tried to wink back, but ended up closing both eyes at once. He covered his mouth with his napkin and pretended to cough so Miriam wouldn't notice his smile.

What Ginny couldn't know was her father's brand of humor sometimes bordered on cruel. You had to look closely in his eyes to see if he meant harm. Even so, most times you couldn't tell. A punch to the arm that was a little too forceful. An insult veiled in a joke. He might compliment Miriam's new dress only to say she'd packed on too many pounds since they'd married. He might praise Ginny's good grades in school, but chastise her for not making friends.

The other guards clamored to be around Joe because his personality was big and brazen. His unwavering confidence had attracted Roscoe as well. But Joe kept things unsettled, which worried Roscoe. A prison wasn't a place for a guard with a hair-trigger temper or a taste for cruelty, especially under the guise of a good laugh.

"Mama says we're moving to Grandma's or maybe into a new house all our own, and we won't be coming back to the prison again," Ginny said, clearing the plates from the table. Her spindly arms managed to hold on to the plates with ease. "I'll get the cake and candles."

Miriam pursed her lips. "What happened to your face?" she asked Roscoe.

"Was nothing."

"Nothing, huh. Looks like a damn lot of something."

"I said it was nothing," Roscoe said. "Part of the job. Leave it be."

"I'm glad Ginny and I are leaving this hell-hole," she said. "This place killed Joe."

"You know the prison didn't kill him," he said. "It was his own goddamn fault."

"I won't have you speak this way in my house." Her words, masked in a whisper, raged like a scream.

"Let's not do this now." Roscoe brought his hand to his forehead, tracing the tender spot that still brought on headaches.

Ginny reentered the room, the cake blazing with too many candles to count. Her playful rendition of the "Happy Birthday" song stood in contrast to the sorrow pounding in his chest. It'd be so much easier to cut ties and not risk any more hurt, but this dinner was part of making good on his promise to Joe that he'd look after his wife and daughter.

The night Joe died was the last time Roscoe had heard the plea, as if the danger of their mission that evening implied one of them might not make it out alive. Or maybe Joe's recklessness always kept his mortality top of mind.

"Make a wish," Ginny said, setting the cake on the table in front of him.

He closed his eyes and blew with all his might.

"Don't tell us or it won't come true," she added.

Roscoe would never reveal the wish to Ginny because it was a hope she'd never have to feel as he did: that Joe deserved what he got.

When Ginny had gone to bed, Miriam pointed to the front door. Roscoe followed her to the chairs on the porch and sat down.

"I guess your birthday wish was you'll never have to see me again." She lit a cigarette. Roscoe hadn't seen her smoke before.

"Cut the crap," he said, pulling his pack of Pall Malls from his shirt pocket. "I'll look after you two even after you move to town."

Roscoe sidestepped the real meaning of her comment. Things had been strained between them, even before Joe's death. One evening, about two months ago, he'd stopped by the house to tell Miriam that Joe was working the night shift at the Waiting Room. Miriam had opened the screen and pulled him into the darkened living room. She pressed herself against him, pinning him against the wall. She'd groped at his belt with one hand and rubbed the front of his pants with the other. He'd not had a woman in more than three years and he hardened at her touch. Miriam responded eagerly, seeing it as proof of his desire. He'd grabbed her arms roughly and asked her to stop. When she wouldn't, he shoved her away, but harder than he'd intended. She lost her balance and fell to the floor. He'd not stayed to ask if she was all right.

"That girl will be the death of me," Miriam groused. "Know what she said to me the other day? I told her Joe was in Heaven and she said we couldn't know for certain what happens when we die. Blasphemy."

"Ginny's a good kid," Roscoe said. "She's just trying to work it all out in her head. Got to be hard for a young 'un."

"It's harder on me."

Roscoe felt contempt for Miriam's self-pity. She hadn't loved Joe and Joe hadn't loved her, at least in the end. Roscoe thought Joe stayed in the marriage solely for Ginny. Her mama was stingy with love and generous with criticism, but Joe adored his daughter. With enough drink and some ladies on the side, he'd settled into a marriage he could stomach.

"Warden Gates gave me permission to bring Ginny to the execution." She took a long drag of her cigarette and used the nub to light another.

Roscoe was as shocked at the comment as the casual, off-handed way she'd delivered it.

"What in God's name are you thinking?"

"Keep your voice down," she said, coolly. "She's mature for her age. She needs to see someone suffer for her daddy's murder. For closure."

"For closure? For goddamned closure?" Roscoe shook his head, fighting the urge to choke Miriam. He couldn't bear the thought of Ginny suffering at this madwoman's hands. "You can't do that to her."

"I'm not doing anything 'to' her. And it's none of your business."

"It is my business," Roscoe said. "I'm Joe's best friend and he'd never let Ginny be hurt in this way."

"Some best friend."

"What the hell does that mean?" Roscoe asked.

"Joe counted on you to protect him. That's what best friends do."

Her hateful smirk only made him angrier. "You don't know the whole story," he said.

"I know enough."

That's what worried Roscoe. Miriam had bits and pieces relayed by three other guards who were protecting their own hides as well. He suspected they'd been less than truthful. And they'd beat the shit out of him to make sure he didn't tell the truth either.

Roscoe stood and made his way down the steps. "I'm going to talk to the warden in the morning."

"Go ahead. But he won't go against my wishes."

Roscoe was already in his truck when Miriam called from the porch. "You're at the top of the warden's shit list. Maybe you should worry about that."

Chapter 10

Tropical storm Arlene tore into Louisiana, dumping thirteen inches of rain near the coast and half as much inland in just two days. It was enough to turn the prison's dusty roads into muck and to compel Ginny to drive to the prison kitchen each morning for more than a week. Dot wasn't averse to walking in rain, but the wind accompanying the storm drove her half-crazy. She gladly accepted the rides.

They appreciated the extra time at the kitchen table each morning with their cups of coffee and sweet rolls. Even after the rains stopped, they continued taking the car to safeguard the new ritual.

Yesterday, Dot had moved the typewriter onto the kitchen table, suggesting they work on the cookbook in the mornings. Their first brainstorming session wasn't going well. Mostly, she just chastised Ginny for poor penmanship and inattention to detail.

"I can't make out your handwriting." Dot sifted through several recipes Ginny had laid out on the table. "Some of these aren't even recipes."

"Those are just guidelines," Ginny argued. "I carry around the steps in my head."

"Women new to the kitchen won't be reading

your mind. You got to write out every step or you'll be responsible for a lot of disasters and wasted groceries."

"You're being overly dramatic."

Dot crossed her arms and looked at Ginny over the top of her glasses. "You're going to have to make each and every recipe. I'll write down the steps as you go along and you can type it up after. We could start this weekend."

Weekends were spent with Roscoe. Ginny didn't relish giving up that time to Dot, with whom she already spent every waking hour during the work week. Not wanting to hurt her feelings, Ginny muddled over how to couch her response.

"You probably don't want me intruding on the time with your boyfriend, huh?" Dot asked. "Fine. We'll work on the cookbook in the evenings and I'll let you lovebirds have your time alone."

"Well, I don't see him much during the week."

"Ginny, I said it was all right. Lester's wife may not like me, but she looks forward to me taking care of the boys on the weekends to give her a break. Lord knows what holy hell would ensue if Granny Dot no longer cooked Sunday dinner for those little ones."

She poured Ginny another half cup of coffee and topped it off with heavy cream. She'd been sneaking extra fat into everything Ginny ate or drank, even offering the skin from her portion of roasted chicken one evening.

Ginny poured the contents of the cup into a small saucepan and lit the burner beneath it. "You've cooled down the coffee by adding cold cream. It has to be hot."

"It has to be hot," Dot mimicked. "Well, as long as you drink it, I'm satisfied."

They had another twenty minutes before they had to leave, so Dot started making piles of the recipes while Ginny sipped the now-scalding drink.

"What are you doing?" Ginny peered across the table.

"Sorting by type of recipe. You know, main dish, side dish, dessert."

"Uh-huh. Then what's that pile?" She pointed to a few pieces of paper at the edge of the table.

"Those are the discards," Dot said.

Dot had appointed herself as lead on the cookbook project just as she'd done with the house renovations. Roscoe's words came back to Ginny. *She was kind of bossy, but we settled into our roles.*

Her enthusiasm was charming, but she couldn't steamroll Ginny, who leaned across the table and grabbed the recipes. She was curious as to why Dot had deemed them unworthy. Scanning them quickly, Ginny added each to an already existing pile. For whatever reason, Dot weeded out the recipes served to the death row inmates.

Their work in the prison kitchen had a rhythm to it. Once in that groove, nothing could throw them off course. Problems cropped up, to be sure, but they met each head-on and rarely became flustered. The challenges in a kitchen, though, were by their nature fixable. Not enough milk? Use broth or water. Produce from the prison fields rotten? Serve something that wasn't yet spoiled. Supplies running low? Serve half rations.

Roscoe's afternoon visit to the kitchen set off an alarm in Ginny, as if a problem without an easy fix was about to upset the delicate balance. She gripped her apron.

"Afternoon, you two." He nodded in Dot's direction. "Ginny, can I speak with you in the hall?"

Knowing Dot would be tempted to listen, Ginny pulled Roscoe's arm until they were safely out of earshot.

"I had a bad feeling when you showed up. What is it?" she asked.

"Samuel LeBoux's grandmother called earlier. She and Sam's girlfriend would like to visit his grave today."

It wasn't that Ginny put the incident with Samuel behind her. That night—the way he died—would be with her forever, as would her guilt she'd not followed through with what Aida and Eileen had asked of her. But she never imagined a scenario that would bring them face-to-face again.

"I don't know if I can—"

"I'm going to meet with them. Not you," he said.

"But they asked for me, right?"

Roscoe chewed on the skin of his thumb. "It doesn't matter. It's best if I show them the grave. I'll make an excuse for you."

"They'll suspect something's wrong if I'm not there." Ginny tried to make sense of the worry lines creasing his forehead. "What? You think I'm not stable enough?"

"Now, Ginny . . . I didn't say that. But it's too risky. I'm already going have to lie to them. Best not to drag you into it."

"I won't tell them Samuel killed himself. I just want to be there."

Roscoe looked puzzled. "Sam didn't kill himself. I thought you knew."

Her mind conjured the images that never leave her, not even in her sleep: the gore, the torn flesh at Samuel's throat, the vacancy in his eyes as he slumped into Roscoe's arms.

"I saw him. He killed himself because of me."

"Let's go to my office," he said. "We need to talk."

• • •

Roscoe asked Tim to hold all calls and not to disturb them under any circumstances. His brusque orders only heightened her confusion.

"I know what I saw, Roscoe."

"When I sat with you, all those nights, I was sure you were listening," he said. "I told you John staunched the blood with his shirt and that we got Sam to the infirmary in time."

"He lived?"

"Oh, Ginny. You know better. We rescheduled the execution for the following week. He was stitched up and mended just enough for us to carry out the sentence."

He explained that John and another guard had helped him clean up the room. Then he'd hurried back to his quarters to change clothes.

Ginny shook her head, unable to process such horrific news. Roscoe used his thumbs to wipe the tears from her cheeks.

"God, Ginny. I scrubbed and scrubbed, but Sam's blood was everywhere," he said, shuddering. "I swear I kept seeing traces of it in the sink and around the tub no matter how many times I cleaned it."

He said when a member of the press and some of the other guards showed up for the execution later that evening, he'd told them there'd been a problem with the electric chair and the execution would be rescheduled.

"You know John's as loyal as can be, but that goddamned Wally . . . I had to bribe him to keep his mouth shut," Roscoe said. "It would have been my head if the prison board found out."

"Will the bribe work?" Ginny snuffled back her tears, now worried about what would happen to Roscoe if Wally talked.

He shrugged his shoulders. "No telling. Our differences run deep, from back in the day when your daddy and I were guards."

Because of the severity of Samuel's wounds, Roscoe said he had to call in a doctor from New Orleans. Still one more thread that, once pulled, could be his undoing.

Ginny's head felt impacted from the crying and she breathed through her mouth. Roscoe handed her his handkerchief.

"It was better for me—for us—that Sam went to the electric chair," he said. "If he died from the neck wounds, there'd have been an investigation. We'd have both been fired."

Even though he was right, it seemed unusually cruel to save a man only to kill him later.

"Surely it was the longest week of that boy's life," she said. "How alone and angry and frightened he must have felt."

Roscoe slumped back in his chair. "The wound to Sam's neck made eating impossible, so he'd grown extremely weak. Even so, he was calm at the end. I sat with him often, reading Scriptures."

Because her daddy's killer had struggled vigorously against his restraints and hollered out his innocence, Ginny's child mind was certain all death row inmates acted the same way right before the levers were pulled. After she started working at the prison, this theory was proved wrong. Sure, some men did struggle, but others just closed their eyes and wept quietly. Still others fixed their mouths into a hard, tight line. Their eyes shone with anger, maybe at the State of Louisiana or themselves.

"Mrs. LeBoux called a couple times asking to see the grave. I said you were visiting an ill family member and I'd meet her. She insisted on waiting until you were back."

"I'm back." Not physically or emotionally strong. Not rested. But she was back.

"It's a bad idea, but I won't stop you," he said. "Go splash some water on your face and blow your nose. They'll be here within the hour."

She nodded and returned to the kitchen to let Dot know she'd be out the rest of the day.

Aida shuffled down the hallway toward Roscoe's office. Arthritis stooped her shoulders and gnarled her fingers. She gripped a cane in one hand while Samuel's girlfriend, Eileen, grasped her elbow. They'd left the baby at home with Samuel's sisters. Aida looked decades older than she had the last time Ginny had seen her, when she moved so easily about her kitchen and porch.

Ginny hugged her. The robust embrace was that of the woman she'd met back in Jonesville. Eileen was still too shy to accept a handshake. Roscoe held his hat instead of offering his hand to either of the women.

"This is Warden Simms," Ginny said to them. "He'll escort us to the cemetery."

"Good afternoon, ladies," he said.

Aida stared at Roscoe a good long time; long enough to make him shift his feet uncomfortably. Ginny wondered what Aida hoped to glean from his face. It was leathered by sun and time and a grueling job, and it wasn't one that gave up truths easily.

"We can all fit in my car," Ginny said, ending the awkward exchange.

Roscoe walked a few steps ahead, stopping several times to allow them to catch up. Ginny worried Aida might not be physically up to walking in the cemetery. Eileen saw the worry in her face and whispered, "She'll do just fine."

Once in the car, Roscoe was more quiet than usual. He started to chew at his thumb, then seemed to think better of it. Ginny felt she had to fill the silence, so she described how inmates are involved with the funeral proceedings, from building the pine coffins to giving the eulogies.

"The coffin is transported via a horse-drawn

carriage," Ginny added. "And several inmates walk beside, singing hymns."

She wanted them to know how poignant and solemn the processions to the cemetery had become over the years. The inmates took the send-off of their brothers seriously and wanted no involvement of prison personnel. Her description of this custom felt inadequate and a disguised apology for the state electrocuting their loved one.

Eileen wept freely, but Aida stared out the window, her lip movements almost imperceptible. Ginny guessed she was praying. When the car stopped, Aida looked confused, as if roused from a nap.

Roscoe led the way to Samuel's grave, although a marker hadn't been placed there yet. The ground was sunken slightly. Rains from the recent tropical storm had also cut deep channels in the dirt walkways between the rows of graves. Its ugliness shamed Ginny.

"Why's it look like that?" Eileen asked.

"The ground is settling above the coffin, ma'am," Roscoe said. "We'll fill in with more dirt soon. And add a stone cross like the other graves have."

Aida and Eileen held each other for several minutes, not saying a word. Roscoe and Ginny stepped back a few feet. It felt natural to reach for him, but he put both his hands in his pockets, reminding Ginny that she was his employee.

"Mrs. LeBoux? Miss Eileen? Why don't we go back to my office," Roscoe suggested. "I'm sure you have some questions."

Ginny shot him an angry look for interrupting their solitude, but Aida agreed it was a good idea; that indeed, she had questions.

Tim brought four cups of coffee into Roscoe's office.

Roscoe waved his off. "Acid's getting to my stomach," he said. "Shall we get started?"

Ginny felt a slight pang that she didn't know this small thing about Roscoe—and whether she was the cause of the physical distress.

Eileen clearly felt ill at ease, but questions played across her face. Ginny took her hand and said she should feel comfortable saying anything she liked.

"I want to ask about Thaddeus . . . what Sam said when you told him he had a son."

Ginny's stomach lurched as she tried to formulate a believable lie. She jumped when Roscoe spoke for her.

"I told Sam about his son, and he was right glad to hear the news," he said. "We were reading together from the Bible. A passage about Jesus and the little children. His hope was the boy might know of him one day, but not about his crime."

Eileen's relief was visible, but she asked why Ginny hadn't been the one to show Sam the photo.

Ginny was reeling from Roscoe's decision to lie, so he spoke for her again. "Ginny was in Florida with her sick aunt. I promised her I'd tell him."

"Then you didn't prepare the stew?" Aida turned her question to Ginny.

"I did make the stew . . . and left instructions for my kitchen helper to bring it over," she lied. "But Sam wasn't feeling well and asked for plain toast. You can imagine it's sometimes difficult for the men to eat before."

"Yes, yes, I understand," Aida said. "We appreciate you trying, Ginny. I could tell you had good intentions. You wanted to do something special for Sam."

Perspiration ran down Ginny's back and the coffee now seemed ludicrous on such a hot afternoon. The office was stifling despite the efforts of the small, metal fan rotating in the corner. She needed to get out of there before the truth escaped her lips in a torrent.

"We worried when we didn't hear from you, Ginny," Eileen said. "You promised to tell us Sam's last words. We didn't know what happened."

"I left so suddenly for Florida . . . my aunt, you know . . . she was dying and I had to drive my mama. I'm sorry. I should've called . . . or wrote." The lies tumbled from her mouth, the babbling almost unstoppable.

"Ginny, looks like the afternoon heat got to you," Roscoe said, standing. "Why don't you get some air? I'll show our guests to their car."

"Perhaps you're right," she said, wiping her face. "Aida . . . Eileen . . . I'm sorry about Samuel. I really am."

Ginny ran from the room and any other questions they could ask.

In her flustered state, she'd gone to the women's barracks, forgetting that all her things had been moved to her childhood home. Ginny's insides roiled with nausea and her tongue was dry and thick in her mouth, but she managed to get to the house. She stood over the kitchen sink, splashing water over her face and chest, then put her mouth near the faucet to try to quench the ungodly thirst. Ginny gulped and gulped, but her tongue still felt like sandpaper.

The faucet continued to run as she vomited the water into the sink.

She'd been lying in the bed for three hours, sleep escaping her. It was dark before Roscoe came to the house. He pulled the vanity chair to the bedside, but didn't turn on the lamp.

"You all right?" He laid a hand on her hip.

"We lied to them. About Sam's son."

205

"I didn't lie about Thaddeus," he said. "I told Sam."

She sat up in bed. "Why didn't you tell me?"

"God, Ginny. I did. I told you lots of things when you were holed up in your room."

Some of that month was crystal clear, like the heated conversations between her mama and Roscoe. But most of that time was lost to her forever. Her inability to recall his words seemed to cause him a deep sadness.

"Sam asked me to give you a message," he continued. "I guess you don't remember that either?"

"No! Tell me what he said, Roscoe." Her heart would surely burst waiting for an answer.

"He said he forgave you for bringing the supper. He didn't want you to carry that night with you the rest of your life."

The news unleased the unspoken grief that had pressed against her heart, threatening to suffocate her all this time. Roscoe scooped her into his lap and cradled her gently. Except for an occasional "shhh," he let Ginny cry long into the night.

Horace Beauchamp
Inmate Number 4603
Crime: Murder
Execution Date: December 22, 1956

Horace likes that she calls him Mr. Beauchamp. He supposes it's 'cause he's the oldest man to be executed at Greenmount. Like that deserves some kind of respect.

"We've talked about a few things you might like," she says to him. "Have you decided?"

He's known for a long while that he wants a fruit-and-nut cake like his mama baked at Christmas when he was just a little thing. But Horace enjoys Miss Polk's company, so he's been pretending to be indecisive. She's come to call on him three times, but he knows he's pushing his luck. Guards aren't likely to let her come again.

"I hate that they scheduled an execution so close to Christmas." She seems awful tired. Sad, too.

"As good a time as any. Wouldn't make a bit of difference to me if it was the Fourth of July," he says.

But it does matter to Horace. Even though he's seventy-nine years old, he remembers

Christmases long past. He wants those memories to be like pieces of hard candy; each recollection so sweet it lingers on his tongue.

Knowing you're meeting your Maker in a few days makes it hard to concentrate on much else. Even though his childhood has faded mostly into shadow, a few details still shine through: the small cedar tree in the front yard his mama would decorate with bits of string, pinecones, and blue jay feathers; and the woolen sock that served as a stocking—one so worn out it couldn't be mended anymore. On Christmas morning, it'd be stuffed with an apple, a handful of walnuts, and two or three pieces of licorice.

For three straight years—he can't remember which exactly—his mama worked as a cook for a French family in the Quarter. The missus there gave small loaves of fruit-and-nut cake as gifts to the neighbors. His mama would bring home those that were left to bake a little too long; those whose edges were so burnt that even soaking with brandy wouldn't bring them back to life.

"I made up my mind, miss," he finally says. "It's fruitcake I'd like."

She smiles as if she's looking straight into his mind and sharing the recollection with him. She's there, right beside him on the front stoop, nibbling the small pieces to make them last. She shares the disappointment that twists in his gut when he realizes he's eaten too quickly. She also shares the anger he feels when he learns his mama's been let go from the job that made those cakes possible.

"That's no problem at all," she says. "I'll bake it right away so it has some time to sit. I'm sure I can find a little brandy for soaking. Just don't tell anyone."

Horace's heart flutters to know they share this secret.

"What do you remember most about the cake?" she asks.

"I expect I wouldn't know. I was just a young 'un," he says. "I do recall it was dark as molasses and had pecans. It surely was the best thing I ever tasted."

"Well, I'll be careful to find ingredients that were around when you were a boy." Miss Polk's eyes seem less focused, as if she's gone away to her kitchen and is already measuring out the flour.

His eyes well up from anticipation. This makes it hard for him to see the floor as the guard leads him back to his cell. Only later does he realize he's forgotten to ask Miss Polk to please burn the edges. Horace hopes he can trust the guard to give her the message.

Chapter 11

Daylight nudged Ginny awake, not Dot's typical knocking or rough shaking of her shoulders. Roscoe hadn't stayed the night after revealing the details of Samuel's passing. He'd said he didn't feel right with Dot in the same house even though he'd slept in Ginny's room at the barracks occasionally. Truthfully, she'd wanted to be alone anyway.

By now, Dot was probably finished preparing the morning meal, so Ginny didn't bother to jump up and race to the prison kitchen. Instead, she grabbed her robe from the foot of the bed and headed to her own kitchen to scavenge for breakfast.

"Sleep well?" Dot's presence at the kitchen table startled Ginny.

"Why aren't you at work?"

"Breakfast's done. Lunch is prepped," she said. "I wanted to check on you. Here, have some coffee."

"I better have some food as well," Ginny said. "Yesterday was so crazy I didn't feel up to eating."

"Roscoe told me. About yesterday, that is. Actually, he asked me to come back here to check on you this morning."

Ginny wished everyone would stop worrying so much about her, but she couldn't blame them considering her roller-coaster emotions and erratic behavior.

"You knew about Samuel, too?" she asked.

"Of course. I was in your room when Roscoe told you," Dot said. "I guess that was during one of your blackouts."

Those troubled Ginny the most. She couldn't fathom why her mind allowed her to hear some of what went on around her, like her mama's piercing criticisms, but not Roscoe's explanation of how Samuel had died. The brain's ability for self-protection made Ginny shudder.

"Let me make you some eggs and bacon." Dot got up from the table, but Ginny headed her off.

"No, please sit. I'll just have some bread and butter."

Dot joined her, saying it wasn't polite to let her eat alone. She heaped spoons of fig preserves on Ginny's bread as well as her own.

"I got other news to tell you," Dot said. "Anna quit. I heard she gave Roscoe a tongue-lashing on her way out."

The prison nurse had kept mainly to herself, so Ginny didn't know her well. The women in the prison didn't have the collegial relationships many of the guards shared. Truth was, Anna intimidated Ginny. The nurse had a real education and her work seemed important. Plus, when Anna was with Roscoe, they appeared equals, not an employer and subordinate.

"What happened? Why'd she leave?" Ginny was too curious to wait to hear Roscoe's side of things. Dot's version would have to do.

"It was about Sam," Dot said. "Or, rather, that was the last straw. A guard near Roscoe's office heard the woman ranting about how she believed Roscoe when he promised things would change at the prison. She said she'd wanted to leave since those men cut their heels all those years ago."

Ginny grew more and more defensive with Dot's retelling of the confrontation. Roscoe had done the best he could. The changes may not have been as dramatic or as public as reformers might have liked, but there'd been progress. And Ginny had seen the toll it'd taken on him.

"Well, shit." Ginny left her uneaten bread on the plate and went to dress.

Ginny could think only of getting to Roscoe. Some days she figured their love was something of a miracle, but other relationships seemed just as miraculous. Couples survived the Depression and world wars and childrearing and infidelities and any number of daily hurdles threatening their momentum. Ginny's and Roscoe's challenges were different, and mostly unspoken. But they'd bound them tighter and tighter over the years, even when they didn't realize it. Maybe that bond began when she was a little girl. It was only recently, though, that she'd begun to think of them as one unit and not two separate people. And right now, Ginny sensed he could use her support.

The dress she threw on needed ironing. How ridiculous, though, that in the past she'd worried about things like wrinkled clothes or hosiery with runs, or cakes that fell or whether it'd be a rainy winter. Those trivial concerns just masked the unchangeable things that bred hopelessness: like murderers and rapists who would kill and rape again given the chance, starving inmates who work half the day with bleeding feet and hands, and guards whose humanity was erased permanently by a system decades older than the hills.

Ginny's hurried steps turned into a run, until she found herself in Roscoe's office, blocked by Tim's earnestness.

"I have to see him," she said. "Right away."

"He's on the phone, ma'am. He can't be disturbed." Tim appeared poised to throw himself in front of the closed door to Roscoe's office should she lunge for it.

Roscoe's angry voice rose and fell. As loud as he was, Ginny couldn't make out much, except he didn't want some inmate transferred to the prison.

"Who's he talking to?" she asked.

"Superintendent," Tim said. "We're supposed to be getting a new death row inmate. Some guy who killed a family in New Orleans. Shot seven people, even a little baby. The trial ended yesterday. They're speeding up the execution."

While the crime was heinous, it wasn't out of the ordinary to have extremely violent offenders at the prison. And because the guy had been sentenced to the electric chair, this was the only place in the state he'd be housed.

"Why is Roscoe so riled up?"

"Don't know," he said. "I can't make out what he's been yelling about, but he's been on the phone for fifteen minutes. If I were him, I'd think twice about talking to the superintendent like that."

Anna's resignation could have triggered this foul mood. The prison had a hard time attracting qualified medical staff, and he probably didn't look forward to hiring her replacement.

"Do you mind if I wait?" Ginny sat down on the chair in front of Tim's desk, straining to make out what had now become mostly a tirade of curse words.

"Maybe we shouldn't eavesdrop," Tim said, turning toward the door.

When Roscoe slammed the phone into its cradle, Tim and she both stood.

"May I go in now?"

Tim shrugged, sensing it was futile to stop her.

She knocked soundly and opened the door a crack. "Roscoe?"

He looked up from his desk only for a second before stuffing papers into a satchel and grabbing his hat from the coat rack. He hadn't shaved for a couple of days and the stubble was startlingly gray.

"I can't talk now," he said.

"I'm sorry about Anna. You know, leaving her post so suddenly."

"It wasn't sudden. She threatened to quit every other week."

He brushed past Ginny, leaving a file folder on Tim's desk. "I'll be back tomorrow after dark. John's in charge until then. Make sure he gets this. He'll understand."

"Roscoe?"

"Leave it be, Ginny. I'll explain when I get back."

Roscoe walked down the hallway, his boots clicking angrily against the tile. His aggravation made her think twice about chasing after him. Her uncharacteristic hesitancy was every bit as unnerving as Roscoe's mood.

"Where's he going?" she asked Tim, who'd poured her a cup of coffee.

"Baton Rouge, of course. It's the fifteenth."

Ginny looked at him blankly.

"His hearing with the prison board is this

afternoon," he explained. "Surely you knew."

Roscoe hadn't said a word and this embarrassed her.

"Oh, yes, the prison board," she lied. "I guess I forgot."

"That's to be expected, ma'am," Tim said. "What with you being sick these past weeks."

Her shame only grew with the realization that everyone in the prison was aware of her "spell." They just didn't know the reason for it because Roscoe had covered up Samuel's mutilation.

"I sure hope he doesn't lose his job," Tim continued. "He's the best boss I've ever had."

She thought to remind him that Roscoe was his first and only boss, but left instead.

With such an agitated mind, Ginny wouldn't have been able to sit still at the house, so she headed to the kitchen to help Dot with lunch. When Ginny described the exchange in Roscoe's office, Dot shared her worry that he'd been brought up before the prison board.

"Why didn't he tell me, Dot?"

"Do you have to ask, considering just three days ago you were still refusing to talk or eat?"

Dot was right. Ginny's drama had eclipsed everything going on in his world. In true Roscoe fashion, he'd tried to protect her rather than seek her support or advice. He would be at the hearing in less than an hour, fighting for his job.

"I wonder if this is about Samuel, or the last suppers. Oh, shit . . . the renovations to my parents' house. Maybe that was the last straw."

"No sense wondering about the whys," Dot said. "He and the superintendent bust heads on a lot of things. Might just be his time is up."

Thinking she could cost Roscoe his job made her sick to her stomach. All these years, Ginny thought of the prison board as mostly impotent and their warnings, without teeth. But they had the power to sack both of them. And while Ginny could start fresh anywhere, she doubted Roscoe could do anything else. She tried to picture him on a tractor, or maybe helping a customer at a feed store. It was a silly exercise. Her mind could only conjure him in his drab tan prison uniform and worn boots, the brim of his hat stained with sweat. Or on a horse, surveying the inmates working the fields. Or making the sign of the cross when he signaled an execution to commence.

"You could call him tonight," Dot suggested.

"He didn't even say where he was staying."

"You going to let that stop you?" she asked.

"I suppose not." After they finished the afternoon chores and evening meal, Ginny knew just where she'd go.

The admin building was mostly empty at six, but Ginny counted on Tim to stay late, even without

Roscoe around to see his brownnosing. Yet, when she got to the office, the door was locked.

"Goddammit." She looked around to see if anyone had heard. The halls were empty, the only noise coming from outside in the parking lot.

Ginny pulled a bobby pin from her hair and worked at the lock. It looked so simple in the movies, surely fiddling with it a few moments might do the trick. When the door swung open, she shouted in fright.

"What the hell?" John, the guard from the Waiting Room, towered above her. The bobby pin hadn't worked. He'd opened the door from the inside.

After listening to her incoherent excuse, he ushered Ginny into the office and closed the door behind them.

"What's gotten into you, trying to break into the warden's office?"

"Why were you in here with the door locked?" she asked, going on the defensive.

He shook his head. "Not that I owe you an explanation, but Roscoe left a file for me to read and I didn't want to be disturbed. And yet, here you are."

Contrition wasn't a strong suit, so Ginny didn't bother to try. "Roscoe left in such a hurry, he didn't even tell me where he was staying. I thought Tim might know. When I found the door locked, well . . . I . . ."

"You did what you always do," he said. "Break the rules."

His statement struck her as harsh. "Break the rules?"

"Never mind. Try the Howard Johnson. The prison board usually puts folks up there when they're visiting." John walked through the outer office and into Roscoe's private office, assuming she'd leave.

"Wait a minute," Ginny said, following him. "What do you mean, I break the rules?"

His visible irritation stoked her curiosity, even if she probably didn't want the answer.

"I like you, Ginny. I do. But you take liberties and now Roscoe's ass is on the line."

When he sat behind Roscoe's desk, her heart almost broke. It was like looking into the future and seeing someone take Roscoe's place. Wrong size, wrong age, wrong stoop of the shoulders.

"Liberties?"

"Come on. I'm surprised it's taken this long," he said. "Someone reported you and Roscoe. They told the board he made exceptions to the rules for you . . . like those death row inmate meals. And now, that house of yours is a daily reminder to everyone that you have special privileges."

Each example cut a little deeper until Ginny felt the truth would bleed her out completely.

"And Jesus, the mess with Samuel? There was no keeping that a secret," he said.

"I never meant—"

"Of course you didn't," he said, bitingly. "I know he told you Sam refused a meal. He mentioned it might even be hard on you. But you still went against him."

Her hand reached for the chair back to steady herself. She would not cry in front of John. She'd not let him think she was using tears to gain sympathy. It wasn't deserved.

"Yes, you're right. Just please tell me how to fix this," she said.

"Ginny, there ain't no fixing anything. A lot of the men don't respect him. Others will follow suit once they find out about the board hearing," he said.

"And you, John? Do you respect him?"

He ran his hands over his face as if buying time to formulate an answer she could stomach. His hesitation hit her low in the gut, which was already twisting with long-overdue shame.

"I do respect him. Always have," he said. "But I'm one man. There's very few in Louisiana who think change is a good thing when it comes to this place. The next warden won't be like Roscoe."

Next warden. John wasn't holding out any hope that the hearing would go well.

"Won't you take the job?"

"Not in a million goddamn years. Now, will

you leave me to my work? I'd like to get home to my wife at a decent hour."

She nodded and headed back to the house that could be part of Roscoe's undoing.

1934

Moonshine and Madness

Joe's dark spells on Monday mornings were almost always the result of his weekend drinking binges. Roscoe learned to steer clear and often drove to Catahoula Lake to fish on Saturdays, sometimes sleeping in the cab of his truck overnight to avoid being roped into drinking with him.

Seeing as how he hadn't been to dinner at Joe's and Miriam's in three weeks, he gave in and showed up on the doorstep with a bottle of busthead whiskey. Joe had taken a shine to sour mash during Prohibition and kept several bottles stored under loose boards in his closet so he'd never run out, but Roscoe figured he better bring a peace offering.

Miriam smiled and kissed him on the cheek, but then whispered angrily, "You're a son of a bitch to bring that in my house."

"Nice to see you, too, Miriam." He placed his hat on the rack near the door and smoothed his hair.

Joe's eyes were already glassy when he stumbled forward to offer a handshake. "Well, old buddy, finally decided we were good enough to eat with, huh?"

The end table and lamp had been overturned and several framed photos were now lying broken on the floor.

"Something happen here?" He scanned Miriam's face for an answer as well as any sign she'd been hit. It wouldn't have been the first time. On occasion, he'd busted up rows between the couple and ended up with a shiner himself.

"Not any of your goddamned business, friend of mine," Joe said, sitting on the sofa. "Is that for me?"

Roscoe handed him the bottle and sat down next to him. Miriam excused herself to set the table in the kitchen.

"Man, you got to lay off the hooch, if not for Miriam's sake, then for Ginny's." Roscoe kept his voice low so Miriam couldn't hear.

Joe pressed a finger into Roscoe's cheek, leaving a painful mark. "Don't tell me how to raise my girl."

At only three years old, Ginny was smart as a whip and headstrong, but sensitive, too. He couldn't bear to think of the things she'd witnessed in this house. It made his blood boil to imagine Joe raising a hand to his daughter.

"She already in bed?" Roscoe asked. "I thought I'd say hello."

"Now you after both my girls?"

It was an accusation Roscoe was used to. Joe didn't have to be very drunk to start in on how he'd seen Roscoe eyeing Miriam's ass or that he knew they met secretly behind his back.

"I'm not after your wife. And I don't know a thing about child-rearing. I just care about your family," he said.

Joe leaned over and planted a kiss on his cheek. "You're a good friend, Roscoe, old boy. A good friend. Now where's that food?"

The pot roast was so dry that each bite stuck in Roscoe's throat, threatening to choke him. Miriam wasn't the best of cooks, but she always set a nice table, so he complimented her on it just to keep the conversation pleasant.

"She was a real looker when we were in high school," Joe said, pointing a knife at his wife. "Man, the other guys were jealous when we hooked up. Should've known by looking at her mama that she'd turn out to be a lardo."

"You're being an ass," Roscoe said. "Why don't you shut up?"

"Make me. Go on, show me you're a big man." Joe pushed his chair back, the dull knife still in his hand.

His Jekyll and Hyde personality wore on Roscoe. When sober, his friend had a wicked sense of humor and was as loyal as a coon dog. He often took shifts for other guards, without pay, so they could tend to family business. Roscoe remembered dinners with Joe and Miriam where they laughed easily, enjoying a game of rummy or dominoes. Some nights, the couple couldn't keep their hands off each other and Roscoe felt like a voyeur. But when drunk, Joe said and did things that made Roscoe daydream about killing him. Miriam would be better off at her mama's place and Ginny wouldn't be afraid anymore.

"Let's just finish the meal," Miriam pleaded.

"You call this a meal? Pig slop is more like it." Joe dropped the knife on the table and staggered back to the sofa, landing facedown on the cushions. Within seconds, the muffled snores began.

Roscoe stared at his plate, hoping Miriam wouldn't cry. Comforting her felt awkward. There was nothing to say anyway. Her husband would be a different man when he'd sobered up. A repentant man. And that always seemed to be enough for her.

"Take the booze when you leave." She stood to clear the dishes.

"Leave my plate," he said. "I'm not finished."

"You don't have to eat it, Roscoe."

"I'm so hungry I could eat shoe leather," he said, taking another bite of roast and carrot.

She sat back down, her eyes a little brighter. "Well, you're in luck. It's on the menu tonight."

He laughed with her, then described the ornery ten-inch bluegill he caught on his last fishing trip.

With Joe snoring in the other room, Roscoe thought it didn't hurt to stay for dessert and coffee. Miriam may burn a roast beyond recognition, but she could bake a hell of a pie.

"It's peach," she said, placing a large slice in front of him.

"One of my favorites." He grinned broadly, rubbing his hands together like a kid.

"You say that about every pie I bake."

"They're all my favorites then."

He gladly ate while she talked about things only she cared about: the fabric she'd just bought in Boucherville to make play clothes for Ginny, her suspicion that the wife of a new guard was part black, her gut feeling that summer was sure to be the hottest one on record.

She refilled his coffee cup and he didn't stop her, even if it meant he'd be up all night. Miriam seemed to drink up any kindness offered, so he asked for another slice of pie and listened patiently as she recited a list of repairs the ramshackle house needed and how Joe had neglected the place far too long.

Roscoe pushed back from the table and rubbed his full belly in appreciation. He was about to tell Miriam it had been her best pie yet when he noticed she'd begun to weep. Her chest heaved with silent sobs as if she struggled to contain some horrible sorrow.

"Miriam? What is it?" He hesitated a moment, then dragged a chair to her side and placed a hand on her shoulder.

She shook her head, signaling for a moment to gain her composure. Yet, each time she opened her mouth to speak, she brought two hands up to cover it.

"Tell me, Miriam. Has he hurt Ginny?" It was the only horror Roscoe could imagine warranting such a crying fit.

"No. He'd never . . . He adores that child," she said, gulping in air. "It's what happened in the Red Hat cellblock."

After several escape attempts last year, thirty men had been moved into a separate cellblock, the strictest in the prison. They called it the Red Hat because those inmates working in the field were forced to wear straw hats painted red. It made it easier to spot and shoot runaways.

Earlier last week, Roscoe had witnessed Joe mete out his own brand of peacekeeping in the unit after an inmate threw his shit bucket at him. The place had been suffocating that day—temperatures so high that some inmates stripped naked and lay on the floor to try to cool themselves. Joe pulled the offender from his cell and bludgeoned him with a nightstick until his face was a mass of meat, bone, and blood. Then, looking like a deranged person, he'd dragged the dead man up and down the cellblock as a warning to the rest of them. When Roscoe had tried to intervene, two other guards held him back.

"Miriam, that's not something you need to worry about," he said. "Put it out of your mind."

But Roscoe hadn't been able to forget it either. The savagery in Joe's eyes burned so hot Roscoe knew it'd never be extinguished. He'd seen it before—guards who lost all sense of reason and decency.

"The drink has affected his mind," she said. "I've heard the stories. Moonshine making people go mad. No telling where he's been getting his booze all these years."

"I won't let him hurt you and Ginny."

Joe's justification had always been that the inmates were animals, undeserving of better treatment. He said there'd be chaos if the guards didn't keep the upper hand. Roscoe had to believe him incapable of that kind of violence against his own family.

"Oh, sweet, naïve Roscoe. You come around every once in a blue moon with a present for Ginny, or to have a piece of pie and shoot the shit. You can't protect us any more than we can protect ourselves."

He cringed at the resignation and truth in her words.

"I promise you," he said. "I'll come around

more often. And I'll make sure Joe cuts back on the whiskey. Things will be different."

She grabbed their empty plates and coffee cups, and placed them in the sink.

"I'll help you with the dishes," he said, getting up.

Miriam turned on the radio that sat on the counter near the stove. The sweet melody came across scratchy and distant on the cheap model. He recognized it as Duke Ellington but didn't know the tune by name.

"Have a quick dance with me instead." She took off her apron and extended her hand.

Roscoe thought it was the least he could do.

Chapter 12

Roscoe hadn't checked into the Howard Johnson, and Ginny didn't feel like calling every motel in Baton Rouge to track him down. What could she possibly say to make things better? *Did it go well? I miss you? I'm sorry?*

Dot was right. Roscoe had made his own choices all along: to hire Ginny, to fall in love with her, to place her wants before his. Yet, blame lay heavy on her shoulders. Ginny had pressed for the job. She allowed the affair to happen. She pushed and pushed and pushed in a system that put a bull's-eye on the back of anyone making waves.

With Dot gone for the weekend, the house was empty, but Ginny's mind was inundated with doubts and regrets vying for her attention. What seemed a magical place just a day ago now felt garish and obscene, especially in contrast with the other housing. Everything John said had been true. She was Roscoe's special pet, perched on a pedestal towering above the muck. The rest of the prison knew she had special privileges, and Roscoe's authority was diminished because of it.

Instead of the radio soothing her, Ginny found the songs too chipper and grating, so she turned it off. Neither reading nor working on the cookbook appealed to her. She almost thought of visiting Miriam for the weekend, but came to her senses quickly.

Her thoughts turned to the mutilated scrapbook she hadn't looked at since Dot helped piece it back together. She dragged a chair from the kitchen to the bedroom closet where the scrapbook lay at the very back of the top shelf under some sweaters. The bulb in the closet had burned out, but enough light shone from the overhead fixture in the bedroom. What Ginny hadn't counted on was not being able to reach it. Standing on the chair, even on her tiptoes, she could barely touch the edge of the book with her fingertips. Dot had been the one to shove it up there during the hasty move from the barracks. She'd said she wouldn't let Ginny keep it unless it was somewhere Roscoe wouldn't happen upon it accidentally. No one was going to go to the trouble of looking in that dusty old closet and Ginny shouldn't have either.

The chair rocked slightly as she stepped down. The floorboard under the front chair legs had bowed just a bit, piquing her curiosity. Pulling the chair away, she knelt before the board and pressed until she confirmed it wasn't nailed down. Her fingers alone couldn't get a purchase on either side to pry it up. Ginny hurried into the kitchen to retrieve two butter knives, which did the trick. The board lifted out like a piece of sheet cake.

The dirt crawl space beneath the house wasn't visible, so she figured her daddy had rigged a compartment of some kind. But why? The thought of reaching an arm into the hole gave her the shivers. A flashlight wasn't available because she'd used it walking to the kitchen one especially dark morning and left it there accidentally.

Ginny sat back on her haunches, contemplating her options, when Dot's voice rang out.

"What in heaven's name are you looking for?" She towered above Ginny, hands on her hips.

"Jesus!" Ginny yelled, losing her balance.

"He's not hiding beneath your floorboards, so you're wasting your time." She laughed at her own joke. Ginny couldn't be mad. Dot might just be curious enough to reach down in there for her.

"It looks to be a secret compartment," Ginny said. "Why are you back?"

"Tried to purchase gasoline in town and realized I forgot my pocketbook," Dot said. "Let me have a look."

Dot dropped to her knees and put her face close to the hole as if she might be able to ascertain its purpose by smell and hearing.

"Guess you don't have a flashlight?" she asked.

"Nope," Ginny said.

Dot leaned on her side so that she was laid out

flat. In that position, she could maneuver the length of her pudgy arm into the space.

"Be careful," Ginny said.

"Nothing in here to be afraid of 'cept maybe some spiders or a mouse. Don't be such a child."

Dot closed her eyes.

"I got something. Feels like glass." She withdrew her hand, now wrapped about a bottle of amber liquid. "Hooch," she said triumphantly. "Must be left over from your daddy's drinking days."

All of his days had been drinking days. Although, in the weeks leading up to his murder, his episodes of drunkenness were less frequent. Ginny knew this to be true because she'd carved a tick mark in the wall near her bed for the nights he called her mama bad names. She'd marked an X for the nights he hit Miriam. The change in him came on gradually, though. Ginny couldn't pinpoint exactly when she started to think he'd become a different person.

After the miraculous change in his personality and drinking habits, there were many nights that he, her mama, and Roscoe would play cards or dominoes until way after Ginny's bedtime. She fell asleep to the comforting sound of laughter instead of her daddy's usual cursing and stomping around. Her stomach tightened at the memory. Those days seemed fragile and fleeting, and she often braced for the old daddy to make an appearance, especially when Roscoe left for the evening. After her father died, Ginny remembered being angry with him for leaving them when he'd just started to become the type of father she wanted.

"I felt something else in there." Dot thrust her arm back under the boards and fished around until she pulled out a large bundle of fabric. It'd been white originally, but dirt and time had made it dingy. She sneezed three times in quick succession.

"Bless you. Now what the hell is that?" Ginny knelt down and took the cocoon from Dot while she stood and brushed the cobwebs from her sleeve.

Unrolling it carefully to keep the dust down, Ginny soon saw it was two pieces. One resembled a long robe. The other piece was smaller and cone-shaped.

Dot moved backward so suddenly, she fell against the bed. Her face was like a child's after a bad dream, twisted with fear that couldn't be eased.

"What's wrong?" Ginny asked. "You look like you've seen a ghost."

"Much worse." Tears formed at the corners of Dot's eyes and she swiped at them angrily.

Dot agreed to stay for coffee. Ginny didn't want her on the highway at night, given the state she was in, and Ginny didn't want to be alone either. She'd uncovered a shameful part of her daddy's past, one that was tightly intertwined with Dot's own family's history. Ginny fought the urge to vomit.

"Those goddamned hooded rednecks." The cup rattled as Dot set it down on the saucer.

"I can't believe it," Ginny murmured.

"Oh, I can believe it," Dot said. "As children, we could never walk alone, even in daylight. My brothers and I spent many a sleepless night, afraid that the white ghosts were coming for us. My father said those spineless bastards could kill, rape, burn. Ain't nobody going to care if a black man or woman died."

Ginny felt she owed Dot an apology for her daddy's actions. Although Ginny had no idea how violent or extreme they'd been. Knowing what the Klan was capable of, especially in Louisiana, she feared the worst. All the images of her father she'd stored in her mind were now superimposed with the robe and hood now lying menacingly on the kitchen table.

"I'm sorry you had to see these," Ginny said.

"It's not like you ever forget about those bastards." Dot's laugh was bitter, yet tinged with palpable fear. "My folks didn't talk about it much except for the warnings to be careful. But we all knew of people who'd been hurt or died.

But even in church, when we mourned them, we didn't mention the Klan outright."

Ginny's eyes welled to think the victims kept their grief as secret as Klansmen kept their identities.

"Please just throw those things away," Dot said. "Burn 'em. Don't keep them in this house another second."

"I can't. Not just yet."

"Why in the hell would you want to keep them?"

Ginny took a sip of coffee and noticed her hands shook as badly as Dot's. "I want to see Mama's reaction when I visit tomorrow."

Dot ended up staying the night. She'd been too unnerved by the discovery, her old fears heightened by the darkness outside. Ginny slept very little. One persistent nightmare woke her over and over. She had been standing underneath a large tree, in the dark of night, clothed only in a thin nightgown. Hooded men with glowing torches surrounded her. One looped a rope around her neck. Her daddy's hazel eyes shone through the eyeholes. In the dream, Ginny started screaming, "I'm white, Daddy. Don't do it. I'm white."

Daylight did nothing to ease her shame or nausea. Thinking her father could be a murderer made her want to hide under the covers like a little girl. Not knowing the truth, though, would only sicken her mind and heart with assumptions. If Miriam could confirm the worst, Ginny vowed to lock the horrors away and never think of him again. She'd burn the robe and hood and with them, any connection she had to her father.

The road to Boucherville was empty at dawn, especially on a Saturday. With the windows down, the wind whipped at her hair and lifted the edges of the robe, which rested on the seat beside her. Originally, Ginny thought to stow it in the trunk. Instead, she let her daddy's sins ride in the front to stoke her resolve.

Her mama's house was dark and still. The door was unlocked, as it always was. Miriam feared nothing, unlike Dot's family, who were hypervigilant, especially when Klan raids were prevalent.

Ginny walked through the silent rooms and down the hall. Her hand hovered over the doorknob to her mother's bedroom. Once Ginny turned that knob, her life would change forever. She reminded herself that the discovery of the robe had already altered her life, so she entered.

Miriam lay with her back to the door, the yellow chenille bedspread pulled up over her ears. Ginny's father used to joke that this lifelong habit was sure to lead to suffocation, especially in the heat of a Louisiana summer. Her mama had insisted that her ears felt a chill, even on warm nights, and it comforted her to have the fabric shielding them.

Gone was the fire Ginny had felt in her belly on the drive over. Earlier, she'd envisioned a loud confrontation, even flinging the robes in Miriam's face and demanding answers. Now, she stood before her mother wanting comfort more than confirmation.

Miriam groaned softly and turned toward her daughter, arms stretching like a cat's. Her sleepy eyes focused and refocused until she recognized it was only Ginny. Her presence hadn't startled Miriam at all. It was as normal as it had been when Ginny was a child, tugging at her mama's covers and begging for pancakes for breakfast.

"My God, Ginny. What time is it?"

Miriam's yawn spurred her own. "Six-thirty maybe."

Her mama sat up in bed. Her slip had twisted and bunched, revealing a part of her breast. She pointed to her bathrobe at the end of the bed, so Ginny tossed it to her. Her face, unburdened by makeup and worry, looked more youthful than Ginny remembered it ever being.

"Something happen between you and Roscoe?" Miriam pulled the robe around her and walked out of the room.

Ginny followed her into the kitchen, the Klan robe tucked beneath an arm. "Why would you assume something like that?"

"It's too early to fight," Miriam said. "I'm making coffee."

The words threw Ginny off-kilter. Her mama was always raring for a fight, especially where Ginny was concerned. Baffled, she sat down.

"What's that in your arms?" Miriam lit a cigarette and blew a ribbon of smoke out of the corner of her mouth.

"Why are you smoking?"

"I've smoked off and on for years," Miriam said. "If you'd come around more often, you'd know that."

Her fight was returning. Perhaps she'd been too groggy earlier to go on the offensive.

"Well, I'm here now. And I need to talk about this." Ginny laid the bundle on the table.

"And that is?"

Angrily, Ginny grabbed the robe and held it against the length of her body. Miriam glanced only briefly before pouring their coffee.

"Well?" Ginny asked.

Her mama blew a cloud of smoke in her direction. "Well, what? So you found out Roscoe was a Klansman."

Ginny raged against Miriam's accusation. "This is Daddy's, not Roscoe's. I found it under a board in your old closet."

"What were you doing in the old house?" Miriam asked. "I figured that rickety place would have fallen in on itself by now."

She couldn't have known Roscoe had given it new life and that Ginny lived there. If Ginny had shared that information—and she never would have—her mama's spite would have poisoned the good in the gesture.

Her mama's indifference irritated and confused her. "It doesn't matter how I found it, Mama. I want to know . . . I need to know—"

"Need to know what, little girl?" Miriam interrupted. "That your Daddy really didn't wear that robe? That he wasn't a part of the Klan? Why aren't you having this conversation with your boyfriend?"

"Please leave Roscoe out of this."

"Why? He and your daddy both wore the hood in the old days. Hell, Roscoe might still."

Angry tears poured from Ginny. "You're a lying bitch!"

Miriam crossed the room in two strides and slapped her face. "I've had about all I'm going to take of your disrespect. You show up here only when you want something. And even then, can't wait to get away. If you don't like the answers you're getting, go look somewhere else."

Ginny's cheek stung like hornet fire, but her mother's words stung equally. Her fury shocked Ginny into uncharacteristic silence. Sitting down at the kitchen table, Ginny cradled her face. She knew Miriam wasn't lying, but how could she not rail against this unbearable truth? Her world was more than upside down and inside out. It was a mutated, unrecognizable version of itself. Within seconds, Ginny was homeless and motherless. Roscoe had abandoned her without even knowing it.

"Ginny?" Miriam placed a cup of coffee in front of her daughter and sat down.

"Huh?" Ginny looked at her through changed eyes and with a changed heart. A stranger was offering her coffee and she didn't know how to act or what to say.

"Stop acting so shocked. You're going to be all right," Miriam said.

What would "all right" look like? Everything would be different as soon as Ginny left this house. Driving, eating, sleeping, breathing, working.

Miriam was right when she said Ginny always hotfooted it out of her house once she got what she came for. And that's what Ginny should've done. But here she was, unwilling to make a move or utter a sound. Her shaking hands gripped the coffee cup. She was able to take a few sips of the scalding liquid, which warmed her throat and stomach.

"It didn't make him a bad man, you know," Miriam said.

Whether she meant her husband or Roscoe didn't matter. In Ginny's eyes, it did make them bad men. She never bought the idea that the Klan was just a reflection of the times in which they lived. Plenty of men chose not to participate in the violence, even if they hated the colored. Hatred in one's heart was different from the kind carried out in church burnings or lynchings.

"How can you be so goddamned accepting?" Ginny implored. "Are you okay with what they do? The people they hurt are our neighbors."

Miriam's doughy face was expressionless. "It is what it is. Don't act like this is some big surprise. You're the daughter of a prison guard and you've worked at Greenmount your whole adult life."

"And that's supposed to mean what?"

Now Miriam appeared mostly exasperated with Ginny. "Back in the day, it was a given that most prison personnel were in the Klan. I assumed it ran all the way up to the state corrections board. Probably still does."

"Did Daddy kill anyone?" Ginny offered up the question to a woman known for her uncanny ability to hurt her daughter, but Miriam was the only immediate link to that time.

"We didn't talk about those things," her mama said. "Women stayed out of that business."

"You didn't ask?"

Her laugh came out like a bark. "Ask? Like, 'How was your evening, dear? Kill any niggers tonight?' "

"Don't be so ugly," Ginny pleaded. "I want to know if you think he killed anyone."

"Of course, I do." She said it so matter-of-factly, she might as well have slapped Ginny a second time. "The man had a vicious streak, and booze only gave him permission to act on it. I'm going to make us some eggs."

Ginny's mind reeled at this nonchalance. Miriam pulled eggs from the icebox and a skillet from the cabinet next to the stove. She looked like an actress in some television program cooking breakfast for her normal family on a normal morning.

"Scrambled or fried?" A freshly lit cigarette dangled from her mama's lips, which had upturned just enough to make Ginny think it was a grin.

Stumbling into the bathroom down the hall, Ginny vomited a burning, coffee-tinged bile.

The smell of frying eggs made it impossible for Ginny's stomach to right itself. She leaned back and pressed her cheek against the cool, porcelain tile of the bathroom wall. At some point since Ginny arrived, she'd kicked off her sandals. Her toenails needed clipping. Traces of the Vixen Red polish remained. She couldn't imagine herself doing mundane tasks like clipping nails or scrubbing toilets or cooking breakfast ever again. Normal didn't apply to anything now.

Miriam came in and sat on the closed lid of the toilet. "Get it out of your system?"

Ginny didn't bother to answer. Retching couldn't relieve her of the helplessness that took up residence in her gut. Her fear was that it would now grow like a tumor, uncontrolled until it consumed the whole of her.

Her mama got up and left, but she wasn't gone for long. When she returned, she sat cross-legged on the floor in front of Ginny. She'd brought clippers, an emery board, and polish remover. The sight of Miriam working on Ginny's toenails left her even more speechless than the earlier slap. At first, the tenderness was almost too much to bear and Ginny jerked with every touch. Her mind suddenly latched on to a memory of the two of them sitting on the front porch, doing each other's nails. As a child, Ginny's hands had been clumsy. More polish ended up on Miriam's skin, yet she always praised Ginny for a fine job. Was Ginny's mind playing tricks on her? Memories of her mama were usually a catalog of hurts and disappointments.

"Why didn't you leave him?" Ginny finally asked.

"Same reason you won't leave Roscoe," Miriam said. "Love."

"Is that enough?"

"Has to be, doesn't it? You want some new polish or leave 'em bare?"

Ginny nodded, which Miriam took as a yes for the polish. Soon the tiny nubs of nail were a bright shade of coral almost offensive to the eyes. Ginny wiggled her toes as she'd done as a child, inspecting the work.

"Good?" her mama asked.

"Thank you," Ginny whispered.

"Let's eat those eggs." Miriam pulled Ginny to her feet. "You're still too skinny and I don't need you fainting and ruining my Saturday."

Miriam let Ginny wash the dishes, even though Ginny braced for the usual criticisms. *You're using too much dish soap. Is that water hot enough? Scrape the plates first or you'll clog my drain.*

Ginny didn't have to worry about the temperature of the dishwater today. She intentionally made it almost too hot to bear because it forced her to feel something. Physical pain seemed almost laughable compared to the ache in her heart.

While Ginny washed, Miriam sat at the table with the morning paper, clipping coupons.

"Please tell me you're not heading back to the prison to give Roscoe hell," she said. "You ought to cool off a bit first."

"Since when do you care about our relationship?" Ginny said, drying her hands.

"Cut the crap. You've been with the man more than four years. I know by now that it's serious."

"Then why do you always give me shit about him?" Ginny asked.

"Any mother would want better for you," Miriam said. "He's almost twice your age and will probably never marry you. You're not getting the kind of life I hoped you'd have."

Not once had Ginny ever dreamed of being a bride, unless she counted the times she wrote Douglas Fairbanks Jr. and asked him to wait for her until she turned fourteen. She didn't fill a hope chest with kitchen items and linens, anticipating the day she'd have her own home, picket fence and all. In high school, Ginny went on a grand total of five dates, all with the same guy. She'd given him her virginity, which apparently meant there'd not be a sixth date because she was "that kind of girl."

"Did you have the life Grandma Nan wanted you to have?" Ginny asked.

"Hell, no," Miriam said. "She called your daddy's family poor white trash even though we didn't have a penny more ourselves. And when he started working at the prison, I didn't think I'd hear the end of it."

After she and Miriam had moved into town, her grandmother never once disparaged Ginny's father in her presence. Had her mama really endured criticisms as harsh as the ones she doled out to Ginny?

"I don't remember Grandma saying an unkind word about Daddy," Ginny said.

"Why would she? After Joe's murder, she felt the problem went away."

Ginny's recollection of her grandma Nan was that of a soft, overweight woman who hugged so fiercely the air left your lungs in one swoosh. Nan powdered her silver hair instead of washing it regularly, and thus smelled more heavily of talcum than perfume. Her purse was always fair game to pillage, the spoils being hard candies, pennies, hairpins, and shopping lists.

"Surely, she wasn't that hateful," Ginny said, wanting to protect the fragile memories of her grandmother.

"After your daddy's funeral, when all the guests had left the house and we were cleaning up, she took my hand and said, 'When you look back, you'll see that man's passing was the luckiest day of your life.'"

Ginny's heart seemed to miss a beat. The strongest urge was to hug her mother, to tell her she was sorry. But sorry for what? Ginny was part of a multigenerational chain of disappointments. If she decided to have children, it wasn't a certainty she'd be a kind and loving mother herself.

"I can throw that away for you." Miriam pointed to the Klan robe.

"No."

"No? Why on earth keep it?"

Ginny mulled over her knee-jerk response. The

robe was something physical she wanted to show Roscoe. Something that could bolster her resolve. Without even thinking it through, she'd already decided to leave him.

Chapter 13

Ginny turned her car onto Highway 61 and drove without a destination in mind. At least she was moving, doing something other than foundering in her grief. Yes, grief was the only way to describe it. Roscoe was dead to her, as was the hope that they would have a future together. She couldn't picture working at the prison anymore; that part of her life was stolen, too.

Occasionally, she swiped at the tears clouding her vision, but didn't care if she saw the road clearly or not. She was suffocating, both from the knowledge that Roscoe had been, or still was, part of the Klan, and that there was no going back to how things were before the discovery of the robe and hood.

She wondered how her feelings differed from those who physically lost a loved one. Did they feel their lives were over? Who or what could they blame? Ginny didn't know where to direct her anger. Miriam had done nothing but confirm the truth. Roscoe had only lied by omission. No. She was angry with herself. Mostly for thinking happiness was within her reach. Her parents certainly proved that happiness had nothing to do with love. Miriam had never been happy, but said she stayed in her marriage for love. Ginny didn't think she had what it took to overlook something so huge just because she loved Roscoe. Her greatest fear, of course, was that he had hurt people—maybe killed people—and yet could appear the gentle man she thought he was.

Lost in thought, she hardly noticed the merge onto Highway 425. An hour had passed since she left her mama's house and she now found herself in the sleepy town of Ferriday. Ginny hadn't been able to eat the eggs her mama had made. A piercing headache taunted her that she'd waited too long to eat. She pulled to the curb in front of a small diner whose window advertised a blue-plate special.

Sitting at the counter, Ginny was aware of the other patrons and their stares. The mirror behind the soda machine told her why. Her unbrushed hair was frightful. Her dress was nothing but a plain cotton frock suitable for housework, but not public display, and she'd pulled on her loafers without stockings or socks. She hadn't been headed anywhere but her mama's, so she paid no mind to how she dressed.

"Morning, miss." The man behind the counter poured her a cup of coffee she hadn't ordered. "Lunch service won't start for ten minutes, but I can make an exception."

His kind eyes were welcome considering how self-conscious she felt.

"I appreciate that," she said. "What's good?"

"Since I own this place, I better say everything is good, but I'd highly recommend the meatloaf today." He winked and motioned for a waitress to join them.

"Betty, take care of Miss . . ."

"It's Polk. Ginny Polk," she said. "I'll have the meatloaf, an extra roll, and a slice of whatever pie is the freshest."

The waitress smiled. "A big appetite for a tiny gal. I like that."

Ginny was astonished that food held any appeal, but the smells of the diner were intoxicating. Simmering soups and gravies, freshly baked breads, roasted and pan-fried meats. She imagined sitting there for a few hours, just breathing in the comfort only food could provide her. Earlier, in the car, she'd envisioned her life in some sort of limbo without eating or sleeping or interacting with other human beings. Maybe she expected to have to retreat to a safe place in her mind as she'd done after the incident with Samuel. But here she was, talking and living and surviving.

When her food arrived, she dug into it with ferocity. To hell with the diners who stared. She'd never see them again.

Betty refilled her coffee cup and set down a small plate with two rolls on it.

"I hope you don't mind me asking, but are you

okay?" The waitress's voice was low. No one else at the counter could hear.

"Okay?"

"Well, you look a little worse for the wear," she said. "And we don't see many young girls out on their own. I saw you drive up in that car by yourself."

Young girls.

"Well, I didn't get much sleep. I haven't eaten in more than twenty-four hours. And this morning, I got some of the worst news of my life," Ginny said, stifling a small burp. "I believe I'm doing all right considering."

"Considering," Betty echoed.

"And, I'm twenty-nine," Ginny added. "I could show you my license, if you like."

The waitress laughed, deep and long. "I'll take your word for it. Holler at me when you want that pie. The rhubarb is the best, but the cherry is a close second."

Ginny's breathing had slowed considerably since entering the diner, and her mind no longer twisted with the what-ifs and whys that tortured her earlier. The calm was at once discomforting and luxurious. She focused on her meal and the conversations she could hear around her.

A few stools over, two older men were having a spirited discussion on who caught the largest bass the previous weekend at Catahoula Lake.

Catahoula. Roscoe's thinking spot. The one place he retreated when life got unwieldy.

When she visited Samuel's family in Jonesville, she saw signs to the lake on Highway 84. It was less than an hour's drive away from the diner.

"Betty? Can I get the pie and these rolls to go?" Ginny asked.

Those times Roscoe said he was heading to Catahoula Lake, Ginny knew he really meant the Little River, which fed into the 30,000-acre, saucer-shaped sump. The river always teemed with fish, even when lake levels plummeted in late summer. He'd described his special spot over and over again and how to access it from a dirt road that meandered until it reached a hairpin bend in the river. He had said that even though the road was marked, he rarely saw anyone else at the fishing spot he so prized.

Ginny pulled the car well off the dirt path and under a copse of river birch. She was surprised to find a beat-up Ford pickup parked several yards away, hidden mostly by the wide trunks of the bald cypress trees at the water's edge.

Grabbing the paper sack that held the buttered rolls and rhubarb pie, she made her way to the river. To her right and farther down the bank stood a black man, ancient as the trees sheltering him. He grappled with a tangled fishing line. She nodded and smiled, and he returned the greeting.

The ground was too saturated for her to sit. Ginny felt awkward, standing there with sack in hand. She looked both up and down the river, not really searching for anything, but wondering why she thought it had been a good idea to have come. As she turned to go, the old man waved her over.

"Name's Crawford." He had a mouthful of large, straight teeth as white as the hair on his head. His smile overwhelmed all other features.

"Ginny," she said, holding out her hand.

"I'd shake, but my hands smell of bait," he said. "Nice to meet you anyways."

An awkward silence settled over them until he said, "You got bait in that there bag?"

She looked down at her hand. Juices from the pie had soaked through the bag's bottom. "This? No. Just some leftovers from lunch. I'd be happy to share if you'd be willing to sit a spell on your tailgate."

He grabbed his fishing pole and a tin pail that held his tackle. "Lead the way, miss."

Crawford pulled the tailgate down and swiped his handkerchief across it before motioning for her to sit. He retrieved from the front seat a red-checked dish towel wrapped around a sandwich.

"This here is onions and lard on my wife's famous homemade bread." He admired the one-inch slices of bread enclosed around the thin layer of filling.

"Famous, huh? I have two buttered rolls and a

slice of rhubarb pie," she said. "I'll trade you the pie for half your sandwich."

Ginny had forgotten that her mama would sometimes make onion-and-lard sandwiches for her daddy to take to work. As a child, she'd turned her nose up at the mere thought of it. Now, it teased her appetite back to life, even after the large plate of meatloaf she'd consumed just an hour before.

"I'm surprised to see you out here." Crawford stuck half the pie in his mouth, then sucked stray crumbs and filling from his fingers.

"Didn't know I was coming, but I had some thinking to do."

He cackled so loudly she almost choked on a bite of her sandwich.

"What is it about white folk needing a place to think," he said. "This man I know, a prison warden from down near Boucherville, come out here every once in a while. Says he's fishing, but mostly he just sit quietly or talk to me. Sometimes he sleep in his truck overnight."

This time, Ginny did choke and Crawford looked at her with alarm. He handed her a mason jar full of water and she gladly accepted.

"A warden?" she asked. "Roscoe Simms, by chance?"

"I'll be damned," he said. "You know Roscoe?"

She considered how much to share. "I work at the prison, too."

Crawford found the coincidence as astounding as she did and kept slapping his thigh to emphasize his delight. Then, he shook his head, sadness replacing the smile. His eyes became his strongest feature then. Amber-colored with two dark spots in the white part of one eye.

"What's wrong?" she asked.

"I feel for the man," he said. "That place has worn him down but good. He ain't cut out for that work."

Ginny drummed her fingers nervously against the metal tailgate. "Why do you say that?"

"He told me 'bout all the changes he want to make. How nothing seemed to get better no matter what he did. You friends?"

"He's my boss, but yes, we're friends," she said, even though she didn't know what they were anymore.

"Then you know he don't belong there." Crawford stuffed the rest of the pie in his mouth. "That was damn good. Even better than my wife's."

"Do you know him well?" Ginny asked.

"Lord, yes," he said. "Him and me been fishing for almost twenty years. Way back before he became warden. After they offered him the job some eight, nine years ago he knew it was a mistake to take it. Every time I told him he should quit, he'd just shake his head."

Ginny struggled to understand how Roscoe

could strike up a friendship with a black man and still be part of the Klan. She wanted to know more about this grandfatherly man and his place in Roscoe's life, but she feared any more prying. Already Crawford had given up information he probably shouldn't have.

Still, she wondered why Roscoe hadn't mentioned her—or if he had, why Crawford didn't guess who she was. Knowing Roscoe, he kept their relationship private. He'd always been worried what would happen to both of them should the prison board find out.

The hearing. It was yesterday. She hadn't given it a thought since finding the Klan robe. This shamed her. No matter what became of them, Ginny cared about Roscoe. She hoped the hearing hadn't turned into a witch hunt. Who knows what kind of state he was in right now, or if he'd already returned to the prison.

"He may not be warden much longer," she said softly.

"Why you say that?"

Ginny regretted revealing that much. "I know it's weighed heavy on his mind. Just as you said."

Crawford lost his train of thought and lapsed into a one-sided conversation on the perks of this particular fishing spot, then into the way his wife prepared the crappie he caught—dusting it with cornmeal and cayenne pepper before frying. No flour or egg, he said. That made it gummy.

His voice rose and fell to match his expressions. Ginny nodded occasionally, but paid little attention to his animated stories. That is, until he brought the conversation back to Roscoe.

"Good thing Roscoe made his peace with the Lord." Crawford picked at his teeth with a small twig. "I think that's the only thing keeping him going all these years. He said he ought to be in that electric chair hisself. Praying over those souls, as well as his own, is the only thing he can do."

A line of sweat trickled down between Ginny's shoulder blades, causing her to shudder. Crawford knew something. Something that shamed Roscoe so much he thought he should die for it. She feared if she asked point-blank, the old man would realize he'd overstepped. The despondency Ginny felt after finding the Klan robe was nothing compared to the panic coming over her now.

"You more than his friend, Miss Ginny, aren't you?" He stared at her solemnly. She wished to see his infectious smile again. She wished he'd tell her a happy story. Maybe one of those fish tales, where the length of the bluegill or bass grew with each telling.

"Yes, I suppose I am," she whispered.

"Then you know a man's never the same after he take someone's life," Crawford said. "You just ask the Lord for forgiveness and try to live the best life you can."

Never the same. Ginny gripped the edge of the tailgate with both hands. She wanted to leave, but feared she'd not be able to stand upright. She'd given her body and her heart to Roscoe. She thought she knew him; all the little pieces that no one else had access to. And yet, she knew nothing of the two horrific pieces that came to light in only the last twenty-four hours.

"I'm amazed he only killed one man while doing his job," he continued. "Everyone know what go on at that prison. Lotta killing nobody even care about."

Ginny's heart raced after this latest revelation. On the job? When had it happened? Whom had he killed? She now had two things to confront Roscoe about, but wondered why she felt she needed any explanation. The past couldn't be rewritten. She doubted he could offer any explanation that would make her consider a life with him.

"Thank you very much for the sandwich, sir," Ginny said, finally getting up. "Best I be getting back."

"All righty then." His smile returned. "Come on back sometime when Roscoe goes fishing."

She longed to be able to say she would. The idyllic spot could have been her and Roscoe's special hideaway instead of the place where she learned an awful truth.

Peabody Lejeune
Inmate Number 5903
Crime: Aggravated Robbery
Sentence: 50 Years

The other inmates pretty much leave Peabody alone these days. At seventy-five, he's no longer got reason to be afraid in his cell. Ain't nobody bother with a shriveled old man. His days are not about survival anymore. They're about peeling potatoes.

His spine is crooked from three decades of bending over in those godforsaken fields. If he'd been transferred to the canning plant, he'd be standing all day. Sitting on a wooden stool inside the kitchen is as close to being set free as it comes.

"Stop your daydreaming," the big black woman tells him. "You still got a bushel to go."

Peabody hates that old nigger, but he keeps his mouth shut. Miss Polk takes too much sass from her, but it ain't his place to point out something that's clear as day.

"Don't be so hard on him, Dot," Miss Polk says. "He's an old man."

When Dot leaves her shift early, Peabody is relieved. He's able to carry on a proper conversation with Miss Polk on those rare occasions when the darkie is gone.

"Someone dancing with Gertie next week, eh?" he says.

"Yes. The execution is Tuesday," she says. "Why do you ask?"

"Just wondering what that boy wants for his last meal."

Before he falls asleep at night, Peabody makes a game of figuring out what he'd ask for if he was going to the electric chair. This week he's got it narrowed down to jambalaya or hoppin' john. 'Course Miss Polk makes damn fine biscuits and gravy. His list changes all the time, but he believes the act of thinking keeps his mind alive in a dead place like Greenmount.

"That's personal," she says. "I don't think we should talk about it."

"Everybody gonna find out anyway," he says. "Guards talk. Prisoners talk. Don't see no harm in you telling me now."

Miss Polk gives him a curious look like she can't decide whether to be mad or disappointed.

"Pecan pie," she says. "And a glass of milk."

Peabody's mouth waters. He's never included sweets on his list, but he's rethinking it now. He remembers the pies his wife would bake for the church suppers. Once a week, he'd round up hog lard from the meat plant for her. Made the flakiest damn crusts.

The last pie she baked for him had been a mulberry pie. Those tart berries required double the sugar, she'd say. He remembers the day perfectly. He'd been out drinking with his brother the night before and didn't make it home until about eleven the next morning. By that time, Angeline was fit to be tied. She stood on the front porch, the still-warm pie in her shaking hands.

She'd quoted Scripture at the top of her lungs and told him he was a worthless excuse for a husband before throwing the pie at him. He grabs his elbow now, recalling the pain when the tin pie plate hit the bone just so.

"Something wrong?" Miss Polk asks.

"Nah, I'm fine. I was just thinking I'd ask for hoppin' john as my last supper."

This time he's sure the look she gives him is disappointment.

"You should be grateful you're not on death row," she says, and turns back to the stove.

He considers telling her she doesn't know what it's like to live in a dead place for thirty years. That frying in that chair sometimes seems like a mercy. Instead, he picks up another potato to peel.

Chapter 14

Roscoe hadn't stayed a second night in Baton Rouge. His truck was parked in front of Ginny's house when she returned from the lake. She sat for a moment, picking at the worn leather spots on the steering wheel. It wasn't that she was afraid of him, but she was definitely frightened. Maybe her dread was worse than the truths to be revealed. Surely once the bandage was torn off, the open wound would hurt, but it would heal.

Music drifted out of the front window. Roscoe wasn't one to listen to the radio, except maybe to a baseball game. While odd, it gave her no clue as to what type of mood he was in.

Ginny's hand shook when she opened the screen door. She wanted to slap herself for disobeying her strict order to remain cool and collected.

"Evening." He leaned against the doorjamb separating the living and dining rooms. Although his arms were crossed, the pose didn't seem defensive in spite of the more formal greeting. He wore jean pants and a plaid short-sleeve shirt. She rarely saw him in anything but his uniform.

"Hello," she said.

Her eye caught the small phonograph on the table where her typewriter usually sat. It was her mama's portable RCA Victor, not something Miriam would part with easily. Beside it was a stack of 45s, also her mother's. Things Ginny had coveted but was never allowed to enjoy.

"You've seen Mama today," Ginny said. "I imagine you stole that thing because she'd never let someone pry it from her hands."

Roscoe crossed the room in three long strides. His left hand took her right. He placed his other hand on the small of her back. It took her a moment to realize what was happening. Roscoe had never danced with her, but he was intent on it tonight of all nights. Their bodies didn't touch, like strangers dancing. Ginny wondered why he chose Nat King Cole's "Unforgettable."

"Miriam and I both thought you'd like to have the player," he said. "She hoped the music would make you feel better."

He smelled of tobacco, so she guessed he was smoking again. Ginny was surprised she didn't smell whiskey on his breath, too. Surely, he knew the conversation they'd be having, unless her mama had kept her mouth shut about the robe. Ginny could almost use some whiskey herself, but she didn't keep any in the house, not even for the nights Roscoe stayed over.

"So, now you and Mama are discussing how to make me feel better," she snapped. "That's priceless."

"Miriam is worried about you," he said, gently

266

guiding their steps. "*I'm* worried about you."

Ginny bit her lip hard. She needed to stay angry. Words failed her, though. She wanted to scream in his face and beat his chest with her fists. Instead, she was in her muddy loafers, dancing with him on a worn-out rug he'd chosen for the room.

"I'm sorry, Ginny," he whispered.

"What exactly are you sorry for." She glanced up at his face, but he looked straight ahead.

"Miriam told me what you found. She doesn't know all the facts."

Ginny pulled away from him and jerked the needle from the record. "Are the facts in dispute? You're saying you weren't part of the Klan?"

The set of Roscoe's jaw and his hesitancy in answering irritated her.

"Well?" she shouted.

"Not in the way you're thinking."

"What the hell does that mean? You're either in or you're out." Ginny paced, one hand on her forehead.

"That's where you're wrong," he said.

Her thoughts became a tangled mess. She didn't know what to ask or what to demand. While she had no expectations as to how this evening would play out, it was now disappointing her on so many levels. Ginny felt pathetic. She'd allowed him to hold her, to dance with her. For the first time, no less.

"Did you hurt anyone?" A gasp trailed her question because of its enormity.

"No, I did not," Roscoe said. He hadn't hesitated with that answer. His hands rested on his hips, challenging her to ask another question or maybe bracing for it.

"Did you stand by while people got hurt?" There was no point in staving off the tears. Ginny knew this answer and wished to God she didn't.

"My being there saved more than were lost," he said quietly.

Surely he knew this fact would devastate her nonetheless. When he made a step toward her, she held her palm out, signaling him to back away. God, she was tired. And hungry again. It was as if her body was saying that food was the only way to fill the holes the pain had hollowed out of her.

"Are you still—"

"That was twenty-five years ago, Ginny. A lifetime ago," Roscoe said. "I'm not the monster you're afraid I am."

She sat on the settee and wept freely now, not bothering to wipe her face. Her mama used to slap her for crying so openly. This memory of Miriam's inability to mother her only made her feel more alone in the world.

Roscoe sat next to her. Ginny didn't push him away when he nudged her chin, urging her to look at him.

"I can't believe I'm the one to cause you the most hurt you'll feel in your lifetime." His body shuddered as if giving him permission to release the emotion he'd held in, yet no tears fell.

This statement shocked her. She pulled her chin from his grasp and wiped her face. "My life is far from over, Roscoe Simms. What makes you think there aren't worse hurts ahead for me?"

"I know it from the way you look at me."

Roscoe stood and retrieved his hat from the dining room table, but didn't put it on. He waited a moment, perhaps thinking she had something else to say.

Ginny didn't speak until he opened the screen door to leave.

"I know you killed a man," she blurted out.

His head bowed just slightly, but he didn't turn around.

"I was out at your fishing site today. Near Little River. I met Crawford," she said.

When he turned and looked at her again, he pointed at her feet. "I wondered why your shoes were muddy."

"To hell with my shoes," she said. "I want to know more. I *need* to know more."

"I don't care what the old man told you," Roscoe said. "I'm not talking to you about that. Ever."

His brusqueness startled her. Ginny figured no

matter what her questions tonight, he'd oblige. She was certain he'd be overcome with remorse, spewing apologies for hurting her and vowing to make up for it. She chastised herself for such asinine thoughts. If he'd done those things, would she have agreed to make a go of it? And if he asked for forgiveness, was it even hers to give?

"I'm not the warden anymore," he said when she failed to say anything. "They gave me a couple of weeks before I have to clear out of here. They said a new warden wouldn't want me around, undermining his authority or something like that. John will fill in for now."

Roscoe was leaving. Not only her, but the prison as well.

"What will you do?"

"Jesus, Ginny. I just found out I was sacked yesterday," he said. "Then, when I stopped by Miriam's on the way home today, she told me about what you'd found. I haven't had a chance to breathe, much less think."

"Why'd you even go there?" Curiosity and jealousy pricked at her simultaneously.

"Really? That's what you want to know?" He pointed his hat at her, as if daring her to push him further.

She cupped her hand over her mouth to hide her trembling lips. Push and push and push. That was what she did, wasn't it? There was nothing left to say. Yet, the thought of him stepping over that threshold and never returning flooded her with despair.

"I'll tell you why I was there." His voice cracked and he coughed to hide it. "I was telling your goddamned mama that I was going to marry you and I didn't give a shit what she thought about it."

Ginny's senses abandoned her. She stood in a vacuum, separate and apart from everything around her. She could see Roscoe waiting for her to say something, feel something. Ginny hadn't thought her heart could break further, but it had. Earlier, her losses seemed too great to bear. Now, they seemed catastrophic.

If she hadn't been curious about the loose board in her closet, if she hadn't found that robe or confronted her mama or stumbled upon Crawford at Roscoe's fishing spot, she might have been cooking dinner in her little house when Roscoe got back from Baton Rouge.

He might have told her the news about losing his job. She would have comforted him and said they'd figure it out together. It was then that Roscoe might have knelt and asked for her hand. She would have been dazed by his proposal, maybe even a little frightened. But she would have said yes.

The slam of the screen door was like a bucket of ice water dumped on Ginny's head. She ran out into the dirt yard as Roscoe was pulling away in his truck.

"Then, this is it?" she called out. "We're done?"

Roscoe stopped backing up. The emotions in his face blurred from anger to defeat to sadness. "That's up to you, Ginny Polk."

The dust from his wheels mushroomed up around her, stinging her already burning eyes.

Ginny woke to someone stroking her hair. The gauzy feeling in her head hinted it could be a dream, maybe about her daddy offering comfort after a nightmare. Her eyes eased open slowly. Miriam was kneeling on the floor beside the settee where Ginny had fallen asleep.

"You're paying me back for those, hear?" Her mama pointed to the pieces of records lying on the living room floor.

"Mama? What are you doing here?" Ginny roused herself enough to sit up. Her head ached and she still felt disoriented. Even more so because of Miriam's tenderness.

"Roscoe stopped by today," she said. "I swear I wasn't going to say a thing about the robe. Then the fool started in about asking you to marry him. I figured it'd be pretty awkward considering what you were going to confront him about."

When Ginny didn't answer, Miriam looked alarmed.

"Oh, shit. He did mention he intended to

propose, right?" she asked. "He said he was coming straight over here."

"Don't worry, Mama. He mentioned it. As he was leaving," she added.

Ginny couldn't be angry with her. She was right to tell Roscoe that Ginny had found the Klan robe. If Roscoe had blurted out a marriage proposal first thing, Ginny didn't know how she would have reacted. The conversation had been confused enough as it was.

"Did you wait for him to leave before breaking these, or were they part of your fight?" Miriam bent to pick up the black pieces of plastic, setting aside those with the label of the record visible. "I'm not kidding when I said you're paying me back."

Her mama smiled. A real smile, not one with a hard edge meant to chastise Ginny for the destructive act.

"Why are you being nice to me?" Ginny couldn't help but ask. It'd been such a strange and disturbing evening. There was only so much she could take. Games weren't one of them.

"Oh, baby girl." Miriam sighed and walked into the kitchen. From there, she called out, "I'm making coffee. I already checked your cupboards to see if you had anything stronger."

It was dark outside, but definitely not anywhere near dawn. Ginny had the drunken feeling one gets when roused in the middle of the night.

"What time is it?" she asked.

"Almost midnight," Miriam said. "You were out cold when I got here. I walked right in without you stirring."

Ginny never locked the door. Her windows stayed open all night on the off chance a slight breeze might make sleeping a little more bearable. The only people who could possibly enter her home were guards or escaped convicts. The likelihood of either of those invading her sanctuary for any reason—evil or otherwise—was small.

Sanctuary was the first word to pop into her head to describe the place, but it wouldn't feel that way anymore. Not without Roscoe.

Ginny heard her mother rattling around in the kitchen. "The cups are in the—"

"I know where the dishes should be," Miriam said. "This was my house once, remember?"

Drinking coffee on a warm, muggy evening was unappetizing to Ginny, but she accepted the cup held out to her. It gave her something to do with her hands and something to occupy her mind other than this unsettling version of her mother.

Miriam sat in the low, upholstered chair and set her cup on the end table beside it. "The place never looked better. Roscoe do all this?"

"Dot helped."

"Ah," Miriam said.

Ginny had no idea what the "ah" meant, but

she wasn't going to engage. Her mother didn't approve of their friendship. One, because Dot was black, and two, because Dot had become almost a mother to Ginny.

"I looked around earlier, while you were sleeping," Miriam said. "That's a lovely bedroom set you have. What I'd give for a mirrored dressing table like that."

Suspicious of the compliment, Ginny managed a smile nonetheless. Her first instinct, though, was to lash out at Miriam for snooping. Going on the offensive was the best way to defend against her mama's usual cruelty. Even now, Ginny's senses were on high alert. She braced, wondering Miriam's motive for driving all the way from Boucherville so late at night.

"So, you two split up?" Miriam asked. Her face gave away nothing. She could have just as soon asked if the Dodgers won the World Series.

"I don't know." Ginny had thought the break with Roscoe would be clean, even if devastating. It was supposed to be accusations followed by confessions followed by an agreement to part ways. Instead, her feelings had been muddied by Roscoe's gentleness at first, then his refusal to offer more explanation.

"Not so easy to judge someone who loves you, huh." Miriam peered over the coffee cup in her hand.

"You think I'm judging Roscoe? He was in the

Klan. He deserves to be judged. I don't care how long ago it happened."

Ginny stoked the anger that failed to fully ignite earlier. She didn't want her mama to sway her toward compassion or forgiveness, even if those things kept popping into her own head.

"He said he never hurt anyone, Mama. That he prevented some people from being hurt." Ginny set her cup on the rug and slumped back into the cushions on the settee.

"Sounds reasonable to me," Miriam said.

"What do you mean?"

"Roscoe wasn't like your father," she said. "He was gentler, more levelheaded. I don't know why he and Joe were friends. Sometimes I think it was to protect Joe from himself."

Earlier that day, Miriam had confirmed the vicious streak that led her husband to kill others without reason or remorse. Ginny no longer held out hope that he hadn't been a killer.

"Daddy hurt people."

"He did."

"Then why—"

"Then why stay with him?" Miriam asked. "Hell, I don't even know the answer. Partly to spite my mama. Partly because I couldn't picture myself without a man and he seemed as good as any in the beginning. Of course, I didn't picture it lasting the eight years that it did."

"But how could you stand to look at him? To

share his bed?" Ginny ventured further than she intended, but this unprecedented honesty between them spurred her to risk more.

"Jesus, Ginny. There's no answer for that," she said. "I just did. And with every year, it got easier to ignore what I didn't want to see."

The answer didn't satisfy Ginny. She wanted her mother to share something profound that could help explain how Ginny could both love and hate Roscoe; how she could still want him in her life and in her bed, and at the same time, want him to pay for his past.

Ginny consciously decided not to mention to Miriam what Crawford had said—that Roscoe had killed a man while on duty. She didn't have enough information to sort it through herself, much less share it with someone she still didn't trust fully.

"You're a grown woman," Miriam finally said. "You got to decide your next steps. I never had to make a decision. Your daddy's murderer made it for me."

Suddenly desiring her mama's advice left Ginny flustered. If Miriam told her to never speak to Roscoe again, she'd want to do the opposite. Same as if she told her to run after him and marry him on the spot.

"You don't have to make a decision tonight," Miriam said. "Why don't you go to bed?"

Ginny yawned at the thought. She was dead

tired and very near the edge of hysteria at the same time. Her bed would at least provide a few hours of respite before having to think again.

"Would you consider staying the night?" Ginny was unsure why she asked. Perhaps because she'd never felt so alone in her life.

Her mama picked up their empty coffee cups and put them in the kitchen sink. She then went to the front door and locked it.

"I'm happy to stay the night. You have any cold cream?" she asked.

Chapter 15

Dot grabbed the long metal ladle from Ginny and nudged her aside.

"You're going to burn that stew," she said.

Ginny's mind wandered. She'd just relayed to Dot all that had taken place over the weekend and was alternately baffled and saddened. Her mama had stayed for breakfast Sunday morning and then left with a promise to visit later in the week. Not once had she uttered a barb or dig. She'd even suggested they go on a driving vacation together, to "put all that Roscoe business" behind them. Miriam had used the word *them* like Roscoe had betrayed her as well. That was the closest she'd come to offering advice.

An odd smile crossed Dot's lips. "I don't know what's more unbelievable: Roscoe being in the Klan or your mama offering to stay the night with you. I think I've heard everything."

"It's not funny," Ginny said.

"No, child. It's sure not," she said. "But you said yourself that you done with crying."

Ginny couldn't say that was exactly true. Every few hours she felt overcome with the desire to weep like a mourning widow or cackle like a madwoman. She was worried her mental state was in jeopardy, but wondered how a crazy person would even recognize that in herself. She hadn't before.

"Why aren't you angry at Roscoe?" Ginny pressed. "After all, it's your people we're talking about here."

Dot stopped stirring. "It's not my people we're talking about here. You don't know what happened all those years ago. The man told you he ain't hurt nobody and that he stopped others from being killed."

"I don't know that's—"

"You do know it's true," Dot admonished her. "You know that man better than anybody at this prison. Even I can see he doesn't have a violent bone in his body. Look what he's done for this place."

"Then I should forgive him?"

"I'm not saying that."

Ginny grimaced. "Then what are you saying? You've never been shy about doling out advice."

Dot shifted the massive soup pot to the back burner. "Am I the only one who sees we got work to do? I'm going to start on those mashed potatoes."

When Dot turned to head to the larder, Ginny touched her arm gently to stop her. "What is it? What's upsetting you?"

Because several guards were waiting for dinner to be served, Ginny motioned Dot to follow her from the building. They sat, side by side, on the cement steps.

"Do you really want my advice?" Dot asked, swiping at her wet eyes.

"Of course." Ginny braced for what would surely be hard truths. Dot had offered her advice freely over the years without regard for hurt feelings. She felt that honesty was a responsibility and that you did your loved ones a disservice by mollycoddling them.

"While I'd miss you something fierce, I think you ought to quit this place," she said. "Take all this bad business as a sign. Roscoe is starting fresh. So can you. Either by yourself or with him, if you can forgive what he's done. Don't matter. But you ought to go."

Ginny felt a wave of grief almost as strong as those that pummeled her over the weekend. She couldn't imagine leaving her job or Dot. She found it hard to contemplate her future at all. She sure wasn't ready to entertain something as drastic as abandoning the two constants she had left.

Dot picked at bits of food and grease that stippled her apron, then clasped her hands together as if to calm their agitation. "You can't go ignoring all the signs," she said. "First, the mess with that LeBoux boy. Then your spell. Finding that damn robe. Now, Roscoe leaving. There'll be a new warden soon. Why not cut and run?"

Cut and run. That's exactly what Ginny felt like doing. But she also felt tethered in place. Maybe not by the prison, but definitely by the unfinished business with Roscoe.

"It's not your job to worry about me. That's too much to ask of anyone."

"Who else is going to worry about you then?" Dot asked.

Guards made their way across the compound. It was the shift change and a dozen or so men would want their supper soon. Several moved in single file past them on the steps.

Ginny cupped her hands around one of Dot's and smiled. "Maybe that job should fall to Mama seeing as we're best friends now."

Dot's throaty laugh warmed Ginny instantly. No need to make a hasty decision. They had work to do.

After supper was over, two inmates washed the tin trays that meals were served on, so Ginny made her way to the larder to take note of what staples needed ordering. She loved the quiet, dark space hidden beneath the hubbub of the kitchen. Its black dirt floor gave off a comforting smell she never grew tired of. Rows and rows of canned beets, green beans, and tomatoes were arranged neatly on wooden shelves. The order of it appealed to her, as did the coolness of the space, which was welcome after she'd been hovering over a hot stove.

She made herself a note that grits were running low and tucked it into her apron before climbing the stairs up to the kitchen. John, the guard filling in as interim warden, was waiting for her.

"Good evening, Ginny," he said.

"I didn't see you at supper," she said, locking the metal door behind her. "I expect you're mighty busy with your new warden responsibilities."

John winced. "I'm not the one who fired Roscoe."

"I apologize for my tone," she said. "All the changes are just so brand-new. It's hard for me to imagine this place without him."

"We agree on that score," he said. "I had hoped he would have stayed a little longer. The prison board gave him a couple of weeks, but he insisted on leaving today. Said it was best to clear out before they hired his replacement."

"He's gone already?"

John looked puzzled. "I figured you knew. Something happen between the two of you?"

"That's not really any of your business." She tried hard to tamp down the hurt of being told this news by someone other than Roscoe himself. Ginny hoped John would leave her be so she could process Roscoe's abrupt departure without an audience to her emotions.

"I expect it's not," John said. "But I do have

prison business to discuss with you. Maybe you should join me in Roscoe's—I mean the warden's office when you're finished here."

He turned and left. She quickly unlocked the metal door to the larder and scurried down the stairs. It was the only place she could cry in private before facing John again.

When Ginny arrived in Roscoe's old office, John had already poured a splash of whiskey in a coffee cup for her. The cup in his hand probably didn't hold coffee either.

The smell of it reminded her of both her daddy and Roscoe; how their breath had imparted the pungent smell of peat, but also the sweet scent of cut hay and vanilla. She gulped it down hoping its fire would fortify her.

"The news must not be good if you've resorted to booze first thing."

"You've worked a long day," he said. "You deserve it."

"I work long days almost every day," Ginny said. "I suspect something is very different about this one."

John laughed and motioned for her to sit. "Dunner was here today."

The state's Superintendent of Corrections hadn't wasted any time. Roscoe's hearing had taken place just three days prior and Dunner was already stirring things up, she guessed.

"And I should care why?"

"Ginny, I'm not Roscoe. I don't have the patience for your smart mouth." John poured himself a generous drink. "Dunner recommended that you be fired, too."

"What do you mean by recommended?"

"It means that two other prison board members convinced him otherwise," John said. "One of those board members, Herbert Levy, will likely be the next warden."

The name sounded familiar. Ginny couldn't remember if Levy had been at the disastrous prison dinner she'd forgotten about until an hour before it was to start. If he was the large, kindly man who came to Roscoe's defense that evening, she thought he might just be an amiable replacement.

"When do you think he'll start?"

"Within the next couple of weeks," John said. "But that's not why I asked you here, Ginny. Your job is going to change and I wanted to be the one to break the news."

"Well, if you have to 'break the news,' it's not going to be pleasant. Just give it to me straight." She tensed her stomach as if she could grunt down the apprehension twisting there.

"You'll be working at the warden's residence," he said. "Levy and his wife would like you to be their personal cook. You'll still oversee things in the prison kitchen, but won't work there."

"I don't understand," she said, but she did. They'd put her in her place for being a trouble-maker. The one who dared fall in love with a warden; the one who dared to show a shred of decency toward death row inmates.

"At least you have a job," he said. "Look at the bright side."

Given that she'd had only a minute to digest the news, she didn't see a bright side. She'd gone from being in charge of a large, institutional kitchen where she was her own boss to being someone's house help.

"What if I won't do it?" Ginny considered her options. Maybe if she just talked to Levy, he'd understand her objections.

"Then you don't have a place here," John said.

Cut and run, her churning stomach warned. But where to go and what to do were still questions she couldn't answer.

"I'd like Dot to be in charge of the day-to-day then," Ginny said, absently. "She knows the kitchen backward and forward. She'd be a good supervisor, too."

"Well, that's up to Levy," John said. "Of course, you can make that recommendation."

Ginny stood, her fingertips tracing the edge of the desk. It'd never be John's desk or Mr. Herbert Levy's desk. It was Roscoe's. Touching it now grounded her and made her feel some connection to him as the changes to her life continued to mount.

"Thank you for telling me the news first. I appreciate not being blindsided by a stranger," she said. "I need to get back to my house now. I'm so tired I could drop."

John stopped her before she made it to the outer door of the admin offices.

"Ginny? I'm sorry I forgot to mention this, but you'll have to move back to the women's barracks. The board said you couldn't live in your folks' old house. It'll be needed for the assistant warden they're hiring."

With her back to him, Ginny closed her eyes and took a deep breath. She would survive. What was one more hurt on top of all the other hurts? Her mind hadn't shattered completely yet, and that gave her some confidence that it wouldn't.

"I forgot to mention that Mrs. Levy said you're welcome to live at the warden's residence," he added. "She said they will be adding on a couple of rooms for house staff."

Ginny nodded to let him know she'd heard. She walked down the hall, consciously counting her steps, until her feet ordered her to run.

Chapter 16

Mr. and Mrs. Herbert Levy had announced their arrival a month ago with much fanfare. The first order of business was a dinner party hosted for the prison board and some of the guards at the prison. Ginny had declined the couple's offer to live in the residence and instead moved her things back to the small pink room in the women's barracks. She could have just as soon slept at the warden's house considering that she spent most of her waking hours there anyway.

Prior to the party, she'd worked her fingers to the bone for three days under Mrs. Levy's keen supervision. Eugenia Levy was the consummate hostess when she lived in New Orleans, and she wasn't about to let the desolate nature of a prison stop her from throwing a grand bash. Canapés, pâté, and hot and cold hors d'oeuvres were passed by what she called the "trusty, docile prisoners who could clean up well."

Those who couldn't clean up well were tasked with painting the exterior of the house, adding new shutters, and planting shrubbery and turf. "This brown dreariness just won't do," she'd said.

Like a general in battle, Eugenia oversaw the work of dozens of people, shouting orders and requisitioning supplies when necessary. No one questioned using the inmates this way. For decades, the prison had hired them out to farms as day labor even though the state expressly forbade it.

"You look a thousand miles away." Eugenia handed Ginny a grocery list to review.

While the warden's wife said the housekeeper could do the shopping, Ginny insisted that she take on that chore. Her reasoning was that she had a better eye for picking out the best cuts of meat or the freshest produce. In truth, it gave Ginny a means of escape, even if for an afternoon.

"Oh, I'm just thinking I might take an extra hour or two next time I'm in town," Ginny said. "My mama's birthday is coming up and I thought I'd look for a present."

"The shopping in Boucherville is just dreadful." Eugenia grabbed the list from Ginny to scribble down a few additions. "Baton Rouge isn't much better. You ought to plan a trip to New Orleans sometime. I mean, when there's nothing going on at the residence."

There was always something going on at the residence. Mrs. Levy treated the prison like a freak show to attract acquaintances curious about the workings of a penitentiary. Whereas another woman might have been horrified at the prospect of living so far from civilized society, Eugenia transformed the place into a weekend retreat.

Like New Yorkers scurrying off to the Hamptons, a flock of New Orleans friends arrived each of the last three weekends for tours, unabashed drinking and feasting, and games of croquette and horse shoes on the newly transformed lawn.

"I'd like to increase your salary," Eugenia said. "You look like you could use a few more dresses. We talked about you purchasing some foundation and other necessaries."

Not long after the Levys moved in, Mrs. Levy made it clear that a woman must take her grooming and appearance seriously. It pained her that Ginny didn't own the slips, girdles, stockings, and other foundation any respectable woman should—even someone of her station. Eugenia spent almost as much time on her own appearance as she did hosting parties. She was impeccably dressed and coiffed by eight each morning, and ate child portions at meals to maintain her rail-thin figure.

"Yes, ma'am," Ginny said. "I'll see what I can find in Boucherville first."

Dot had found it amusing that Ginny now worked for a woman more irritating than her mama. When Ginny spent time in the prison kitchen as overseer, she talked almost nonstop about Mrs. Levy's peculiarities and demands. Dot would just giggle and whisper "cut and run."

Both Dot and John had been flabbergasted that

Ginny agreed to the new working arrangement in the first place. But when Mrs. Levy doubled Ginny's salary, she saw it as an opportunity to save up as much as she could in hopes of building a new life elsewhere. Running off willy-nilly seemed foolhardy. Ginny didn't know where to go. She wanted time to plan.

Roscoe had helped in that regard. He'd not called her once or let her know his whereabouts. By giving her space, she figured he was making it easier on her to choose a future without him.

"Why, look who's paying us a visit," Eugenia said, pointing out the window. "The warden is here in the middle of the day."

Eugenia never used her husband's first name in front of Ginny or the housekeeper. She referred to him as the warden or Mr. Levy.

"How's the homestead?" Warden Levy called out when he reached the porch. Whenever he came to the residence during the day, he'd announce himself loudly as if giving Mrs. Levy fair warning. It was like he suspected she might be walking around naked with a gin and tonic, or harboring a lover, and he was giving her the opportunity to hide her vices.

"What brings you home, Mr. Levy?" Eugenia pecked her husband on the cheek when he entered the kitchen. "Shall I make you some lunch?"

"No time, darlin'," he said. "I'm here to see Miss Polk."

"Me?" Ginny looked as surprised as the warden's wife.

"Could you give us a few minutes to ourselves?" he asked Eugenia.

She hesitated a moment as if he'd insulted her, then gained her composure and left the room with a fixed smile on her face.

The warden sat down at the kitchen table across from Ginny. Herbert Levy had been the kindly man who'd complimented her pork neck stew the evening of the fateful prison board meeting. When he started the job, he'd recognized her immediately and thanked her profusely for staying on to help his wife. He even joked about the superintendent's wife getting all uppity at the failed board dinner, without realizing the night had been one nail in Roscoe's coffin.

Levy had proven to be an easygoing, considerate type, but his commanding presence left no doubt who was in charge.

"Is there something wrong, sir?" Ginny cut her eyes to the swinging door to the dining room. Mrs. Levy was obviously rearranging items on the buffet, hovering close enough to eavesdrop.

"Well, there's a troubling issue I want to talk over with you," he said. "It has to do with those meals you used to cook for the death row boys."

She was shocked to hear him mention the dinners. He hadn't been on the job two days before he'd told her there'd be no more special meals prior to executions. While he never mentioned the incident with Samuel LeBoux specifically, she guessed he'd learned about it from the guard Roscoe had paid to keep his mouth shut. Surely, it played a part in Roscoe's dismissal.

"A prisoner was transferred here just a short time ago. Name of Jasper Sires," he continued. "A violent man. He murdered a whole family down in New Orleans. Despicable."

"I don't understand," Ginny said, noting the tension in the warden's features.

"He's causing a lot of trouble in the Waiting Room." Levy's jaw clenched visibly. "Some other inmates told him about you cooking those last suppers. When he learned we didn't allow it anymore, he started riling up the men."

The warden said the twelve men in the death row barracks went on a hunger strike, throwing their rations at guards. For hours on end, they howled and hurled their meager furnishings against the cell walls. Prisoners tasked with emptying the slop buckets refused to enter the barracks for fear of being doused with excrement.

"Those bastards aren't responding to beatings," he said. "We tried putting Sires in solitary, but he'd made an impression on those men. They don't care if you beat them, hose them down, starve them. Nothing works."

"I still don't see how this involves me," Ginny said.

"I'm wasting all my energy trying to restore order." He shook his head. "The superintendent and board will be touring the prison soon, to see how things are going under my command. The situation could prove embarrassing for me and Mrs. Levy."

Ginny's stomach tightened as she started to see a clearer picture. He was reinstituting last suppers.

"Sires's execution is less than two weeks away," he said. "I'm going to allow you to cook whatever he wants. Things just need to calm down long enough to get through one inspection by the board. Then those fucking miscreants aren't getting a goddamned thing out of me no matter how they misbehave. They'll pay dearly for thinking they can cross me."

She startled at Levy's cursing. There was no mistaking the depth of his anger and frustration. He'd obviously pictured a different start to his tenure. And he wanted to keep his post enough to do whatever it took to convince the board they made the right choice.

"I'm happy to oblige," Ginny said. Deep down, though, she wondered if she hadn't been relieved that the meals were outlawed. The mere mention of them had nettled her. She laid a hand on her knee to stop its bouncing.

"Sires wouldn't let a guard relay his request," Levy said. "He said he had to see you personally. I'll have John fetch you later today."

Ginny nodded.

Levy appeared hesitant to leave. His eyes roamed the kitchen countertops. "Any chance you have some leftover mulberry pie?" he asked. "I swear the best part of this appointment has been partaking of your desserts."

"It's in the pantry, sir," she said, standing. "I'll fetch some wax paper and wrap you up a couple of pieces."

Ginny's nerves upset her bowels and brought on a headache that shot across her brow and down her neck. She hadn't spoken with a death row inmate since Samuel. She wasn't afraid of Jasper Sires, the man, but she was afraid of what personal demons she'd unleash by going through with the warden's request.

She also hadn't spoken with John since he'd been relieved of his duties as interim warden. The assignment lasted only a week at best, but he'd made it known he didn't want the job from the get-go.

When he knocked on the residence's screen door, he looked as putrid as she felt.

"You ready?" John offered no other greeting.

"I suppose," she said. "How've you been?"

"Does it matter?"

Ginny walked to his pickup and got in, curious about his shortness with her. He made no move to start the engine, but fidgeted with the key ring.

"You shouldn't be talking to this guy."

The cab of the truck was too small for an angry conversation. She thought about refusing to ride with him and just walking. "It wasn't my idea," she replied hotly. "The warden told me I had to."

"You could have objected," he said. "He wouldn't have fired you. Everyone knows how much his missus likes having a personal chef at her beck and call."

She winced at his tone. It was clear he thought she was Eugenia's pet.

"Before Roscoe left, he asked only one favor of me," John said. "He told me under no circumstances were you to talk to Jasper Sires. He was so torn up, he made me swear."

Roscoe must have worried she didn't have the mental fortitude, not after her breakdown. Still, John's description of Roscoe's state of mind told her he had larger concerns. Was it that Jasper was such a violent offender? Did Roscoe fear for her physical safety?

"That's nonsense," she said. "I'm in no danger. You'll be there. I suspect you'll have other guards, too?"

"I had to tell him, Ginny. I'm sorry."

"Him who?"

"I called Roscoe when I learned the warden's

intentions. He's fit to be tied." John perspired like a man with a deep fever. "He's not allowed back on the grounds, so he begged me to stop you."

She rolled down the window to the stuffy cab. "You have a phone number for Roscoe? Why didn't you tell me? Where's he staying?"

Ginny had asked John on more than one occasion if Roscoe had been in touch or if he knew his whereabouts, but John had said no.

"Roscoe asked me not to give you his number, or tell you where he was staying. He said you needed time to think things through and seeing him would complicate matters."

Her cheeks colored to think how much of their personal business Roscoe had shared.

"Did he tell you—"

"I didn't ask what happened between the two of you," he said. "It's not my business. He's a friend, so I did as he asked. No questions."

"We best get on with this," Ginny said. She knew she could prepare this one last meal and then she'd get serious about leaving, even if it meant staying at her mama's for a few weeks.

"You can still refuse," John said. "For Roscoe's sake."

She didn't owe Roscoe. He hadn't even given her a way to reach him in case she wanted to talk things out. They hadn't settled a thing the night she confronted him. He'd shut her down when she wanted to know about the inmate he'd killed.

Just because she wanted details didn't mean she judged him for it. Ginny was hurt that he'd kept something so life-changing from her. The circumstances had to have justified his actions. But given that she judged him for associating with the Klan, he might have thought her judgment boundless.

"Take me to the Waiting Room," she demanded. "Let's get this over with."

John turned the truck key and put the vehicle in reverse. He tore out of the warden's driveway, digging deep ruts in the gravel Mrs. Levy just had brought in from Baton Rouge.

Jasper's feet and hands were in heavy black chains when he shuffled into the corner room. Ginny had pulled her chair a few paces back from the table where he sat. Her mind went straight to how easily Samuel had lifted the table with his shoulder and hurled it at her. She took shallow breaths to bring her to the present.

The present, though, felt almost as horrifying as the night Samuel mutilated himself. Looking at Jasper, she could only see the faces of the family he'd murdered. The couple and the four oldest children had been shot. An infant was bludgeoned to death. She was surprised to find herself searching for words to a prayer. She'd hoped the children were unaware of what was happening that night. She shuddered to be in the presence of so much evil contained in one human being.

"You the cook lady?" His teeth were straight, but yellowed by chewing tobacco.

"You expecting any other visitors?" she sniped.

He laughed so long and hard that one of John's junior guards hit Jasper on the shoulder to shut him up.

"I hear I can have anything I want to eat," he said.

"Within reason."

"What that mean? The death row boys always got what they wanted." Jasper was angry now, as if he'd been fooled into thinking his tirade had worked.

"I mean that I'm not going to barbecue you an entire side of beef or order caviar up from New Orleans." Ginny noted that this prisoner meeting was very different than any she'd had in the past. She felt disgust, not compassion. Something in her had changed in the past few weeks. It was getting easier to imagine her decade at the prison as an aberration. Everything after would surely resemble a normal life.

Jasper slouched in his chair so that his shackled feet stuck out on her side of the table. She consciously scooted her chair back a few more inches.

Tim, the young guard who used to be Roscoe's assistant, stood vigilant in one corner of the room, but he looked as uneasy as Ginny felt. He was the last person who should be working in the Waiting Room, and she wondered if he'd asked for the assignment.

"Listen here," Jasper said. "I want fried chicken, okra with tomatoes, and cornbread. Fry up that entire bird. I'll eat every scrap and then suck the bones."

Ginny's stomach convulsed. She rarely cooked fried chicken. Ever since Silas Barnes's wife brought a basket of it to his execution twenty-one years ago, the aroma brought on a nausea that could last for a day. She got through her entire childhood not having to eat it because Miriam found it difficult to get the breading just right. As an adult, Ginny rarely cooked it herself unless it was specifically requested for one of the prison board dinners.

"Miss Polk?" A second guard touched her shoulder. She didn't know his name. "If you have the information you need, why don't we just go now?"

"Polk? Your name is Polk?" Jasper no longer slouched but leaned forward, interested in the guard's revelation. "What are the chances? I know of a guard Polk that used to work here. He dead now and good riddance. Son of a bitch."

She blinked, unseeing. He couldn't mean her daddy.

"That's enough now." John stepped forward

and motioned for two of his guards to pull Jasper to his feet.

"How old you be? That man Polk could be your daddy," he said, straining his head to still look at her. "Ain't this the darnedest thing."

Ginny stood abruptly. "Stop! Let him talk."

The guards looked to John for instruction.

"Meeting's over," John barked.

"What do you know about my daddy?" She was angry now. Angry that he was more than just the last dead man she had to cook for. Angry because Roscoe knew something about this man and did everything in his power to ensure Ginny didn't meet him.

"I know how your daddy died." Jasper's sneer showed he was well aware of the power he held. "That was what he got for trying to lynch black folk. Silas Barnes was my uncle. He didn't have anything—"

A loud crack rang out as John's billy club came down on Jasper's head once, twice, three times. Blood rushed from the wound, coating Jasper's face in a slick red mask. His sinister yellow teeth taunted her as he laughed. When the blood reached his lips, he spat at the guards subduing him. "Just ask my aunt. She know the whole story. You just ask."

"Get him to his cell," John yelled. "Now!"

In the mayhem, Ginny hadn't realized that Tim grabbed her upper arm. She pulled, but he wouldn't release his grip. "Stop it! Let him speak. Please let him speak," she pleaded.

The second guard grabbed her other arm and they forced her into the execution room and away from the shouting Jasper. His words grew incoherent as the beating continued.

Tim insisted on escorting her to the women's barracks, but she told him it wasn't necessary. Ginny wanted away from everyone who had anything to do with death. She quickened her step, forcing Tim to keep up.

"Miss Ginny? Miss Ginny, are you sure you're all right?" Tim's question was directed at her back.

"I'm fine," she said, gritting her teeth. "Leave me alone."

"I want to be sure you're okay." He bent over, hands on thighs, to get his wind back. "The warden . . . I mean, Mr. Simms . . . asked me to make sure."

Ginny stopped dead in her tracks. "What's this about Roscoe?"

"When he was leaving, he said to keep an eye out. That you'd likely be wanting to talk to the death row prisoners. He was worried about you."

Even gone, Roscoe seemed inextricably tied to her life. "What exactly did he say?" Ginny asked.

"Only that he'd rather you not talk to Mr. Sires. But that if you did, he wanted extra guards there."

"Did he know that Jasper was Silas Barnes's nephew?" she demanded.

"I wouldn't know, Miss Ginny."

She was overwhelmed by the steps Roscoe had taken to prevent her talking to Jasper. He must have feared Jasper would figure out who she was and make the connection to her father.

"What else?" she demanded.

"He tried to slip me some money, but I wouldn't accept it." Tim blushed. "I respected Warden Simms. He was a good man. I told him I was sorry he had to leave."

The sun hung low in the sky. Earlier, she thought about helping Dot with supper, but greens and grits were the farthest thing from her mind. Her father's death had always been a murky thing—a subject skirted and twisted until the asker felt embarrassed for inquiring. Her mama never talked about it. Roscoe never talked about it. Most of the current guards were hired well after 1938, so there was no institutional history of his passing. The warden at the time— Gates or Graves?—was long dead. And now, a despicable man—a murderer of the evilest sort— held the key to whatever shame was attached to Joe Polk's untimely death.

"Why are you even working in the Waiting Room?" she asked. "That's not the place for you."

Tim kicked at the dirt with his boot. "Warden

Levy wanted his own assistant and there really wasn't another opening. But I think he was just hoping I'd quit."

"Why do you say that?"

"I overheard him telling John I was slow, that I don't have what it takes to be in corrections," he said. "Warden Levy said the Waiting Room would scare me senseless and that I'd be begging to quit after two weeks."

While Ginny agreed Tim shouldn't be working at the prison, she didn't find him slow. And she hated to see the deep wounds those remarks had inflicted.

"Well, he doesn't know you at all then." She shielded her eyes from the intense orange of the sunset. They were still sensitive from the headache that came on earlier in the day and that still stood vigil.

"Thank you, ma'am," he said. "I guess I'll get back to work if you don't want me to walk you back to your room."

He'd only taken a few steps before Ginny called out. "Would you mind doing me a favor?"

He nodded. "Anything."

"I'd like you to ask Jasper Sires where his aunt is living now. Her name would be Barnes, unless she remarried."

"I probably shou—"

"Roscoe said to take care of me. Doing this one thing is taking care of me." She held her breath, not knowing if she'd asked too much of him and fearful that he'd tell John.

Tim jangled the change in his pocket. He looked at the death row barracks as if asking their permission. "I guess I can do that."

Ginny exhaled her relief. She closed the space between them, requesting one last thing.

"Write down the address on a slip of paper and bring it to the kitchen tomorrow morning when your shift is over. Remember, her name is Barnes," she said. "And, Tim? Don't tell anyone else about this."

Terrence Arceneaux
Night Shift Guard, Death Row Cellblock
October 21, 1957

Terrence's wife regularly scolds him for looking forward to eating leftovers from the last suppers. He secretly wants to tell her he wouldn't desire another woman's cooking if she could prepare a piece of meat that didn't taste like burned shoe leather.

Sometimes, he daydreams Ginny is his wife and that while he's on shift, she's back at home preparing his favorite dishes: pot roast with sweet potatoes, pigs' feet with sauerkraut, rhubarb pie so tart it makes his jaws clench.

Tonight, Ginny spreads a checkered napkin on the metal table in the corner room before placing a tray on it. Terrence is jealous she takes such care for a man who doesn't deserve it. Not a decent, honest man like himself who would appreciate the love and cooking of a woman like Ginny Polk.

"Good evening," she says to him. "How've you been?"

He forgets to answer because he's staring at her hands. Those long fingers. He pictures himself as a mound of satiny bread dough, her hands kneading and shaping him.

307

"Terrence? You okay?" she asks.

His face colors and his groin aches. "Fine, fine," he says. "Just preoccupied by the execution. What you got there?"

"Red beans and rice, with andouille," Ginny says. "He wanted it extra spicy."

Terrence closes his eyes and tries to imagine what the dish will taste like. Here, in such a cramped room, he can already smell the cayenne and its dominance over the onions and tomatoes. He hopes she'll bring fresh cornbread tomorrow as well. It'd tame the heat just right.

The door to the cellblock opens. Roscoe ushers Antoine over to the table but keeps one hand on his firearm. Can't risk a prisoner acting up. Things could get out of control.

"Eat," Roscoe says. "Don't be shy about it."

The inmate shovels in spoonful after spoonful, grunting in pleasure. He grins at Ginny with his mouth wide open, his rotten teeth a disgusting display. She smiles back, although Terrence wishes she hadn't.

He despises the man. His body odor competes with the smells of Ginny's fine cooking. It's like a slap in Terrence's face. He can't wait until Antoine gets the chair in two hours. The asshole won't be grinning then.

At least the Cajun asked for a decent last supper. Terrence is annoyed when those sons of bitches ask for something foolish like butterscotch candy or plain toast and eggs. What kind of goddamned meal is that? It's a crying shame to waste Ginny's talents.

He turns his attention away from the inmate and back to Ginny. Terrence's stomach knots at once. She and Roscoe are looking at each other like two people who've just done it. Terrence decides he despises Roscoe more than Antoine. It ain't proper for the warden to be interested in Ginny anyway. He's old enough to be her daddy.

Then Terrence's mood lifts. His daydream about Ginny morphs into something new and exciting. He pictures an inmate uprising in the fields that gets out of control. Maybe Roscoe finds himself in a bad situation and doesn't make it out alive. Then, Terrence would be ready to comfort Ginny. Maybe he'd ask her out for coffee and pie in Boucherville. He'd tell her she was a fine woman. She'd offer to cook him a nice meal on his day off. Yes, it wouldn't take long for her to see he was a good and decent man, deserving of her love.

Chapter 17

Eugenia Levy was none too pleased that Ginny asked for a day off with such little notice, but there was no way she could wait even twenty-four more hours to find Mrs. Silas Barnes. Tim had left a slip of paper in the prison kitchen as Ginny had instructed. He'd done good. The note contained Jasper's aunt's name—Olivia—and an address in New Orleans.

She didn't dare tell Dot the true reason for her absence. Ginny's excuse was that her mama wanted to see her urgently. Given that Dot didn't care one lick for Miriam, she'd have no occasion to speak to her.

Although Ginny worried that her Chevy might not make it the two hours to New Orleans and back, she couldn't risk borrowing her mama's Cadillac. John had probably already called Roscoe to tell him about Jasper's outburst. Roscoe had gone to Miriam's on more than one occasion seeking answers. Better not to have Miriam trip up in a lie.

Ginny's nerves were frayed. She'd driven in New Orleans just a handful of times when she and her mama had gone to the city to shop. Miriam would insist that Ginny drive to get over her fear. She hated her mother in those moments. It was that hatred that steeled her nerves and kept her focused until she could get away from the congested streets and smell of canal brine and exhaust. Now, she'd give anything to have Miriam in the front seat, if not to help with directions, to at least offer moral support.

The house she looked for was at the corner of Josephine Street and Danneel. Jasper had been specific in his directions, noting the color of the light green house and the tobacco shop that was two doors down. He'd wanted to be certain she found his aunt.

Ginny was so aware of her shaking limbs she feared Mrs. Barnes would notice, too. She stood in front of a screen door, unable to bring herself to knock. A sane person would have thought things through and seen just how inappropriate and ill-timed this visit was. Instead, she drove two hours to remind a woman of the most painful day of her life. She'd also be reminding her that her nephew was about to die in the same manner her husband had.

The front room was dark, making it impossible to see anything through the screen. She was conscious of the minutes that passed with her just standing on a stranger's porch. Ginny's eyes stayed fixed on a small area of screen that had been patched with a perfect square of newer mesh. She was aware of the fly that buzzed nearby and of the shouts of children playing in the street. She was aware of how odd it felt for her hands to be gloved and her legs to be covered in stockings.

"May I help you?" A man's low voice drifted from the darkened room.

Ginny jumped, dropping her purse on the porch. She knelt to pick it up just as the man opened the door. The frame of the screen clicked lightly against her head before she could stand again.

"I'm so sorry, miss. Are you all right?" he asked.

She rubbed the top of her head out of reflex, but the bump hadn't hurt a bit. "I'm fine. Thank you."

The man stepped out onto the porch, still apologizing profusely.

"It's quite all—" Ginny looked at the man's face and lost the ability to finish her sentence. He had kind, round cheeks and a birthmark on his forehead that was much lighter than the rest of his ebony skin. But it was his lazy eye that had rendered her mute.

She stood only two feet away from Silas Barnes's son, trying to figure out what he was thinking, just as she had more than twenty years ago outside the execution chamber.

"Is this the home of Mrs. Olivia Barnes?" she stuttered.

313

"Yes. Yes, it is. That's my mother," he said. "She's out at the moment, just down at the grocer's. You're welcome to wait for her. Unless I can help you. My name's Willy."

No, Ginny thought, he definitely could not help. Whatever knowledge he had of her daddy's murder, it'd be secondhand, just like Jasper's. Olivia was the one she needed to question.

"Thank you, Willy. But I think I must speak with your mother directly." Her mouth and throat were dry, which made her words raspy and low as a whisper.

"Well, would you like to sit inside? I could get you a beverage."

Her heartbeat was a dull thud, as prominent in her ears as in her chest. He hadn't recognized her. If he had, surely he'd say something.

"Miss, you don't look well. Perhaps a glass of water?"

The noise of the fly was suddenly more aggravating than any sound she'd ever heard. She swatted at the air absently and looked down at the smooth boards of the porch. Several had been replaced and not as weathered as the rest.

"I could come back?" Her words came out as a question. She hoped he might advise what her next move should be.

"Why, that won't be necessary." Willy pointed to the sidewalk. "Here's Mama now."

Ginny turned to greet the woman ascending

the stairs. When Mrs. Barnes met her eyes, she dropped the bag of groceries that had been nestled in the crook of her arm.

"You look like your daddy," she said.

Willy watched intently as Ginny downed a second glass of water. She thought of asking for a third, but her distended belly was upset. She felt so small in the large but sparsely furnished drawing room. Mrs. Barnes, looking completely uninterested in Ginny's discomfort, finally motioned for her to take a seat.

"I'm sorry to bother you, ma'am, but—" Ginny began.

"But you're doing it anyway," Mrs. Barnes said.

Her hair had gone almost all gray and her back was stooped even though she couldn't be more than sixty. Ginny's memory of her was very different. In 1938, Olivia Barnes had been tall and held herself almost regally. Her hair had been raven black, pressed straight with a hot iron and rolled into soft waves. Like Ginny and her mama, Olivia had been dressed in her Sunday best at Silas's execution.

"Mama? How do you know this woman?" Willy sat by his mother's side on the sofa. He seemed to pick up on her agitation. The worry played out in his brow.

"If I'm not mistaken, her name is Polk," she

said. "Unless you're married. I don't see a ring on your finger."

"Yes, I'm Ginny Polk. I work at the prison."

Mrs. Barnes's lips turned into something like a sneer. "Like father, like daughter."

"I work in the kitchen," Ginny said, even though that wasn't exactly true anymore. There was no sense trying to describe what she was now that she worked at the warden's residence.

"Your nephew—"

"We don't want to talk about Jasper." Willy was on his feet again. His hands curled into fists at his sides. "We want nothing to do with him."

"It's all right, son," Mrs. Barnes said, patting his arm. "She's not here about Jasper. She's here about your daddy."

"Daddy?" he asked. "What about Daddy?"

Ginny gulped. The woman's hostility was understandable, but it unnerved her nonetheless. Ginny was an intruder and mining their grief for selfish reasons.

"Why now, after all these years?" Mrs. Barnes continued.

"I know it's wrong of me to be here." Ginny removed her gloves and now twisted them into a compact mass.

"Mama, tell me what's going on," Willy begged.

Mrs. Barnes looked from her grown son to Ginny and back again. "Your daddy was executed for murdering her daddy. Only thing is, Silas wasn't the one who done it."

As a child, Ginny had almost fainted from the horrific smells of the execution room. She had covered her ears, trying to block out Silas Barnes's screams as he begged for his life. He maintained his innocence to his last breath. His eyes had been wild with desperation. Spittle dripped from his lips and tears had streamed down his face.

Her mama had said all guilty men claimed they were innocent in those last moments before the switch was thrown. But that wasn't true. Ginny had witnessed eighteen death row inmates die. Only Silas had screamed out. She'd never heard anything like that again. Except in her nightmares.

"Your nephew said that Silas didn't do it. That you know the whole story." Ginny panicked to think she was this close to the truth and Olivia Barnes could deny her.

"Nobody wanted to hear the truth then. Nobody wants to hear it now."

"I do," Ginny insisted.

Willy paced, shaking his head in disbelief. "You're that girl. The little one with the curly hair. You smiled at me that day."

She had? Ginny only remembered the sad, crooked smile he'd given her.

"Your mama had the devil in her to make you

317

watch." Mrs. Barnes's mouth drew into a tight line of judgment. "And your daddy? He was an evil man. He got what he deserved. I'm not sorry to say so."

Those were Jasper's words as well. Ginny's throat tightened, making swallowing difficult. She drew in deep breaths through her nose to tamp down the feeling she was suffocating.

"Your daddy and those other men, they came to our home in the middle of the night, dressed in their white robes and shooting their guns in the air." Mrs. Barnes's eyes grew glassy and vacant. "They had no business on our property. They were going to take Silas or burn our place down. I couldn't let that happen."

"You don't have to say any more about it, Mama." Willy was back by his mother's side. His tears flowed freely and Ginny wondered how much he remembered from that night. Maybe he'd been told the story over the years and was just recalling those memories now.

No one had bothered to tell Ginny the details. Two guards had shown up at their house to tell Miriam her husband was dead. Ginny had been hiding in the dark kitchen while the guards spoke softly to her mama in the living room. They'd said Silas Barnes had been caught in the act of robbing a bar. Her father and several off-duty guards were there drinking beer after their shift had ended. They said Silas shot her daddy in cold blood.

Willy tried to place an arm around his mother, but she shrugged him away.

"Your daddy had his gun on Silas, so he didn't see me," she said. "But I had a shotgun, too. I intended to cut him down right there. I wasn't even thinking what would become of my little boy. Then your daddy caught sight of me. He was going to kill me."

"You shot him?" Ginny managed only a whisper.

"No," she said, leveling her eyes at Ginny's. "One of the other Klan members shot him in the back. I'm alive because someone had bad aim. But they blamed it on Silas. Guess they were protecting one of their own."

"Why didn't you tell someone?" Ginny asked.

"You think I didn't want to?" Mrs. Barnes's face twisted with rage. "Who was going to believe a black woman? I had a son to protect. They told me to keep quiet. They made sure I kept quiet."

Ginny recoiled. She'd heard more than enough, things she could never unhear. So many lives were ruined because of her daddy's heinous acts. She was looking at two of them, and their pain was almost too much to sit with.

"They done things to me worse than death, Miss Polk. Worse than death." Mrs. Barnes stood and turned her back to Ginny. She traced a finger over a black and white photo sitting on a shelf on the far side of the room. A father holding his baby son, beaming with pride.

When Silas was in the electric chair, Ginny hadn't noticed that he shared the same lazy eye his son had. But she recognized it in the photo now.

Willy coughed and both women turned their attention to him. "You need to go now, Miss Polk."

"Yes. Yes, of course." Ginny felt unsteady on her feet. She walked as a drunk person trying to appear sober. "I'm so sorry for your loss. I'm sorry about my daddy."

Willy held the door open for her. She didn't look back at him or his mother.

"I'm sorry 'bout both our daddies," he said, and closed the door.

1938

A Choice
Between Wrongs

Roscoe lay in the bottom of the pickup bed, his teeth rattling with every bump in the road. He put his arm behind his head to cushion it and tried to focus on the stars. Joe was next to him, leaned against the cab of the truck. He banged his fist on the back window whenever the men in the front seat started hooting and hollering.

"Don't those bastards know anything about keeping quiet?" Joe took a draw on his cigarette. "Shit. You'd think the warden would know better."

They'd swung by the guard barracks at midnight to rouse Roscoe from a deep sleep. He kicked and scratched as they dragged him through the dark hallways. Wally, one of the older guards at the prison, had punched him in the kidney to still him. When Roscoe collapsed in pain, the guard helped him up, whispering into his ear, "You're coming with us, nigger lover."

Roscoe toed the white bundle Joe had thrown at his feet. By the light of a full moon, it looked pale blue, as did the landscape around them.

Trees and shrubs, fences and houses all took on a nightmarish hue. The world slept, unaware of the five men and their night run.

"I don't want to be mixed up in this," Roscoe said.

"Just go along with it." Joe slapped his friend's stomach, causing him to grunt. "That is, if you want to keep your job."

Roscoe could think of little else except his job. He needed to stay close to Miriam, to protect her and Ginny when Joe's drinking got out of control. He wasn't in love with the woman, so the need to protect her puzzled him. In some ways, he was protecting Joe. Roscoe loved him. Sure, he wanted him to cut back on the drink and go back to being the friend he had been. But Roscoe also feared that Joe would reach a place beyond redemption if someone didn't stop him. That had been a job in and of itself, and the sole reason Roscoe was even in that pickup bed.

God, how he wanted to leave the shit hole behind. But whenever those thoughts picked at Roscoe's brain, his stomach clenched with defeat as it did now. He had nowhere else to go.

"Hey, buddy?" Joe asked. "You'll take care of my gals if anything happens to me tonight, right?"

"Talk like that tells me you know this is wrong. All wrong." Roscoe chewed the side of his thumb and spat a piece of skin into the darkness. He'd already bitten most of the nails on his right hand to the quick.

"Maybe the guys are right. You are some kind of nigger lover." Joe laughed and flicked a finger at Roscoe's ear a bit too hard.

Roscoe rose up and took a swing at the shadowy figure next to him. Because of the rocking of the truck, his fist only glanced off Joe's chin, knocking the cigarette from his lips. Regaining his balance, Roscoe threw another punch, connecting with Joe's shoulder.

Joe scrambled to his knees and managed to straddle Roscoe in a single move. He punched him squarely in the face just once, but with terrific force, then crabbed his way to the other side of the pickup bed.

"Don't you fucking lay a hand on me again, buddy. I'll kill you if you do." A half-assed laugh followed Joe's drunken threat. He rubbed his knuckles vigorously.

Roscoe touched his mangled nose. His fingers came away sticky with blood, its sheen almost black in the dim light. He let out a slow breath, trying to tamp down the rage. *No, buddy, he thought, I may kill you first.*

The truck slowed and pulled onto a dirt road lined with gum trees that blocked out the clear, starry skies. The engine rattled to a stop and the men in front jumped out. Jacked up on adrenaline and whiskey, they seemed unable to control their movements as they pulled the white robes over their heads. Joe tossed one to Roscoe and muttered, "Do it," before a cone-shaped mask obscured his face.

Warden Gates handed Joe and Roscoe each a shotgun from the rack behind the seat. The other men checked their pistols before trotting to the lone house at the end of the road.

Roscoe's gut cramped so bad he thought he might have to shit in the woods. He knew, though, that Joe and the others would think he was making off into the night. If it came down to it, crapping his pants was preferable to the beating they would give him.

He kept at Joe's heels while Wally and the warden took the lead. Roscoe hadn't noticed the torches the other two guards carried until they stopped in the yard to light them. A line of pointed shadows stretched toward the porch that wrapped around two sides of the house.

"Get out here, Silas," Wally barked, then raised his shotgun in the air. The boom startled Roscoe. His sweaty grip on his own shotgun tightened.

"We know you got that pregnant white gal in there," the warden shouted. "Come on out or we'll burn you out."

A tall, well-muscled man opened the front screen door, his hands raised. He wore a white sleeveless undershirt and loose pants that weren't buttoned. Even by torchlight, Roscoe could see the slick sweat that covered his face and chest.

"Don't want no trouble," Silas yelled. "That girl had nowhere to go. She came to our church looking for help. My wife's taking care of her."

"Her daddy says different," Joe called out. He shuffled his feet, causing his robe's hem to flutter. Roscoe knew this nervous tick well, but he didn't know who the girl was or how Joe knew her father.

"Girl's daddy the one who got her in a bad way," Silas countered. "She safe with us. Ain't no harm come to her."

"We don't know what you're doing to her in there," Joe shouted. "Could be keeping her against her will."

"I'm a man of God. Why would I hurt that girl?"

Silas kept his hands raised, but they now shook. His grimace was almost unnoticeable. But Roscoe saw it. The set of his jaw said he was bracing himself. He knew that violence awaited. But neither he nor Roscoe knew what form it'd take.

The hood on Roscoe's head was suffocating. The sweat from his hair and forehead stung his eyes. He poked two fingers through each eyehole to wipe it away. He willed himself not to blink; not to tear his attention away.

Joe inched toward the house, shotgun raised.

He used the barrel to motion the others to do the same.

"Goddamn this," Roscoe muttered.

"Keep your mouth shut, boy," the warden warned.

"Let's leave this man be," he begged. "We have no business being here."

As Joe and the other men turned their attention to Roscoe, they failed to notice the woman easing slowly around the corner of the side porch. Time slowed as Roscoe took in every detail of the ghostly figure: the long white gown she wore, her bare feet, the night kerchief she'd tied around her hair, the shotgun raised to her shoulder.

"Olivia, no!" Silas shouted, and lunged for her.

Joe whipped around, raising his gun in one fluid motion. Two blasts went off in quick succession. The blur of white robes disoriented Roscoe. The warden and two guards rushed the porch and overtook Silas and his screaming wife.

Roscoe's gaze landed on Joe, who lay facedown, unmoving. The starkness of his white robe was marred by a dark spot whose edges grew until it was almost the size of a silver dollar. Roscoe knelt and rolled Joe onto his back. He wished he hadn't. The gaping exit wound looked like used motor oil and hamburger meat. Roscoe's stomach heaved as he fought for air.

He removed Joe's hood first, then his own. He

closed his eyes and found he could breathe again. The night air smelled sweet, of honeysuckle or gardenia. Almost strong enough to overpower the metallic pungency of the blood seeping from Joe's body.

"I'm sorry," Roscoe said, but those were words he didn't mean. He felt only relief. A relief so huge that it overshadowed the chaos still erupting around him.

When someone called his name, it sounded tinny and distant. He turned just as the butt of a shotgun met his forehead.

Roscoe couldn't tell how much time had passed when he came to. The rope around his wrists was secured to a tree branch so that his body arched unnaturally and his feet barely touched the ground. His face was caked in blood from the wound inflicted by the shotgun butt, yet every muscle pulsed in agony. He'd been beaten but good. Although one eye was swollen shut, Roscoe could make out his assailants. He worked with them every day. That included Warden Gates.

Now that he was awake, they continued the beating in between swigs of white lightning. His body spun on the rope with each punch. He prayed he'd lose consciousness again.

"You sack of shit," the warden said. "Killing a fellow guard. And your best friend."

Roscoe tried to speak, but his mutilated lips managed only a mumble.

"What's that, you son of a bitch?" Gates asked. "I can't hear you."

"I was aiming for the woman," Roscoe lied. "I was aiming for the woman." The salt in his tears seared the torn parts of his face.

"I don't believe him," Wally shouted.

Roscoe spat fresh blood. He didn't figure on dying this way or this young, but he wasn't going to beg for mercy. "Let me down or finish me off."

The warden motioned for Wally to cut the rope from the limb. Roscoe collapsed into a heap, his hands still bound.

He forgot there'd been a second shot. Had Joe or Silas's wife fired? Talking was painful, but he had to know if other lives had been taken. "Are they dead?" Roscoe sputtered.

"The nigger and his woman? Nah, but they probably wish they were." Gates squatted and spoke directly in Roscoe's ear. "So, here's what's going to happen, Simms. We're going to say that nigger killed Joe. You're going to go along with it."

The warden said no more. Roscoe expected him to follow up with a threat, but it was implied. Gates motioned two of the guards over and they threw him into the back of the truck like a sack of potatoes. They hadn't bothered to untie him.

Joe's body lay just inches from Roscoe's face.

He was thankful someone had closed the eyelids. Leaning his head back, he tried to imagine what his pummeled body would feel like at daybreak. He'd never been so thirsty. He just wanted water. God, just a little. Licking his lips caused a hot, red spike of pain. Blackness closed in once more until a muffled cry near the tailgate roused him. He eased himself up to get a better look. Silas lay motionless in a twisted, hog-tied lump, a burlap bag over his head.

Chapter 18

Ginny had always been told that Roscoe was with her daddy the night he was murdered. Yet, he'd sworn he never hurt anyone. If Mrs. Barnes's story was true, then Roscoe stood by while Olivia was raped and beaten. For twenty-one years, he covered up the fact that one of the guards—not Silas—had killed her father. Worse, he let a man go to the electric chair rather than tell the truth. He *had* hurt someone. Several people, in fact, and she was just now realizing the full domino effect.

Emotional pain had a physical quality beyond the fatigue and headaches. It was something that invaded every one of her cells and changed their makeup. It was not alleviated by crying or screaming at the top of one's lungs. She'd done both for two hours. At one point, an irrational fear overtook her. Perhaps God was punishing her for not believing in Him all along.

By the time she reached Boucherville, Ginny was surprised that she felt very little emotion. Her body seemed featherlight as if she purged the heaviness of grief the entire drive back from New Orleans. Her headache had been replaced by a slight dizziness, something akin to the blood rush a child might feel hanging upside down on a tree limb or swinging too high on a swing set.

She could only think of two places to go: the prison or her mother's. Dot was likely to provide comfort and a voice of reason. But perhaps Ginny needed Miriam more. Her mama would relish helping Ginny hold on to her anger. It was such an active emotion compared to sadness. Fueled by anger, she could imagine being propelled forward. Toward what, she did not know.

Both options, though, required energy she didn't have. A third option emerged: sleep over at the warden's residence. Eugenia had offered her a bed on several occasions, especially after late-night parties when Ginny worked well past midnight cleaning up the kitchen.

She passed through the prison's main gate around five. Dot would have supper prepared for the inmates by then, so Ginny didn't bother stopping to check in on her. After all, Dot handled most every aspect of the kitchen now that Ginny worked for the warden and his wife. And Dot had hired her grandniece, Bertie, to help. The young girl was eager, tripping over Dot's feet throughout the day, seeking her approval. And she could bake a mean biscuit.

Ginny left a note on Dot's door at the women's barracks to let her know she was sleeping at the residence. Her excuse was that Mrs. Levy needed her early in the morning and it was just easier to stay there. She slipped a nightgown, toothbrush, and change of clothes into a bag before leaving.

Driving up to the freshly painted home, with its lush green lawn and blooming crepe myrtle, was like stepping onto a movie set. Eugenia had worked magic to create a space that could make you feel you left the prison behind once you parked on the gray crushed gravel.

With the setting sun in her eyes, Ginny almost didn't notice the warden sitting on the front porch.

"Good evening, sir," she said.

"Let's dispense with the sir business," he said, jovially. "I'm off the clock."

It was five-thirty. The warden was rarely home before seven.

"I thought I might have a word with Mrs. Levy." Ginny eyed the glass of iced tea the warden was gulping. Her throat constricted. She couldn't wait to drink something—anything—after the long drive.

"The missus is in New Orleans for the night. She's seeing an old friend and having dinner," he said. "I thought I'd kick off early and enjoy the peace and quiet."

Ginny understood exactly what he meant. Mrs. Levy filled the house with her constant chatter and hummingbird movements, seguing without transition to the next topic. Ginny had taken to ignoring her until Mrs. Levy repeated a question. That was the only way Ginny could determine if

Eugenia was talking just to hear herself talk or if she had a real request.

Seeing as how the woman was still Ginny's boss, she didn't think it proper to commiserate with the warden about his wife's nagging.

"Join me for some iced tea?" He motioned to the full pitcher on the wicker table near his chair.

Normally, Ginny would decline, but her chapped lips and pasty tongue made the decision for her. She nodded her thanks and sat in a wicker rocker. The view out toward the prison compound was colorless and depressing. She'd just as soon go stand out in the driveway and stare back at the house. At least she wouldn't be out there long.

"You're gussied up today, Miss Polk," he said. "Not a workday, I presume."

She looked at the gloves on her hands. Ginny couldn't remember putting them back on when she left Mrs. Barnes and Willy. Suddenly, she felt self-conscious and tugged at the skirt of her dress. It was one that Mrs. Levy had purchased for her in case she decided to start going to church on Sunday mornings. It was the first time she'd worn it.

"Your wife gave me the day off to visit someone in New Orleans. I thought I better clean up a bit."

"Well, you ladies should have driven together," he said. "Although, I know the value in having some time apart from Eugenia."

334

Ginny didn't know what to make of the good mood and jokes. Outside of "good morning" and "good evening," they'd really only had two conversations and those were about the last suppers: the first being that they were no longer allowed; the second being that she'd have to cook one for Jasper Sires.

"Thank you for talking to Jasper. He's calmed down a good bit." The warden picked a stem of mint from his tea glass and sucked on one of the leaves. "I heard he wasn't a pleasant man to speak with. I'm sorry for that."

"That's all right," she said. "I've pretty much seen it all." Ginny wondered if the guards had mentioned anything about Jasper's ramblings. It was clear that John wanted Jasper silenced on the subject of her daddy's murder. She didn't know if the warden shared the same feeling, but she was curious enough to ask.

"Did you know that Jasper is the nephew of the man they say killed my daddy?"

His expression didn't change. "I did. John mentioned it. Although I don't know the details of your father's death. That was some years ago, correct?"

"Twenty-one to be exact."

"Hmmm."

Ginny stared at her scuffed loafers. They were too casual for the clothes she wore, but she figured the day would prove painful enough without her heels and little toes stinging with blisters.

"I've just learned an innocent man went to the electric chair for Daddy's death." She figured there was no real danger in being bold. She'd lost so much already.

"Is that right? And you've got this on whose authority? I wouldn't go believing everything Mr. Sires tells you." The warden's words were no longer lighthearted, and his expression turned to granite.

She hadn't said it was Jasper who said anything. John obviously knew something. The warden knew something. Ginny doubted they had the details that Olivia Barnes had shared, but she couldn't be certain. If John was one of the guards who'd been there that night, he'd know the whole story. Warden Levy had only been a prison board member for a short time, unless he'd done some digging.

"Silas Barnes," she said.

"Who is Silas Barnes?" he asked, agitated now.

"An innocent man that the state put to death. I spoke with his widow today. I finally know the whole story."

The warden stood at the edge of the porch, his hands resting on the railing. "A jury found Mr. Barnes guilty."

"This is Louisiana, sir. I believe a good many innocent black men have been found guilty."

Warden Levy turned and pointed at her. "Miss Polk, you choose to live in Louisiana. You choose to work in a penal institution. Don't go getting all preachy about the failures of our justice system. Your daddy's death was two decades ago. Leave it alone."

Ginny stood, thinking it'd give her courage to continue. It only proved how weak her legs had become.

"It might mean something to the family if Silas's name was cleared," she said. "Maybe one of the other guards who'd been there that night would come forward."

Roscoe was one such guard. He could go on record about what really happened. Yet, even if he wanted to come clean about that night, he'd probably refuse to implicate the others who had been with him. Maybe if she confronted him, his remorse would be so great that he'd consider it.

"I've heard enough. I'm not entertaining any more of your foolish notions. Now, please go see about fixing my supper." His tone straddled the line between angry boss and admonishing grandfather.

Ginny's heart pounded wildly. She felt like David confronting Goliath, except that she didn't have a rock in her hand or God on her side. No matter what the warden said, her accusations weren't foolish notions. Anyone who spoke to Mrs. Barnes would see she was telling the truth.

Sparring wouldn't help Ginny's case tonight, though, so she backed down.

"I believe it's still my day off, sir." She blinked rapidly despite her best efforts to remain aloof. "I'm sure Mrs. Levy left something in the fridge for you since she expected me to be home much later."

He turned and entered the house, slamming the door behind him.

Ginny's heart rate didn't slow until she was covered in flour and smelling of warm milk and yeast. She twisted and pounded the pale bread dough, imagining she was bashing in the face of a hooded Klan member. Cowards. Cowards who deserved to be in prison themselves. Her tears threatened only when she realized her hypocrisy. Even though she was adamant each of them should pay, she was ashamed she didn't mean Roscoe. How could she exclude him, though? Could her love be that strong or that blind?

Ginny recalled the warden's remark from the day before; that her baking was the best part about taking the job. Just to spite him, she thought about throwing away the dough instead of letting it rise. He'd been in the kitchen to make himself a sandwich earlier, so he'd already seen she was baking something.

"Who the hell cares," Ginny said out loud. She scooped up the sticky mass and was about to throw it in the trash when a tap at the kitchen window startled her. Dot motioned toward the side door. "Let me in," she mouthed.

Ginny opened the screen door and Dot pushed past her.

"What's this about you sleeping here tonight?" Dot's hands were firmly planted on her hips. "And why are you baking in your good dress?"

"I was working out some aggression." Ginny held the dough at arm's length. "Let me finish up and we can talk."

Dot knew the kitchen cupboards almost as well as Ginny did. She pulled out a large ceramic bowl with a blue rim and oiled it with the shortening that was on the counter. Ginny dropped the dough in the bowl and Dot covered it with a dish towel.

"What did your mama want today?" Dot asked.

"You know I wasn't at Mama's."

"Then why lie unless you knew I'd try to talk you out of some foolhardy plan."

"Too late for that." Ginny sat at the kitchen table. She'd gotten egg yolk on the brand-new dress. She smiled to think how it would irritate Mrs. Levy if she found out. Ginny considered leaving it draped across a dining room chair on the pretext she was taking it to the dry cleaner's.

"What's funny?" Dot asked.

"Absolutely nothing," Ginny said. "Except that I'm dog tired and can't believe I'm having yet another hard conversation today."

Dot looked hurt. "Do you feel obligated to explain yourself to me? 'Cause I can go right now. And who says our talk has to be hard?"

Ginny relayed Jasper's allegation about Silas being innocent and admitted she manipulated a young guard into obtaining Olivia Barnes's address in New Orleans. When she described the meeting with Silas's widow and son, Dot's eyes grew moist.

"You shouldn't have gone and disrupted those people's lives," Dot said.

"If I hadn't, I wouldn't have learned the truth."

"And what's the truth going to get you?"

Ginny didn't have an answer. Maybe peace of mind. Maybe justice.

"Now, more than ever, I'm positive you have to leave this place," Dot said.

"I've got to do something. It's not right that Silas was punished for a murder he didn't commit."

"There's nothing to be done!" Dot shouted. "Don't you see that? You're going to stir up a hornet's nest, then be surprised when they sting you."

She got up to check on the rising dough even though it'd been sitting in the warm oven less than five minutes.

Ginny wasn't surprised at Dot's reaction and allowed Dot's anger to run its course. She nodded as Dot ranted about her foolishness, the same word the warden had used.

"I thought you'd be on my side," Ginny said, interrupting her.

"Why? Because I'm black?"

"No, because you're a good and just person."

Dot shook her head, muttering to herself. Then she started crying.

Ginny wrapped her arms around Dot as far as they would go and squeezed with all her might. "You've got nothing to worry about."

Dot squirmed until Ginny let go. "Those men . . . whatever they done to Mrs. Barnes kept her mouth shut even if that meant her husband was going to die. You don't think she knew she'd be next? Or maybe her little boy?"

"No one's going to kill me for telling the truth," Ginny assured her.

"Then you're not as smart as you look," she said. "That man's execution has caused you nothing but pain since you was a little girl. And you're going to let it keep on hurting you until the day you die."

Dot was right. Silas Barnes had been a bigger part of her life than even her own daddy. She figured if the nightmares hadn't stopped in twenty-one years, they'd never stop. She'd see Silas's face and hear his protests of innocence until the day she died. Her gut twisted to think she'd known all along that he hadn't done it; that she sensed it in the execution chamber and ignored the suspicion.

"Think long and hard about your next move," Dot said.

As she opened the screen door to leave, she pointed back at the oven. "And you got the temperature too high for rising. You probably killed the yeast."

She left, not looking back. Ginny watched her walk across the shamelessly green grass and then onto the dusty road. She had a long walk back to the barracks.

Ginny woke before the housekeeper or the warden. She slipped into the kitchen without a sound and made herself some coffee to have with the bread she'd baked the night before. Ginny cut off both heels and buttered them generously. They were still her favorite part, and there was no way she'd let the warden's wife throw them away, as she usually did.

It didn't feel like a new day, but rather an extension of the day before. Maybe the rest of her life would go on feeling like one long day full of horrific revelations around every corner. She didn't know, and it tired her to think ahead more than a few minutes.

Since the warden liked sweets, Ginny vowed to spend the day baking pies and cakes and cookies—enough to rot his teeth and strain the buttons on his shirt. Then, she'd leave a note saying she didn't want the job anymore and they could kiss her ass.

She went into the pantry to check she had enough brown sugar. The warden, now awake and dressed for work, followed her into the cramped space. His physical presence had never frightened her before, but it did now.

"I heard you and the kitchen negress talking last night," he said, moving even closer.

The scent of Barbasol shaving cream filled the pantry, even with the door open. Ginny gagged on its cloying dominance.

"The cook from the kitchen, her name is Dorothy." Ginny craned her neck so that she could meet his eyes. There was no way she'd look away.

"Well, Dorothy is a smart woman. You ought to listen to her advice."

"And what advice was that?"

"Maybe your time at the prison has reached its natural end," he said, finally backing up into the kitchen. "Perhaps there are new opportunities you'd like to pursue."

Ginny tried to hide the relief she felt at being released from the pantry. She gave the warden wide berth, though, retreating to the kitchen chair nearest the door. She didn't expect him to be physically violent, but she wasn't going to take any chances. Sitting next to an exit calmed her. She just wished Sarah Jane, the housekeeper, would make an appearance.

"Now that you mention it," she said. "I have been thinking about moving on."

His shoulders relaxed. "Well, that's good to hear. I have a friend who owns a restaurant in New Orleans. His information is there on the table. He might need some help. And there's a women's boardinghouse nearby. You'd have a place to stay until you could save up some of your wages."

Ginny had plenty of her own money. What was there to spend it on these past nine years? She didn't care if she had the latest fashions or shoes. Living in the women's barracks meant she never had to pay rent. She ate her meals in the prison kitchen or with Roscoe at the residence. Or rather, she had. Her nest egg was substantial. It was just she had no clue where it could take her.

"Mrs. Levy won't be very happy," he continued, "but I'll smooth things over."

"I'm sure you will."

He narrowed his eyes, probably wondering what her tone implied.

"I'll give my friend a call later this morning then. If I hear anything, I'll drop by during lunch," he said.

"I'll be here."

He nodded and pushed through the dining room door, almost running into Sarah Jane.

"There's a phone call for Miss Polk," she said, panting. "It's your mother. She says it's urgent."

The conversation with the warden had been so tense, Ginny hadn't even heard it ring.

"Make it quick," the warden said. "The phone isn't for personal use."

Ginny pushed past the housekeeper and ran to the phone in the foyer.

"Mama? What is it?"

Miriam was incoherent, tears garbling her words. Ginny couldn't remember the last time her mother had cried, and definitely not with this level of hysteria.

"You've got to calm down," Ginny begged. "I can't make out what you're saying. Are you hurt?"

Her mama's guttural sobs sent a jolt of terror down Ginny's spine. She couldn't fathom what was causing Miriam's heartache.

"Spit it out, Mama!" Ginny yelled, hoping to shock her into speaking.

"I think I killed him," she finally said. "I think Roscoe's dead."

Ginny dropped the receiver and ran for her car.

Chapter 19

Miriam waited on the porch. She was still in a housecoat, one hand on her forehead, the other at her side holding an unlit cigarette.

"Where's Roscoe?" Ginny screamed.

Miriam babbled on about a gun and not knowing how much damage she'd done. Ginny grabbed her and shook with all her strength. When her mama wouldn't answer, Ginny slapped her once and then again.

"Tell me what happened. Tell me this instant!"

"I didn't intend for this to happen." Miriam's eyes were wide and panicked. "But I'm glad now. I'm glad he's dead."

Ginny pushed her out of the way and entered the house. She moved through each room, shouting out Roscoe's name and checking behind large pieces of furniture in case he was on the floor unable to answer.

"Where is he, Mama?"

Miriam had come inside and was sitting at the kitchen table.

"He left," she said. "I told him he had to stay and tell you what he told me, but he just up and drove off."

Ginny's shoulders relaxed. Her mother was

crazy. She hadn't killed him if he could walk out of here of his own volition.

"Mama, you didn't kill anyone. You're not in your right mind."

As soon as Ginny spoke, she noticed the pool of blood by the kitchen door that led to the backyard.

"Jesus Christ, what did you do?" Ginny saw that a trail of blood extended down the back wooden steps and into the grass.

Shouting at Miriam wasn't helping, so Ginny knelt beside her, placing a hand on her knee. She had to find out what happened. Roscoe may need medical attention considering how much blood he'd lost. It took everything in her to squelch her panic long enough to get Miriam calmed.

"Please, Mama. Tell me what happened. I can't help you if you don't tell me. You haven't killed anyone, but we need to find Roscoe." Ginny spotted the pistol on the floor near the stove. She'd deal with it later.

Miriam's nose ran profusely. She used the arm of her housecoat to wipe her face before speaking.

"Roscoe came over early. Daybreak," she said. "He was banging on the screen door something fierce. At first I thought it had to be you. But you'd have just walked right in."

Unnerved by that realization, Miriam had grabbed her pistol from the nightstand before going to the front door. She said she'd been relieved to see it was Roscoe, until she got a good look at him. Miriam said he looked like crap: bloodshot eyes, crumpled clothes. He'd pushed his way inside the living room and wouldn't stop pacing, no matter how much Miriam tried to calm him down.

"I thought something happened to you, Ginny. That's how upset he was," she said.

"And what did he say?" Ginny pressed.

"He said you'd likely found out something about his past, something that affected me, too. And he wanted to explain. He wanted to apologize."

Ginny guessed that Roscoe had found out about her altercation with Jasper, or maybe that she'd tracked down Mrs. Barnes—especially if Tim was feeling particularly loyal and fessed up. It was strange, though, that Roscoe thought it more important to come clean with Miriam first.

"I already know about Daddy's death." Ginny pushed the damp strands of hair from Miriam's flushed cheeks. "Silas Barnes was innocent. I swear I didn't know until yesterday. Roscoe kept it from us both all these years."

"He was a goddamned coward." Miriam's jaw was clenched tight. Anger replaced her earlier despondency. Ginny was grateful for it. She could handle her mama's rages, but the weeping and hysteria were almost unbearable.

"All of them were cowards," Ginny said. "Roscoe lied to protect one of his buddies. And Silas paid the price."

Miriam shoved Ginny's hand off her leg. "What the hell are you talking about?"

"Daddy didn't die at that bar," Ginny explained. "He and some men from the prison had been on a Klan run. Silas's widow told me one of them shot Daddy accidentally."

"It wasn't an accident, little girl. Roscoe killed your daddy that night."

Ginny backed away as if burned by fire. "I don't understand."

"He said Joe was going to shoot that woman and he had to stop him. He killed my husband. He killed your daddy."

"But Mrs. Barnes said—"

"Roscoe admitted it," Miriam said. "He stood right here in my kitchen and said he was sorry; like a goddamned apology would mean something. Then he said the men near beat him to death. As if I could feel sorry for him."

"So you shot him?" Ginny's hysteria was mounting. She'd not be able to rein it in much longer.

"I was just pointing the gun at him. I wanted to scare him," Miriam said. "He told me to put it down. Then he tried to wrestle it away. I swear it just went off."

Ginny stumbled into the living room. Roscoe

had killed her father. Her mother had likely killed Roscoe. She longed for her brain to come unhinged as it had the night of Samuel's execution. Oh, the bliss of retreating to a place of unknowing. She wanted her mind wiped clean of every memory, good and bad: the faces of all the inmates she cooked for; the way Roscoe's eyelids would grow heavy after they'd made love; Dot's good-natured ribbing and unsolicited mothering; Willy Barnes's lazy eye and birthmark. All wiped clean.

"Roscoe deserved it." Miriam's voice was high and unnatural now.

"Shut up, Mama. Just shut up!"

Ginny had to pull herself together. *Think.*

"What if he went to the police?" Miriam eyed the front door frantically as if she'd be hauled away in handcuffs any minute.

"He wouldn't have gone to the police," Ginny said. "You said it was an accident." She doubted he would choose the hospital either.

Her brain tugged at a long-ago conversation. Roscoe had just come back from a weeklong fishing trip. She'd never seen him as relaxed or happy. In recounting his vacation, a smile never left his lips. He'd said, "I would consider myself a lucky man if the Lord decided to take me when I was on the bank of that river with a pole in one hand and a beer in the other. That'd be the way to go."

Her stomach dropped just as her mind caught up. He'd gone back to the Little River, or he had died trying.

Ginny grabbed the pistol from the kitchen floor. "I have to leave now, Mama. Pull yourself together and clean up all that blood. Don't tell anyone what happened."

The drive to the lake was infuriatingly long. Ginny babbled to herself the whole way, one second hoping Roscoe was still alive, then in the next instant, certain he couldn't have survived that much blood loss. She shook uncontrollably to think the next time she saw him, he'd be dead.

Once at the lake, she parked her car closer to the road fearing her wheels would sink in the marshy ground nearer the water. She leapt from the car and ran toward the bank, her shoes making sucking sounds in the mud. Roscoe's truck was nowhere in sight.

"Goddamn you, Ginny!" she screamed. How could she believe an injured man would drive all that way? She'd ruined any chance of finding him back in Boucherville and would have to live with that decision the rest of her sorry life.

She kicked off her shoes and walked down to the water's edge, feeling the grass and mud between her toes. A breeze lifted the damp hair from her neck. The pistol felt heavy in her hand. Why had she even brought it with her? She turned it over and imagined it in her mother's grasp. Miriam originally pulled the gun out because she feared an intruder. The gun could have become an unfortunately handy way to amplify her anger in that moment. Had her mama intended to kill Roscoe?

Ginny shook off the image and hurled the gun into the water. She'd make sure Miriam didn't pay for her crime. It'd serve no purpose and there'd been more than enough loss. Still, Ginny couldn't imagine ever forgiving her. Her mama's rashness eliminated any chance for Ginny to get the explanation from Roscoe she swore she couldn't live without.

The squawk of a jay turned her attention upriver. The sun glinted off something shiny. The windshield of Roscoe's truck. He'd made it after all.

She ran as fast as she could, the sticky mud hampering her speed and throwing her off balance. The trees almost completely obscured the truck. Why hadn't she looked more closely when she first got there?

He'd left the door open. The steering wheel, front seat, and door handle were smeared with blood; enough blood to tell Ginny he was likely already dead. She swung around, frantically searching the thick copse of trees for any sign of him.

She choked back her horror when she saw

Roscoe's legs sticking out behind a large tree. He'd propped his back against the trunk. His arms lay slack at his sides, his blood-soaked hands resembling red mittens.

"Oh God, Roscoe. Oh God."

Ginny froze. She knew what death looked like. The faces of eighteen dead men would never leave her. Yet, she didn't want to see the life drained from Roscoe's face. She'd give anything for a different last memory of him, but there was no way she could leave him there.

When she rounded the tree, the rise and fall of his chest startled her. "Roscoe? You're alive?"

She knelt beside him and pressed both hands against the dark, wet spot on his belly. It's warm stickiness made her want to pull away, but she feared she was now the only thing keeping the last bits of his life from slipping out.

Surprise registered in his unfocused eyes. "Ginny? How in the hell—"

"Shhh. No need for words," she said. But that was a lie. She'd give anything to have one last conversation. It didn't have to be about him killing her daddy, or letting an innocent man die. It didn't have to be about making the wrong choices and then trying to atone for them. She wanted him to tell her why he always came back to the same fishing spot, and whether or not he was popular with the girls in high school. She wanted to know why he hated Alabama so much, and preferred ham to turkey on Thanksgiving.

"Joe tried to teach your mama to shoot once," he said. "She was terrible."

"Don't talk, Roscoe."

"She didn't do too bad today." He smiled and then winced with the effort. "Don't blame her for this. Promise me. I swear it was an accident."

She nodded. Tears blurred her vision, but she wouldn't remove her hands from the wound. He placed a bloodied hand over hers. The warmth was leaving his body. The color of his skin was all wrong. She longed for the comforting scent of Old Spice to overpower the coppery smell of his blood.

It struck her that she'd never again feel the warmth of his skin after a hot bath, or hear him read Scripture after making love. The stubble of a missed shave would never rub a raw spot on her chin. The perfect spot at the crook of his neck would never welcome her when her heart was heavy.

"About Joe. I had to do it." His breath became a labored wheeze.

"It's done with. You did what you thought was right," Ginny said. She couldn't judge whether Olivia Barnes's life meant more than her daddy's. But he'd have gone on hurting people and Roscoe knew it, too. Ginny remembered what Roscoe had said earlier: "My being there saved more than were lost." She knew this to be true.

"I feel like I've been running a race my whole life." His words were barely audible, so Ginny leaned forward. "I could never get away from it. From the things I did. From the things I didn't do."

Ginny understood. She'd been running a race, too, always afraid to look back at the monster on her heels. Dot had been right. The monster had always been the memory of Silas Barnes's death. No matter how many suppers she cooked, she'd never undo the pain his family endured. She'd never had the power to undo it in the first place.

Whenever anyone asked why she stayed in that hellhole, Ginny always said it was because she loved her job. And she did. But it wasn't the job that bound her to that prison. It was Roscoe all along, even before he'd grown to love her. Even before she admitted she loved him.

He patted her hand lightly. The blood from his wound seeped slower now.

His blue eyes stared past her and past the river that brought him the only peace he'd ever known.

"God knows I do love you, Ginny Polk."

She grabbed his face with both hands and kissed him. The still-warm lips wouldn't respond no matter how hard she pressed. She leaned her forehead against his and closed her eyes.

"Then He also knows I love you, Roscoe Simms."

Chapter 20

The class bell rang and mercifully put an end to lunch service at Carver Elementary. Ginny motioned to the two other women in the kitchen that she was going out for a smoke break. Once outside in the alley, she leaned back against the brick steps. The quiet was heavenly, although her ears still hummed from the cacophony of the lunchroom. Metal trays clanging against metal tables only added to the din of the children's excited voices.

Ginny lit up a Pall Mall. It was the brand Roscoe preferred, although he used to say he'd smoke whatever was cheapest or whatever he could bum from a friend. It had been more than a year since she left him at the lakeside. She'd made an anonymous phone call to alert the police about his body. There'd been an investigation, which closed rather quickly considering the woeful lack of evidence and that Miriam had indeed managed to keep her mouth shut. Ginny was grateful when the newspaper coverage dwindled to nothing.

She touched the St. Christopher's medal at her throat. She'd taken it off Roscoe's body. It was her only remembrance of him, except for his worn Bible. Before she left the prison for good, she checked the dresser back in his old room in the admin building. Someone had cleared out all his belongings except for that damn dog-eared King James version. Perhaps he'd smile to know she'd chosen both as mementos.

When she'd applied for a cook's position at the all-black elementary school, the principal noted the medal and asked if Ginny was a woman of God. Ginny figured she wouldn't get the job anyway and saw no point in lying. She'd said she was still figuring things out and the medal served as a reminder to keep her options open. The principal had laughed. Several months later, the woman had admitted it was Ginny's candor and not the glowing recommendation from Warden Levy that got her the job.

"Principal Marberry doesn't like teachers to smoke." Carol, the head cook, sat down beside her and pulled a cigarette from the pack that lay between them.

"Good thing we're not going to get caught." Ginny wrapped her sweater around her shoulders. It was usually warmer in November, but the air was clammy as a result of an early-morning rain shower that left behind dull gray skies.

She'd adapted quite easily to the rhythm of the school's kitchen. She no longer had to worry about spoiled milk or rotten vegetables. There was plenty of fresh meat and produce. It became apparent that Ginny was the strongest baker, so she took over making bread, rolls, and dessert. There were a few bumps in the beginning. Carol had taken Ginny to task after she'd chided another cook for failing to season a dish properly. Once the hierarchy was made perfectly clear, Ginny and Carol had become friends. It reminded Ginny of how her relationship with Dot had grown over time, to the point that Dot was now the closest thing she had to family.

"What are you reading so intently?" Ginny pointed to the newspaper in Carol's hands.

"I just can't believe marshals are needed to get a child safely to school." She shook her head and folded the paper.

That fall, people weren't taking the forced desegregation of New Orleans public schools very well. Hundreds still gathered every day to protest the admittance of a six-year-old black girl to an all-white elementary school. Flanked by three federal marshals, the girl showed up to school every day, her head held high, despite the jeers and slurs being slung her way.

"I'm proud of her," Ginny said, snuffing out her cigarette. "Things have got to change."

"This is Louisiana," Carol reminded her. "Things won't change overnight."

Warden Levy had warned Ginny of the same thing when she'd brought up the idea of clearing Silas Barnes's name for her daddy's murder. Later, when she asked for a letter of reference, he'd rebuked her for wanting to work at an all-black school. He maintained some things were best left separate.

She sometimes judged Roscoe for not being braver in 1938. He allowed an innocent man to die rather than admit he'd killed Joe Polk; rather than turn in his coworkers for raping Barnes's wife. A six-year-old girl was courageous enough to show people their ignorance, yet a grown man refused to stand up against the Klan.

If she and Miriam were still talking, her mama would probably chastise her for such thinking. After all, it would have cost Roscoe his life to say anything. Even though Ginny looked back on that time with the benefit of hindsight, it didn't stop her from wishing things had been different.

Two white students had been scheduled to enroll at Carver, but their families were harassed so thoroughly that they backed out before the start of the school year. Carol joked that instead of integrating white students at the school, they'd hired a white cook instead.

"Time to clean up the kitchen." Carol slapped Ginny on her thigh and stood up. "And I need your help planning next week's meals."

"I'll be there in just a bit," Ginny said, lighting another cigarette. It was a rare and wonderful thing to feel chilled in Louisiana weather and she was going to savor it a few minutes longer.

• • •

After the pots and pans had been scrubbed, Carol suggested that they play a few hands of gin rummy. It took a bit of prodding to convince Mabel, the other cook, but she finally acquiesced. Carol was good at managing people that way. Mabel could be pathologically shy, hence the reason she'd been so hurt when Ginny told her not to be so stingy with black pepper when making gravy. The impromptu game brought Mabel out of her shell. She even attempted to tell a dirty joke. It fell flat, which made it all the more funny.

Emboldened by the camaraderie, Mabel must have decided it was safe to ask Ginny about her insistence on wearing slacks to work.

"When I worked at the prison kitchen, Dot would give me holy hell for not wearing stockings. She said I looked like a teenager in my socks and loafers," Ginny said. "She'd have a conniption if she knew I was wearing pants most every day. I can almost see the consternation in her eyes."

Carol and Mabel had heard dozens of Dot stories, so they weren't surprised to hear Ginny's reason for bucking tradition once again. They tolerated her eccentricities. It hadn't taken long for Ginny to grow fond of her coworkers. Each day it was easier and easier to believe she could leave behind those years at the Greenmount Penitentiary.

"Hey, look at the time," Carol said, interrupting the laughter. "You best get moving, Ginny."

She was right. Ginny hated getting caught in the after-school stampede of students and parents. The decibel level of the cafeteria was nothing compared to a group of 200 children getting their freedom after seven hours of schooling.

Grabbing her sweater and umbrella, Ginny ducked out of the kitchen into the alleyway to avoid the main halls of the school. It was a short walk to her apartment, and she looked forward to stopping at the corner market to chat with the grocer. He'd often set aside overly ripe bananas for her so she could bake banana bread, or bruised peaches for jam.

She was checking her pocketbook to be sure she had a few dollars when she walked straight into a street sign.

A man walking in the opposite direction stopped to see if she was okay.

"Are you all right, miss?" he asked.

"Yes, yes. Just lost in thought," Ginny said. "I can be clumsy when . . . Willy? Is that you?"

Silas Barnes's son seemed just as surprised to see her. "Miss Polk! It's nice to see you. What are you doing in this area of town?"

"I work at Carver Elementary. In the kitchen." She pointed to the redbrick building behind her.

"Ah," he said. "My little girl just started first

grade this fall. On my days off, I try to walk home with her."

That explained why she hadn't run into Willy before now. He probably came around only rarely, and she made it a point to leave the school well before last bell. Their chance meeting caused the hair on her arms to prickle. The encounter was awkward, but not unbearable. Ginny was genuinely pleased to see him.

"I hope you and your mother are both well," she said.

"Yes, we're both fine. Thank you," Willy said. "So you've left the prison, then?"

Ginny nodded. "It was time."

Willy looked past her, down the street. His little girl would be pouring out of the front doors with her classmates any second. "I should probably be going," he said. "But I wanted to thank you for what you did to clear Daddy's name. I know nothing came of it, but it was brave of you to try."

Lucky maybe, but not brave, Ginny thought. After Roscoe passed away, she had taken a last look inside his truck, although she couldn't remember why. She'd found a note he'd scribbled on a paper sack and then signed. Roscoe had detailed the events of the night of her father's death, including the names of the warden and all guards involved. Ginny knew it was useless to bring it to the attention of anyone in the Louisiana penal system. Just as useless to bring it to the attention of the state's press. So, she'd mailed it off to a reporter from the *New York Times* who'd written a series of articles on Klan lynchings in Louisiana and Mississippi.

He'd been interested enough to dig around. The one person who could corroborate Roscoe's story was Mrs. Barnes, and she'd refused to talk.

"I expect your mother is still quite angry with me," Ginny said. "I had the best intentions."

"I know you did. But she's still afraid. For herself. For all of us. She'll take that secret to her grave."

"I understand."

Ginny knew something about keeping secrets. She'd never tell anyone that the man she loved— the man who asked her to marry him—had killed her daddy. She'd never tell anyone that Miriam had killed Roscoe. The truth could be so outlandish that to speak of it would make them all appear quite insane.

Roscoe had always wondered if she had a touch of her daddy's madness. Despite her fragile hold on reality at times, she knew her madness wasn't hereditary. It was her own doing. She'd made choices that other women wouldn't have— including working for her father's best friend at a prison.

"Going to that reporter must have caused you a great deal of pain," Willy said. "I'm sorry for that."

"Don't be," she said. "I owed your family that much."

They stared at one another without feeling the need to look away. Ginny could envision a point in the future when she'd look at Willy's face without seeing Silas's.

"I hope to run into you again." She turned away quickly so he wouldn't see that her eyes were misting up.

Willy touched her arm to stop her. "Miss Polk, you're not to blame for my daddy's death," he said.

She brought her fingers to her trembling lips. In her nightmares, the eight-year-old Willy Barnes had accused her of killing his father no matter how much she protested. Today, he tried to release her of a burden she'd carried more than two decades.

Ginny nodded and squeezed his hand. Perhaps one day she'd believe him.

FEATURED RECIPES

The recipes that follow have been reprinted almost exactly as they appeared in the vintage sources. In a few instances, instructions have been clarified.

AUNT SUSAN'S CLABBER CAKE
Source: Daily Oklahoman, *1952*
(http://newsok.com/article/2666525)

½ pound butter
2 cups sugar
2 eggs, beaten
3 ½ cups cake flour
2 teaspoons baking soda
3 ⅓ tablespoons cocoa
2 cups clabber milk (can substitute
 buttermilk)

Cream together butter and sugar. Add eggs, one at a time.

Sift dry ingredients together and add alternately with clabber milk to creamed mixture. Bake in greased and floured 14 × 9-inch pan in a preheated 350-degree oven for 45 minutes.

Author's Note: Clabber milk is clotted, soured milk. To make it, leave raw (not pasteurized) milk on the counter in a sealed jar for two to three days in a warm spot until solids appear. Shake it to see if it's turned thick. It should not yet be separated. If the milk is still mostly white when shaken, and has turned thick, then it is done clabbering. Store clabbered milk in the refrigerator. If left on the counter too long, it will separate and turn into curds and whey.

MASTER RECIPE FOR DIGESTIBLE CRISCO SHORTCAKE
Source: Crisco advertisement, 1934

2 cups flour
4 teaspoons baking powder
½ teaspoon salt
⅓ cup Crisco
1 egg
⅔ cup milk, water, or juice

Sift dry ingredients. Work in Crisco (a pure digestible shortening). Beat egg in measuring cup; add liquid to fill cup ¾ full. Add to Crisco mixture. Divide dough. Pat out into rounds to fit bottom of pie plate. Brush one round with melted Crisco. Place second round on top.

Bake in a 425-degree oven for 20 to 25 minutes. Separate rounds. Put filling between.

For individual shortcakes: Cut out biscuits ¼ inch thick. Brush tops with melted Crisco. Put other biscuits on top. Bake in a 425-degree oven for 12 minutes.

SEVEN MINUTE FROSTING
Source: All About Home Baking
(General Foods Corporation,
1933, p. 104)

2 egg whites, unbeaten
1 ½ cups sugar
5 tablespoons water
1 ½ teaspoons light corn syrup
1 teaspoon vanilla

Combine egg whites, sugar, water, and corn syrup in top of double boiler, beating with rotary egg beater until thoroughly mixed. Place over rapidly boiling water, beat constantly with rotary egg beater, and cook 7 minutes, or until frosting will stand in peaks. Remove from boiling water; add vanilla and beat until thick enough to spread. Makes enough frosting to cover tops and sides of two 9-inch layers or about two dozen cupcakes. Make sure the cake is cold and free from loose crumbs before attempting to frost it. The frosting should be cool so that it does not run and soak into the cake.

CALUMET FRUITCAKE
Source: All About Home Baking *(General Foods Corporation, 1933, p. 135)*

1 pound (4½ cups) sifted Swans Down Cake Flour
1 teaspoon Calumet baking powder
½ teaspoon cloves
½ teaspoon cinnamon
½ teaspoon mace
1 pound butter or other shortening
1 pound brown sugar
10 eggs, well beaten
½ pound candied cherries
½ pound candied pineapple
1 pound dates, seeded and sliced
1 pound raisins
1 pound currants
½ pound citron, thinly sliced
½ pound candied orange and lemon peel
½ pound nut meats, chopped
1 cup honey
1 cup molasses
½ cup cider

Sift flour once, measure, add baking powder and spices, and sift together three times. Cream shortening thoroughly, add sugar gradually, and cream together until light and fluffy. Add remaining ingredients. Add flour gradually. Bake in four greased pans, 8 × 8 × 2 inches, lined with greased paper, in a 250-degree oven for 3 to 3½ hours. Makes four 2.5-pound fruitcakes.

SOUTHERN SPOON BREAD

Source: The Southern Cook Book – 322 Old Dixie Recipes *(Culinary Arts Press, 1939, p. 31)*

2 cups cornmeal
2 cups boiling water
3 large tablespoons butter (melted)
1 teaspoon salt
1½ cups sweet milk
3 eggs

Sift the cornmeal three times and dissolve in the boiling water, mix until it is smooth and free from any lumps. Add the melted butter and salt. Thin with milk. Separate the eggs; beat until light; add the yolks and then the whites. Pour into a buttered baking dish and bake in a 350-degree oven about 30 minutes. This should be served in the dish in which it is baked.

BAKING POWDER BISCUITS

Source: The Victory Binding of the American Woman's Cook Book – Wartime Edition *(Consolidated Book Publishers, Chicago, 1938, p. 118)*

2 cups sifted flour
3 teaspoons baking powder
1 teaspoon salt
¼ cup cold shortening
⅔ cup cold milk

Sift flour, baking powder, and salt together and cut in shortening with two knives or a pastry blender. Add milk and mix quickly. Knead for a few seconds on lightly floured board. Pat out to ½-inch thickness and cut with biscuit cutter. Place in greased pan close together for crust on top and bottom only, far apart if crust is desired on sides also. Bake at once in a 450-degree oven for 12 minutes. Makes 12.

PORK NECK STEW

Source: Allrecipes.com (adapted from http://allrecipes.com/recipe/184741/neck -bones-and-lima-beans)

2 tablespoons garlic powder
2 tablespoons onion powder
1 teaspoon cayenne pepper
1 tablespoon rubbed sage
1 tablespoon ground nutmeg
1 teaspoon seasoned salt
Salt and pepper to taste
3 pounds pork neck bones
3 tablespoons oil
1 cup diced onion
1 cup diced celery
1 cup chopped red bell pepper
1 (16-ounce) package dried lima beans
10 cups water, divided

Combine the garlic powder, onion powder, cayenne pepper, sage, nutmeg, seasoned salt, salt, and pepper in a small bowl. Rub ¾ of this mixture into the pork neck bones; set the neck bones and remaining seasoning aside.

Heat the olive oil in a large skillet over medium heat. Stir in the onion, celery, and bell pepper; cook and stir until the onion has softened and turned translucent, about 5 minutes. Add the neck bones; reduce heat to low and cover. Cook, stirring occasionally, for 1 hour, adding water as needed to keep the meat and vegetables from scorching.

Meanwhile, place the lima beans into a large pot and pour in 8 cups of water; bring to a boil over high heat. Once boiling, turn off the heat, cover, and let stand 1 hour.

After the beans have soaked for 1 hour, drain and rinse. Return the beans to the pot, then pour in 2 cups of water. Bring to a boil over high heat, then stir in the pork and vegetables and the remaining spice mixture. Reduce heat, cover, and simmer until the lima beans are tender and the pork is falling off the bones, about 30 minutes.

SHIT ON A SHINGLE
(CREAMED GROUND BEEF ON TOAST)
Source: Department of the Army
Technical Manual, *1957*

24 pounds boneless ground beef
1 pound onions, chopped fine
½ cup salt
1 tablespoon black pepper
1 bay leaf
2 gallons evaporated milk mixed with
  2 gallons water
2 pounds wheat flour, hard
100 slices toast

Brown beef in its own fat in roasting pans on top of range. Remove excess fat during cooking period. Add onions and seasoning and mix thoroughly.

Add 3 gallons of milk mixture to beef mixture and heat to simmering, stirring frequently. Mix flour with the remaining gallon of milk and stir into hot mixture. Bring to a boil, stirring steadily; reduce heat and simmer until thickened.

Serve 1 cup serving over 1 piece of toast. Makes 100 servings.

CHOWCHOW

Source: The Victory Binding of the American Woman's Cook Book – Wartime Edition *(Consolidated Book Publishers, Chicago, 1938, p. 697)*

18 green tomatoes
1 bunch celery
8 cucumbers
5 dozen small green onions
1 pound green string beans
1 cauliflower
3 red peppers
½ cup salt
2 quarts vinegar
1 cup brown sugar
2 tablespoons turmeric
4 tablespoons mustard seed
1 tablespoon cloves
1 tablespoon pepper

Dice tomatoes, celery, and cucumbers; skin onions and remove tops; cut beans into small pieces; separate cauliflower into flowerets; and chop peppers. Arrange vegetables in layers, sprinkling each layer with salt. Let stand 24 hours, then drain. Combine vinegar, sugar, and spices and heat to boiling, stirring well. Pack in hot, sterilized jars and seal. Makes 6 quarts.

Author's note: My grandmother also added sliced yellow squash to chowchow.

CAJUN DIRTY RICE

Source: Cooks.com (http://www.cooks .com/recipe/pv2850nl/cajun-dirty-rice.html)

1 pound chicken gizzards
1 pound chicken livers
½ cup butter
1 ½ onions, finely chopped
½ cup green pepper, finely chopped
½ cup celery, finely chopped
2 garlic cloves, minced
2 teaspoons salt
1 teaspoon pepper
½ teaspoon ground red pepper
3 cups hot cooked rice
½ cup chopped parsley

Chop chicken gizzards and livers very fine. Brown meat in butter in large skillet (or Dutch oven). Add onion, celery, green pepper, garlic, and seasonings. Mix ingredients well. Cover and cook over medium heat, stirring occasionally, until vegetables are tender. Add rice and parsley, mix lightly. Garnish with parsley, if desired. Serve immediately. Serves 8.

Author's note: If you prefer a less spicy version, reduce the amount of ground red pepper by half.

Acknowledgments

Several years ago, I had a conversation with my good friend, Katrina Burtt, who'd stumbled upon a website that listed the last words of Texas death row inmates prior to their executions. She mentioned that some entries also noted what the men asked for as their last meals. One young man asked only for two boxes of Frosted Flakes and a pint of milk. We talked about the poignancy of that image, and how inmates' last requests have more to do with memory and loss, than they do of hunger and pleasure. I remember texting Katrina a week later and saying "I have to write a book about last suppers." She said, "Go for it." So I did. Katrina is the reason I told Ginny's and Roscoe's story, and she has my love and gratitude always.

The book wouldn't have been possible without J.L. Stermer, my agent, and John Scognamiglio, editor in chief at Kensington Publishing. Their enthusiasm for the manuscript (and their insistence that Dot should have a larger role) makes me smile to this day. And I am beyond honored that John chose *The Last Suppers* as the first book released by the John Scognamiglio Books imprint at Kensington.

The only person who's read *The Last Suppers* as many times as I have is my invaluable critique partner, Micki Browning. She and I started our publishing journeys about the same time and we've had each other's backs since then.

So many people read and offered their insights on the book: Hunter Knox, Mari Clark, Kathleen Costello, Kathy Watkins, Evie Bromiley, and Camm Dougherty. Thank you.

I'd be remiss if I didn't acknowledge my grandmothers, Marie Mikulencak and Lena Skrovan. They instilled in me my lifelong passion for baking and served as inspiration as I researched recipes that Ginny and Dot would have prepared in Louisiana from the 1930s to the 1950s.

And last, but certainly not least, thank you to my husband, Andy, who reminds me every day that I'm doing exactly what I'm supposed to be doing—and that I need to start writing that *next* book. I couldn't ask for a more passionate supporter of my writing.

DISCUSSION QUESTIONS

1. As a daughter of a prison guard, Ginny had been a part of the Greenmount Penitentiary since she was a little girl. How does her childhood and father's murder impact her decision to return to the prison as a cook?

2. Ginny becomes obsessed with the preparation of the last meals for death row inmates. In what ways does Ginny come to understand the reasons for the obsession?

3. What do you think motivates inmates to request the last meals they do? Do you believe Ginny cares about their motivation?

4. Discuss the central role that food plays in the novel. Why is it important for Ginny to involve the inmates' families?

5. What role does Dot play in Ginny's life? Do they allow society to dictate these roles?

6. Roscoe said on more than one occasion he didn't do enough to improve conditions at the prison. Do you believe that?

7. How does the time period for the novel (1920s-1960s Louisiana) affect the actions of the characters? Would they have made the same choices today?

8. What purpose does Ginny's scrapbook serve?

9. Roscoe once told Ginny that seeing her at the execution of her father's murderer brought him more sadness than the death of his best friend. Why do you think that's so?

10. What are some of the reasons you believe Ginny began a relationship with Roscoe? Why is it so important that Roscoe say the words "I love you" out loud?

11. Why do you believe Miriam's relationship with Ginny is so difficult? How is it further affected by Joe's death and Ginny's relationship with Roscoe?

12. In uncovering the truth of her father's death, Ginny upsets the lives of many people including Silas Barnes's widow and son. Are her actions justified?

13. After learning about Roscoe's past, Ginny wants her mother "to share something profound" that would help explain how Ginny could still love him. Why do you think Ginny needs to

justify her feelings? And why does her mother's opinion matter?

14. Did reading *The Last Suppers* change your views on the death penalty?

15. Was Ginny's compassion for the inmates and their families an insult to the victims and their families?

Books are produced in the United States using U.S.-based materials

Books are printed using a revolutionary new process called THINKtech™ that lowers energy usage by 70% and increases overall quality

Books are durable and flexible because of smythe-sewing

Paper is sourced using environmentally responsible foresting methods and the paper is acid-free

Center Point Large Print
600 Brooks Road / PO Box 1
Thorndike, ME 04986-0001 USA

(207) 568-3717

US & Canada:
1 800 929-9108
www.centerpointlargeprint.com